HOMBRECITO

HOMBRECITO

Santiago Jose Sanchez

RIVERHEAD BOOKS

NEW YORK

2024

RIVERHEAD BOOKS
An imprint of Penguin Random House LLC
penguinrandomhouse.com

Copyright © 2024 by Santiago Jose Sanchez
Penguin Random House supports copyright. Copyright fuels
creativity, encourages diverse voices, promotes free speech, and creates a
vibrant culture. Thank you for buying an authorized edition of this book
and for complying with copyright laws by not reproducing, scanning,
or distributing any part of it in any form without permission. You are
supporting writers and allowing Penguin Random House
to continue to publish books for every reader.

Riverhead and the R colophon are registered
trademarks of Penguin Random House LLC.

Library of Congress Cataloging-in-Publication Data

Names: Sanchez, Santiago Jose, author.
Title: Hombrecito / Santiago Jose Sanchez.
Description: New York : Riverhead Books, 2024. |
Identifiers: LCCN 2023054876 (print) | LCCN 2023054877 (ebook) |
ISBN 9780593542187 (hardcover) | ISBN 9780593542200 (ebook)
Subjects: LCGFT: Queer fiction. | Bildungsromans. | Novels.
Classification: LCC PS3619.A52246 H66 2024 (print) |
LCC PS3619.A52246 (ebook) | DDC 813/.6—dc23/eng/20231204
LC record available at https://lccn.loc.gov/2023054876
LC ebook record available at https://lccn.loc.gov/2023054877

Printed in the United States of America
1st Printing

Book design by Alexis Farabaugh

For my mother and my brother,
Carl, Larissa, and Johnathan,
and the rest of mi familia.

I

ONE

The boy is ready at the window when the last bell rings. He tightens the straps of his backpack and hugs his lunch box close to his chest. The cars at the end of the schoolyard melt into a line of glistening metal.

Today she forgot she is a mother. Either she's first in line or not there at all. He's worked out the system to these two options.

Tugging the lapels of his uniform, the boy squeezes his eyes shut until they sting. Small pains like these sustain him. He thinks hard, because he has to, he has to picture her face—imagining her there, willing her to his side—then she'll appear. He starts with her eyes and nose, which are identical to his, before he reaches a deep, glowing blank, unable to remember the parts of her that aren't his.

It must have been a Friday, like today, the first time she forgot she was a mother. Because a whole weekend passed before the boy and the brother found her in the kitchen. Small, pale, upright. She greeted them as if nothing had happened. That Monday, on their way to school, the brother sat in the back seat and squeezed the boy's hand each time she peered at them in the rearview. The warped surface of the mirror made her features quiver as if there were another face beneath. In the safety of their room that night, the boy finally got answers. "She went to Tierra Caliente," said the brother, throwing a volley of punches at an invisible target, "to search for your father." It was their secret to keep, he said. No one could find out that she had left or where she had gone; no one at Años Maravillosos or Colegio Champagnat, especially no one in the rest of the family. The brother pivoted slowly, circling their round orange rug with his arms up by the sides of his head, his cheeks and forehead blotched. For as long as the boy could remember, the father came back to Ibagué once a month from his construction sites. But he had not come home in a while. First the father, now the mother. No one was telling him why. Tierra Caliente—he couldn't find it on any map—spread fires in his mind. In the middle of the room, the brother lunged forward, tackling and straddling something only he could see. He punched the rug between his thighs. Again and again and again. His own father lived downtown, he had another brother and sister, a whole other world should this one expire. All the boy could think was *fire*.

Today, the boy's classmates pour around him to the door. One by one, the little caballeros exit the first-grade classroom with a bow to Profesora Cecilia. Only Diego, out of politeness, says *see you next week* to him before disappearing out the door. The boy doesn't play outside at the end of the day anymore. He has no friends left, the better to keep his secrets.

He sits by the window like last time. From his perch, forehead pressed to the cold windowpane, he concentrates on holding the world together. He tracks his classmates running across the court-yard, imagining himself in their limbs, in their heads—*he lives between the world and his own mind*, Profesora Cecilia once said to the mother. When Pedro jumps over the slabs of cement, avoiding all the red bricks of lava, the boy, too, is jumping. When Lucas runs up the slide chute, all the way to the top—the latest stunt—the boy, too, is triumphant. It's his sacrifice, keeping the world in order. But when his classmates reach the fence, falling into the arms of maids and mothers, they don't turn around to look at him. They cross a threshold, unaware that without him their fun would be impossible. Their world would be cast into peril and chaos. His is a thankless job.

"Did your mother say anything this time?" Profesora Cecilia's voice is hollow. He shakes his head and gives his best attempt at a smile, like everything is as it should be, but despite his efforts, the gloom doesn't leave her face. "We'll wait just a little longer." She reclines in her chair, eyes closed, and it's too much for the boy. He can't look out the window any longer. He walks to the back of the classroom and slides into the last desk. This way, when the teacher wakes up, he will be a smaller problem.

He opens the latch of his lunch box, sifts through his leftovers: a banana skin, the plastic wrapper of a straw, the gooey ball of a used napkin.

He learned about restlessness from the mother quite early. In preparation for the father's return from Tierra Caliente, the mother went from room to room for hours each night, erasing every trace of life. She polished every fork, knife, and spoon in the kitchen, only satisfied when she could see her face in the metal. In the bathroom, she stored all the creams and toothbrushes in the cabinets, folded the towels, even turned the candles on the toilets so all the labels—the snow-frosted pines, the rolling yellow fields—faced forward. When he asked why, the mother said: "It's something to do."

This is something to do, he tells himself now, picking up the banana peel. He folds the almost-black skin in half, and in half, and in half, trying to make it a smaller problem, trying to make it disappear. The sweet smell gives an outline to his hunger. Finally, when the peel is a black cube, he holds it up to his lips like he might take a bite. He isn't seriously hungry, though, not yet. But what would happen if no one came? What would be worse, dying of hunger in this classroom or going home with Profesora Cecilia? Would he become her son and she the new mother? And what about the brother, already fifteen? How would the laws work? Would anyone think to find the father? The boy throws these questions around like dice, aware he's only playing a game. This is only, for now, a game.

No more boys, no more maids. No mother. The wind corrals the leaves into a corner of the empty courtyard and then, changing its mind, lifts them back across the playground. As the leaves swirl toward the gate, it begins to rain. The drops slant down in silver lines, hissing like static from the mother's television, until they reach the classroom windows; the sound becomes deafening.

This latest stretch is the longest the father has been away. At the end of each night, the father's side of the bed is always untouched, the sheets a neatly folded envelope and the cushions a pyramid stacked from largest to smallest; the boy squeezes in at the mother's side, keeping to her half, as if at any moment the father will barge in through the door. When the air above the empty span of the mattress vibrates, the boy wonders if she, too, can hear the high ring of the father's absence over every television program. The boy asks her from time to time, trying his best to be brave, when he'll be home. *He's a civil engineer,* the mother says, repeating herself word for word. *He's the real deal, out there in Tierra Caliente, where roads and bridges are most needed, where others are too chicken to work. He'll be back,* she says, *this weekend or the next.*

The first crack of thunder wakes Profesora Cecilia. She lurches forward, rising from her desk with arms outstretched. She feels her way to the light switch by the door. Then the brilliant shock hits the boy—he's been sitting in the dark this whole time. Her eyes survey the room, narrowing when she spots him, and the particular look of disappointment hovering between sadness and revulsion on her face is not new to him. He drops the black banana cube in his lunch box, his fingers sticky with pulp. She unhooks the phone from the wall and a dial tone buzzes over the rows of slick, empty chairs to the back of the classroom where the boy sits, circling his ears like a mosquito. Impossible to swat away, try as he does. The buzz spirals into his ear canals, batting its wings and legs against his brain. Profesora Cecilia dials all the numbers in her phone book, waiting with her fist dug into her chest. He has become a problem she cannot solve again. Her fingers massage her temples, the sides of her jaw. Creeping to the front of the classroom, back to his own desk, he feels like a little demon with red wings and talons disguised as a boy. He opens his notebook to the lesson of the day. Across the page, the cursive letters resemble zoo animals waiting patiently in their cages.

"Manuel? It's me," she says, dropping her words like anvils.

. . .

"I don't care if you're swimming. Someone has to pick him up."

. . .

The boy can picture the brother darting through the water with the force of an arrow. He's been swimming for as long as the mother has been disappearing. Or longer, perhaps. The boy's mind is a scattered calendar, all the months thrown into a box, then shaken.

Profesora Cecilia turns to the chalkboard. He's not supposed to hear this part.

. . .

"Unbelievable."

. . .

He sucks his stomach in until he can fit his fingers underneath his ribs, holding himself in place from the inside.

Her head snaps back; he looks away, as if he's not straining to listen. Oblivious.

He knows his stare makes her feel strange. One of the brother's favorite stories: how they thought the boy was troubled when he was little. He didn't speak, didn't cry, didn't eat. He sat in his high chair, staring across the room into everyone's eyes. If they were lucky, he would believe their hands were planes and accept their cargo into his mouth. On the worst days, they took him to the zoo. There, the boy stretched his lips silently around the sounds the lions and monkeys and elephants made, as if uttering the same cries from his own mouth. Only then were they able to feed him. He doesn't recall any of this, but he's sorry, sorry he was ever difficult.

Profesora Cecilia puts a hand to her forehead, taking a sharp inhale. Then, to the boy's surprise, she says the words he's been keeping himself from thinking: "What's wrong with her?"

. . .

Something is wrong with the mother. She's forgotten she is a mother. He had hoped only he thought this, but here it is, alive and crawling out of someone else's mouth.

Profesora Cecilia paces the length of the chalkboard, the phone pressed between her shoulder and ear, the coiled cord joining her to the wall. She's looking straight at him now.

What does she see? What kind of animal?

"It's not your fault," she says. "Don't apologize for her or anyone."

. . .

"You poor boys."

Profesora Cecilia hangs up, falls into her creaky chair.

In his notebook this time, the boy begins again, because he must, because it's something to do. He draws an oval. He will attempt summoning the mother again. With tense hands, he scratches two *X*'s for her eyes and coils a meticulous crown of graphite curls for her hair.

"Your brother is on his way," says Profesora Cecilia to no one, to the ceiling.

Honks erupt from the street. The boy doesn't know how much time has passed. He shoves his desk away and runs to the window as he did when the father returned from Tierra Caliente, beating his horn down the mountain, the marshal of his own parade.

A silhouette emerges from a cab onto the empty street, lit orange by the lamppost. The sun has gone down and the rain is still falling. The figure runs through the courtyard with purpose, in a white button-up and khaki trousers, his high school uniform, with his coat—too light for this weather—spread like giant bat wings set in silver.

The brother knocks on the window, flicking his head, saying *qué más*, in the secret language only the two of them share. He flashes the boy a thumbs-up. And so the boy gathers his backpack, his lunch box, cramming the unfinished drawing of the mother deep in his pocket. He pauses only at the window to raise his own thumb, slowly, at an odd angle.

"This won't ever happen again," says Profesora Cecilia at the door.

He's not sure whether this is a question or not. He can see the unplucked hairs above her lips but not what she means. He almost shoves her into the hall then but stops himself.

Outside, leaning against the building in all his size, is the brother. Strings of rain burst on his shoulders in bright, electric snarls; the extra fabric in the arms of his jacket swells with wind. His hair, combed down the middle into neat and symmetrical halves, is a perfect mountain of hair. He is elegant, in his way.

"What's the matter?" asks the brother, patting the boy's cheek.

"Nothing." The chlorine lingering on the brother's wrists, sweet and pungent, shoots like a current through the boy. He feels his face glitch or flicker, then the heat before tears. Before it's too late, the boy punches the air in front of himself and ducks an invisible jab.

"Don't worry about her. She's fine," says the brother, offering the boy his hand. The rain splits around his boulder-sized knuckles into smaller streams. "How about a walk through the city before we go home?"

"But it's dark," says the boy, "against the rules—"

Every other time she'd forgotten she was a mother, they had taken a cab to their home in the mountains north of Ibagué, locked the doors and windows, and waited. They ate ham and cheese sandwiches for every meal, pretending each time they sat in front of their plates was the first. For some brief moments, the boy even fooled himself into believing he belonged to an orphaned world, but everywhere he looked, her spirit was there—on the sofa, on her empty bed—reminding him this was home.

The boy shakes the brother's hand. Like they still have a choice. Like the taxi he came in isn't long gone now. Like whatever is going to happen hasn't already started.

The only way to survive this is to be young, ecstatic—to pretend the mother is truly gone this time. Without her they can be anyone.

Mountains border the city on all sides. Their peaks slice open the clouds blown in from the Amazon and the Pacific, staining the city brown with rain. At the city's edge are pastures green with brush where herds of smooth, black cows graze diligently under the sun. A single snowcapped volcano, bear-shaped and fierce, rises in the distance—on the clearest days, the boy can stand on tiptoe in front of his house and look eastward, sighting across the city and beyond the sharp dip of the trees the faint, almost imagined line of the blue volcano. The boy has grown up amid the mountains, in a tract of orange-shingled houses a thirty-minute drive from downtown. Past their backyard is a stream choked with polished, smooth stones, and beyond that, a field of mango and palm trees home to colonies of bats. Their neighbors are doctors and engineers, always coming or going to Medellín and Bogotá for business. Farther up the mountain, in a richer section, compounds and villas house Ibagué's politicians and landowners in their fantasies of a secluded paradise. The boy knows, thanks to the brother, that kings are always above their people—and that they themselves are almost kings, close to kings. He has never needed to ride a bus or jump on the back of a motorcycle. His mother drives a Volkswagen. They eat meat every day of the week.

They have vacationed in San Andrés and Cartagena. Just last year, they spent a week in Miami visiting Abuela.

Here are the boy and the brother a month before the move to America, walking home through the city of night. The brother pushes past the fruit vendors, launching himself into the crowd of umbrellas, and the boy runs after, rain needling his head, playing follow the silver raincoat. The boy prefers walking with the brother. The father, when he's home, makes the boy lead the way through the mercado to their favorite tamale stand, so that every few seconds he has to turn around and make sure the father hasn't vanished the crowd. The mother keeps him at her side when they go to doctor's appointments and uniform fittings, never letting go of his hand or neck, so that while walking they're a single, clumsy creature. The brother always walks ahead of the boy, facing the world of strangers so the boy doesn't have to, so that as the rain lessens, becoming a fine mist, the boy can look at the shirtless men honking at their girlfriends' windows and the men in the video bars arm wrestling over beers. Everywhere he looks, from the grocery stores to the pharmacies, to the clouds of smoke issuing from the swinging half doors of pool halls, there are small groups of men in lively conversations.

His footsteps are heavy with a sense of being in the middle of everything. Free to look at what and whom he wants without shame or consequence, he looks everywhere, even at the soldiers standing at the intersections, one on each corner. He's never prepared for how large the guns across their torsos are. To draw less attention to himself, the boy matches his footsteps to the brother's with the logic of a shadow. At the brother's side, his fears are smaller. He looks up again like he's reading a sign or checking the clouds, doing anything but studying the soldiers. Slowly, in pieces—unibrows, downy mustaches, skin cratered with red pimples—he puts together the faces he sees underneath the rain-studded helmets. These are faces as young as the brother's. These soldiers are still boys. He looks away, pretending he hasn't seen this. He won't ask the brother where they'll hide after curfew. He's heard that boys caught by the soldiers are shipped to faraway cities to become soldiers themselves, never to be seen again by anyone they love; but he won't ask if these stories are true. There's another hour, maybe two, before they have to think about that.

For now, he returns his eyes to the ground, to his feet. Fleets of mice disappear in and out of the telephone bills, the wrappers of chocolatinas, and the napkins stamped by red lips strewn across the uneven sidewalk, stirring, murmuring, crossing between his and the brother's feet along invisible threads. The boys reach larger streets with more people, where it's possible to forget the soldiers under the red neon signs blinking VENTA VENTA VENTA. Potholes filled with the stardust of ground-up glass bottles catch the lights like portals into an underground world. Girls on billboards blow kisses down onto the traffic, and mournful folk songs spill from the bars. Buses boom down the avenue, full of poor people and pickpockets, bad thoughts and the smell of wet onions, pregnant brown girls selling little yellow candies from large plastic bags for a penny or two. He can't look away from the bursts of light the world becomes in the rain.

In the future, when people in America ask the boy where in Colombia he's from, he'll recite a list of facts about Ibagué: It's the seventh-largest city in Colombia; located in the interior of the country, between Bogotá and Cali, surrounded on all sides by the Andes; known for its music and rain. And no one will understand any better where he's from or what he's talking about.

They reach Plaza Bolívar. There's not a pigeon in sight tonight, not a single one. Skipping down the steps, past the sculpture of three Natives sailing a canoe, the boy sees posters with the faces of politicians—on the walls of the bank, the courthouse, the old capitol building. There are layers and layers of them. Some have peeled back to reveal another face beneath—there, an eyeball on a lip. An ear over an eye.

For no reason at all, the brother screams at the top of his lungs. Then the boy, too, is screaming. Both of them scream like maniacs, like men who've lost their limbs in a minefield, like orphans stranded in an empty plaza. Because they want to. Because they can.

Stirred from their hiding place, hundreds of gray and black birds, their bodies swollen with rain, soar into the sky. As the shrieking mass circles, swirls, and swoops furiously around them, the boy remembers like a vision the day the father brought them here to feed the pigeons.

It was sunny, the plaza full. Children flung corn across the square, and the kernels caught the light like gold. The father filled his own hand with corn, and instead of tossing his palmful, he lifted his arm high in the air with that look he got when he tested the mother's patience. Within seconds, a bird perched on his wrist. The mother, haunted by worry, by the world of germs and diseases only she could see beneath her microscope, protested. She slapped the father's shoulder with her purse, calling out his full name the same way she called the boys when they were in trouble, but the father laughed through the blows. The boy wondered whether this was strange or the way things were supposed to be. He took the bag of corn from the father and did as he was told. He filled both of the father's hands until yellow hills peaked in his palms, which he then held out at his sides like a man bound to a cross. Pigeons flocked to him. He was majestic. Perhaps what the boy felt then, without entirely understanding it, was the distance between the father and the mother growing fast, faster than he imagined possible. The boy filled his own hands. The mother tried to pull him into her arms, but it was too late—the birds were already swooping. At first, the boy was exhilarated. The pigeons zipped past his head, wings brushing his shoulders. Tiny claws curled around his wrists, digging gently into his skin. Each pigeon had a heart of its own; he felt each one thumping. Three, four, five, then more came to eat from his hands. They clashed before his eyes in feathery collisions. The mother's voice flared around him, dull as if heard through a storm. The birds pecked at one another's eyes and throats, greedy to claim his arms, but he was too small to hold them all. He couldn't tell the pigeons apart anymore. His skin was swelling red beneath their desperate, flapping bodies.

That night, the mother rubbed his forearms with cooling slivers of aloe, and her face, as before when glimpsed through all the feathers, was disappointed.

Now the brother jets across the street to the recessed walkway below the offices of the national bank, and the boy, giving himself over to joy, follows. From under the enclosure, side by side and both fantastically grinning, they watch the birds shit across the plaza in explosive bursts of white.

At the end of the walkway, they cross the street again, past another soldier, another gun. The pavement turns to rubble as they descend into the blue, fluorescent flames of the neighborhood ahead. No sidewalks here. Some boys play soccer barefoot in the rain. Two cats fight over a tin of Vienna sausage left on the hood of a car. The boy knows the bottom of a hill is a bad place to be, as is any place too brightly lit, but tonight the mother's rules don't matter. He lets the brother steer him down the hill by the shoulders. A shield or an offering—the boy doesn't care which he is. He pounds into the mist forehead first, past the two-story houses, past the grainy walls streaked with mud. His mind is clear, sharp, noticing every change in pressure between his shoulders and the brother's hands.

The security lights over the doorways ignite as they step under the sensors, the rubble becoming their stage. His shadow hides close to his feet. Without the brother having to utter a word, the boy stops in front of a metal gate decorated with swirls and knots in the shapes of flowers. Behind the gate is a red door. Under the light bulb, the scene is bright as day. The brother's face is calm, even amused, looking past the metal flowers through the door to a light only he can see.

The jab between his shoulders means *Knock*. Out of habit, the boy knuckles the door like in the cartoons, five taps followed by two. The mother's words crawl around his mind, though he's tried his best to bury them: "Your brother has always hoped to fall into another family." In the silence, moths rocket past the boy's face into the overhead light. Footsteps sweep across the room on the other side of the door. Past the metal gate, a pair of legs appear—thin, long, dark—darker than his and the brother's. He wants to keep her face out of his head, as if seeing it would be enough to make her the new mother. The girl's hot pink nails straighten her plaid school skirt over her knees and scratch the spot over her lips before resting at her waist; he looks no farther than her mouth when she asks: "What are you doing here? Is everything okay?"

She's trying to sound concerned, older, like a mother, but there's an edge to her voice, something delicate breaking.

The brother jabs him again, meaning *Speak*, so the boy says hello to the girl's skirt.

The knife at his back is unsatisfied, prods him to say more.

"Our-mother-forgot-she-is-a-mother."

The words shoot out of his mouth as if from a wound.

She bends down to his height, forcing him to look at her. Her cheeks are the wide handles of a pot. How did he not know the brother had a girlfriend? He drops his fists like anchors at his sides, afraid he'll be swept away by the tug deep in his heart.

"It's okay," she says, stroking his wet hair through the bars. "Santiago, right?"

She tells him to calm down, to repeat himself—for her, she says—and slowly this time, he pulls each word out of his mouth, one by one, hanging the mother in the air between them. He thinks he's made himself understood when the girl's lips strain into the shape of a smile and her eyes narrow as if recalling the name of a capital city.

"Come inside," she finally says. "I need to borrow your brother for just a minute."

The metal gate bangs shut behind them. The red door remains open. She takes the brother to the middle of the kitchen in the other room, but the house is small and she is loud.

"Seriously? What the fuck is this stunt?" Her arms barricade her chest—the place where feelings live. "I've told you again and again: Your parents fighting isn't my problem. And it's definitely no excuse for sticking your tongue where it doesn't belong!"

The brother steps toward her, settles one hand on her elbow, then the other on her shoulder. The boy can't make out his words from the living room, but he wants to believe it's possible they'll still embrace.

The girl slides out of the brother's grasp and backs away from him until her calves press up against the stove.

"How could you think bringing your little brother would change things? How can I make this any clearer? You. Me. We're done, Manuel."

"Luisa, Luisa, Luisa . . ." The brother says her name, a last resort. He repeats it to her as if somewhere inside her is another girl—the one he longs to see.

An excuse—it's all the boy has been. He turns toward the door, fitting his face between the metal bars. The betrayal spreads—he can't unthink it—staining every part of the story he's been telling himself about this night.

They're screaming at each other now. Their words pass through the boy, but some are impossible to ignore—"What's wrong? I thought you would be happy to see me!" and "Do you really take me for a fool? Everyone knows about her!"—words that also belong to the mother and the father.

He looks up to watch the boys who were playing soccer march down the street. All six are skinny and tan with identical rattail haircuts; their white shirts hang like towels over their shoulders. The one with a metal thorn through his eyebrow kicks the ball ahead, so that it bounces against the side of a parked car, taps a lamppost—rainwater exploding around each impact—and finally climbs ashore on a mound of trash. Before he knows it, the boy is standing outside, like he might yet join their game. He squeezes his eyes shut and tries to go somewhere else—anywhere else but the sidewalk—and the mother's lap is where he lands: He's between her legs, staring up at the triangle of her rigid jaw, his ear pressed against her churning belly. The father's voice wanders down to him, in and out of static, from the phone at her ear. She will tell him everything afterward, how *los muchachos*, as she calls the guerrilleros, had stolen a ton of cement overnight. How the company's guards had accidentally shot a local after a night of whiskey and cumbias. How there are more delays, more months, many, many more months, before the roads will be finished. After every call, her finger traces a spiral on his stomach as she maps out the story of the Guerrilla for him again. "It began in the far reaches of this land, in the jungles," she says, making him squirm when she pokes his armpits and traces his nipples. "And then they spread to the small towns between larger cities." She draws circle within circle, nearing his belly button. "And for now, the only safe place is here."

The gate flies open. The brother is still saying *please* when he's spit out onto the sidewalk next to the boy, still saying *please* when the door shuts; he's a pleading patch of brown skin under the spotlight, saying, "Please." Then, as he rises to his feet, "that bitch." The gravel crunches beneath him as he takes small, backward steps from the house. "That bitch." The boy whispers *curfew*, not loud enough. "That bitch," the brother keeps saying, looking around himself as if there were a way to escape he hadn't considered—a trapdoor, a chute, a ladder, a red button to the next life. In the middle of the street, he picks a handful of stones from the ground and studies each of them on his palm. He stops and drops all but one. He kisses the chosen one, the one now sailing through the air at the second-floor window, the one having the time of its life.

Up the hill, the street is molten and strange, the surface of another planet. The boy pinches his thighs through the lining of his pants to remind them to keep climbing. He doesn't recognize it at first—the pulp at the bottom of his pocket—the unfinished drawing of the mother, of her face that wouldn't manifest. His nails dig into the wet clumps.

"That bitch!" the boy yells at the top of his own lungs.

The shouting, the curfew, the fact that he didn't get a last look at the girl—it doesn't matter. What does is that the night smells terrific, like fried plantains, and the streetlights, they're huge enough to fill entire puddles.

The next morning, in their house, the boy runs from room to room. "That bitch, that bitch," he chants, unlatching all the windows. In the mother's room, he climbs atop the sill, and with a firm grip on the frame he closes his eyes. The mountain breeze swells past him. For the first few seconds he's diving through water. A feeling grips him from within when he opens his eyes and sees the innocent blue streaks of light rippling over the sheepskin rug and the lace curtains, the books on microbiology and the loose lab reports—the floating organisms of this underwater world. He sees the room for what it is: the mother's old room, now buried beneath the sea.

His mission takes him to the kitchen. He heaves his body up onto the marble counter, his shoulders arching as if he were clambering out of a pool. The stone is smooth and cold underfoot. He steps carefully around the plates with the hardening crusts of ham and cheese sandwiches the brother made for dinner last night and again for breakfast today. He pushes the skylight open with a spatula. The wind whips in; the roll of paper towels turns on its hinge, unspooling onto the ground. He goes to pick it up but stops himself. Tidiness doesn't matter anymore. They haven't heard from the mother—as far as he knows she's gone forever. But that's not important now. The brother is apologizing. This day is his apology.

He returns to the living room, where the sight of the brother sprawled on the naked sofa makes the boy feel useful and proud. The plastic cover, cast off to the side, stands like a clear boulder next to the dining room chairs where their jackets hang drying—this, too, is the boy's handiwork. They can hear the churn of the stream in the backyard and the trees wrestling shoulder to shoulder on the mountain. Every now and then, a breeze dashes through the house, shaking the gold-tasseled curtains and rocking the glass trinkets in the vitrine. No inside, no outside. No order. He wishes it were always like this, just the two of them in the living room.

The boy blows on the game cassette's metal spine. Then the brother plugs everything in. Mario and Luigi appear inside their cars on the television, racing down Rainbow Road. Their cars leap over chasms of empty space and stars shoot out of their wheels with loud, righteous sounds. When the brother wins, which is always, they drum their chests with their fists in celebration.

Inside the brother's red plastic lunch box, there are several lighters, a tin jar with a crank, and a small book with sheer pages. The green nuggets, studded with little crystals of light, are already on the table. The brother rolls the cigarette right next to the wooden coasters and the pictures of them in Miami without the father.

"Listen, boy. You're going to breathe easy."

He loves when the brother gives him commands; it's the only way he knows with conviction what he must do.

"I'll hit it and pass it to you," the brother says. "It'll burn at first, but you'll get used to it."

The boy taps his foot to the beat of their victory as the cigarette forms, thin and even like a pencil, between the brother's fingers. When it's finished, the brother lights the scruffy end and blows on the tip until the flame is tamed to a crackling orange. The brother pulls the boy's chin toward him, so close they are almost kissing, then bridges their mouths with the smoke. The boy is caught off guard; he had imagined the smoke swirling down his throat, absorbed into his meat and bones, inside out, until he was weightless and glowing like a speck of dust, but he can only hold it so long before his lungs are spasming. He doesn't know if he's about to laugh or cry.

"Hold it," says the brother, on his feet now, dancing in front of the television where Mario is jumping atop the podium with his golden trophy. The last thing the boy sees is the brother with his arms raised above his head, shaking his hips like a fútbol player after scoring a goal. The boy finds a pink room behind his eyelids. He prickles with the newness of this secret room, its glazed walls pulsing as if to greet him. Somehow he knows he's in the deepest room of himself.

He exhales and the vision fades.

He doesn't know where he has just gone.

"I think I'm high."

"Not yet, boy." A slim flame shoots up from the lighter. "Tranquilo."

The brother inhales, and this time the smoke slips out from the sides of his mouth, unspooling and rising high to the rafters; the smoke collecting, the boy thinks, into the mother's face. He blows up at the ceiling, trying to send her away on his own, until his lungs are tight. He stands on the couch, aware he's breaking another of her rules. The springs squeal under his unwashed feet. He's as tall as the brother, but when he reaches for the cigarette, the brother swipes his hand away.

"One more," the boy says, holding his hand out again.

He wants to see the pink room.

The brother slaps the boy's hand away, just hard enough to assert himself.

"Who's a little man now?" asks the brother. He makes a cone with his hands around his ear. "Huh? I don't hear you? I said, who's an hombrecito?!"

"Me!" the boy shouts. "I'm an hombrecito!"

From a barn across the stream, past the line of trees, in one of the farms stretching over the mountains, a cow moos for the boy. And then there's music, too—growing louder, louder. The boy dances while thinking of being near the brother's mouth again, of finding more and more and more rooms within himself.

The mother's face still hovers there in the smoke. He blows upward at the ceiling at the same time that a strong gust of air comes in through the windows, forcing the smoke apart into a vague, bright blob holding them, the boy thinks, together.

The front door swings open. They whip their necks toward the world outside, a sheet of white in the sunlight. It's impossible to see anything. He can imagine what will happen next. The Guerrilla has reached them, even here in the mountains, the one place where they were supposed to be safe. The guerrilleros will force them out into the jungle, train them to carry guns and sleep in hammocks strung between trees. In his mind, these future days shimmer with possibility. With the help of the guerrilleros they will find the father, rob him of his tools and money, and without a job the father will have no choice but to return home. The mother will no longer need to search for him. *We, the boys, will bathe in the rivers*, he says to himself. *We will be revolutionaries.*

He straddles the back of the sofa like a horse, his legs kicking at either side, beating the wooden mane with his fists. And when he yells across the house, he does so as only a little man can: "We! Are! Ready!"

The world outside materializes from the haze. There, in the driveway, the boy makes out the mother's car with the windows rolled down, the radio blasting a cumbia at full volume. A moment later, the mother reaches the door; backlit, her face is dark, her body compact and neat and sharp. She takes a long step inside, leaving the door ajar. She limps past the boy atop his couch horse. In the kitchen, a finger of light touches her face, right under her eyeball—the open gash there fills with gold. She stomps across the threshold as if crushing a swarm of roaches beneath her heels and squirms out of her dress, inspecting the garment under the light, fingering the hole in its side when she finds it. The dress splits open in her hands, until it's like the hide of an animal, symmetrically filleted. She drops it on the tall, skinny table, over the brother's framed black-and-white communion photos. At the sound of laughter, her head snaps back toward the front door she's left open; the band is saying their cheerful goodbyes over the car radio. She doesn't see him or the brother even though they're right in front of her, watching her. They have become invisible. Her purse hangs heroically from her hand. The radio goes silent. For a moment, recognition flickers across her face, like she's about to come to her senses—she's left the car on, these here are her sons, smoking hierba in her living room—but instead she drops her purse. The compacts and lipsticks and brushes erupt across the floor, shooting under the furniture. The heels come off last, so brilliantly red, so alive, so much like bloody pieces freshly torn from her body that the boy's heart sinks. She stands on the landing in her beige bra and panties, more naked than they have ever seen her. He could look at her like this forever, but she's at the mouth of the dark hallway to her bedroom, disappearing now.

The boy and the brother snap to life. After sweeping the crumbs off the table, the brother stashes the remaining nuggets in his loafers. He points to the windows, and as quickly and quietly as the boy can, he runs to shut them. No need to talk to decide their course of action. The brother leaps up from the couch and leads the way, tiptoeing into the hallway.

They peek their heads around the frame of her bedroom door, turning into detectives. The lace curtains wave in and out of the open window. The mother's inside the bathroom; her shadow moves across the open door like a slip of silk. She runs the bath and rifles through the vanity cabinet. The boy looks at the brother. His stare dares him to go first, but the boy shakes his head, wrapping his arms around the brother's waist. There's no way in hell he's going in there. He's no hombrecito.

After dinner, the boy hears his name hissed like a bad word from the bunk below. The orange-green lights of the neighborhood security van enter the room and disappear. A small dog howls from the next yard over. He hasn't really slept, or if he has, he's dreamed only of being on this bed, like this, still as death.

"Quit pretending," the brother says, appearing beside the top mattress. His voice is a jolt in the silence. "We should check she didn't drown."

The boy's stomach turns. In his center the ham and cheese sandwiches they made for dinner again ball up, hardening like cement. He throws up a little in his mouth and swallows it back down.

They find her in the middle of the bed, a fallen statue, the light of the late-night news sculpting her matronly body. One by one, they slip under the sheets at her sides. Her face is laid bare beneath his. A fingernail has claimed a chunk from her cheek. He can look at the wound, lumpy and alien in its blue sheen, for only so long before he pictures the father falling, falling faster and faster into her flesh.

On the TV, a woman says that yet another town, somewhere else in their country, has been destroyed. The image cuts to a line of green-clad soldiers in Tierra Caliente, stationed at the side of a road, holding their arms at their waists, impervious to flames leaping across the trees behind them. In the next shot, other soldiers are seen from above, indistinguishable from one another, a swarm of ants around a clump of dirt. In the next, they're close again, so close he can see the small shrubs and trees torn from the ground by the men pulling their way up a steep mountain. He imagines the soldiers sneaking out of the screen and onto the bed. It doesn't take much for him to see that the geography of the mother's body under the sheets is like the mountain's. A hundred green men mount her arms and legs, heading toward the slow-heaving knolls of her breasts, toward her face. He leans over the small bloody town of her cheek before they can reach it and plants his lips there, willing the entirety of his being into this kiss. He scans the length of her body; the soldiers are gone, held off by his shadow. When he moves aside, the soldiers reappear, scrambling up her neck, up its tight cords. He thinks, and not for the first time, that he comes from her, that he is made of her. He kisses her again, with more conviction this time, the way she kisses his cuts and bruises, as if love were something tangible, a balm to spread over every injury.

A shudder starts at her head, passes through her. The boy pulls away. He meets the brother's eyes over her body, ready to follow his lead. They remove her hands from her armpits, extend her arms, kiss her from her shoulders to her palms. They kiss up and down the length of her arms. They're breathless, panting. The brother settles a hand on the back of the boy's head to assure him he's sorry, she's sorry, everybody's sorry. And the boy is sure this is something they have done before, in this life or another.

The news broadcast finishes and static slashes across the screen. Washed in the white light, they're still kissing her. He has no clue what they're doing anymore. He doesn't need to know if this is how things are supposed to be or if everything has gone terribly wrong, because this is just how things are. She forgot she was a mother, but it doesn't matter. He begins to chant over her body the one prayer she raised them on, until they are both chanting, their voices raised over her body in unison.

"We belong to each other.

"We belong to each other.

"We belong to each other."

Days later, the mother walks back across the yard with an empty drawer in each hand. She joins the boy and the brother at the window. Together, as a family, they watch the contents of the father's closet float piece by piece down the stream behind the house: red polos followed by the khakis with elastic waistbands and argyle socks stitched with his initials. There is charm in how the Hanes balloon in the water. They watch every piece of his wardrobe disappear around the river bend, past the line of wind-shorn trees, rushing away from the mountains downhill into the city, where if you're not careful, the sun makes a hide of your skin.

TWO

A woman named Tata introduced herself as the father's oldest sister when they landed at the Orlando airport. The boy refused to believe her until she looked at him in the rearview mirror of her van and asked, with the ridiculous English of the father, "Jaguar you?" *How are you?* She used his other words and phrases, too. Mierda, chimba, bacano, tenaz, joda, parceros. She was the first woman he ever heard say, *No seas marica*.

Watching her talk to the mother, the boy waited for the brother to say something, to squeeze his leg, his knee, anything. But the brother, silent ever since his head-turning tears on the plane, stared coolly at the headrest, out the window, anywhere but at the boy.

That night at Tata's, the boy shuddered over the cup of rice, the pork chop, and the slices of pale tomato she served for dinner. He felt the walls of the kitchen contract as the father's face emerged from hers.

Don't cry, he said to himself. *You will not cry.*

Her voice, her face, her food—he knew everything had to be

kept out of him. He didn't even touch the glass of Coca-Cola Tata poured him after dinner or the bread rolls in the paper bag she pushed toward him across the glass tabletop insisting he eat, for her, for the mother.

Neither the boy nor the brother understood more than a word or two from the television despite years of English school.

From the couch, he heard Tata and the mother talk about a woman from their Catholic school days who had moved to Texas after Pastrana was elected president.

"When are we going home?" he asked the brother.

"Never."

"Why?"

"Because of you."

"What did I do?"

Suddenly the brother tapped the boy's nose. "Ring, ring."

"No."

"Come on."

"Fine. Who is it?" the boy heard himself ask.

"El Huracán."

"Manuel, leave him alone"—said the mother from the dining table, and then to Tata—"ever since we got on the plane he keeps telling Santiago a hurricane is going to kidnap him."

The air in the room swirled around the boy. Too many words drifted past.

How could he, she kept asking, *how is this possible, Tata?* "I told him I left Manuel's dad, and I wasn't afraid to leave another man.

I warned him: If he ever did anything like that to me I would take the boys so far away he would never see them again."

The boy still had no clear understanding of what was happening beyond the loathing he felt for her, the father, the brother, for everything and everyone.

The following day, at Disney World, the brother finally spoke: "It's like she wants us to think we're on vacation."

At night, in Tata's guest room, the boy jumped from bed to bed lip-synching to Britney Spears on the radio. "Mami, come watch this," said the brother, turning the volume up. Everyone was laughing, taking in the boy's joy, which seemed to lift everyone else out of their sadness. They looked so happy he could jump like this forever. But then his foot slid off the edge of the mattress. The room hurled itself away from him. The back of his head struck the nightstand. He didn't cry until he saw the blood. A long debate—should they take him to the hospital, how much would an ambulance cost, could the mother solve this herself—spiraled around him. With Tata pressing a towel to his head, the mother cut his hair. When the bleeding stopped, she cleaned the wound and wrapped his head tight in gauze. For the rest of the night the mother stayed at his side, and he lay very still and straight under the fantastic pressure of her hand over his head. The red pulse dimmed, and dimmed, and dimmed.

THREE

The mother was sad again. Santiago could tell because she was at the edge of the mattress, next to his and the brother's feet, humming prayers. From the corner of one eye, he could just see the outline of her new hair, almost as short as a man's, choppy and faintly red.

He was pretending to sleep, as he'd done for a week, a month—hard to tell, exactly, how long they'd been in America. Each morning he woke up when the mother did, before daybreak, but kept his eyes closed, his lips a little parted. This mission was the first he'd ever given himself, a secret even from the brother. He was collecting glimpses of the mother when she thought no one was looking to compare to what he remembered of her in their past, because a part of him—and he hated this part—wanted to believe the real mother was left behind in Colombia.

"Mi tesoro." Before he knew it, she was right by his side. "Ya me voy." The little hairs on his body stood up, all the way from his ears to his toes. "Did angels visit your dreams last night?"

In her small, unsmiling face was the same need as the uncles and aunts in Ibagué who came to the door with unpaid bills and late notices. He wanted this broken woman, whoever she was, to put away her sadness; the poison of this thought surprised him, even as the thought itself felt absurd.

Not knowing what else to do, he stared past her at the blue-black underworld of the room the three shared, wanting to be so still he thought nothing and hurt no one. The parking lot beyond the window was still lit by the floodlights, and if he concentrated, he could believe they were the moon itself, that it was moonlight touching the piles of clothing and shoes and manila folders stuffed with documents and photographs—everything they could fit into their six suitcases—making them look wet, lustrous, like mounds of fresh soil and bones under which a person could hide and never be found.

Just then, the brother let out a wail. Santiago hugged his knees to his chest. He knew what was next. For the millionth time, the brother flailed and screamed across the mattress like he was on fire. Santiago had laughed the first two or three times; he'd been reminded of the Christmas they kidnapped the baby Jesus from the neighborhood's nativity scene, tore him apart in the woods, and scattered his limbs across the treetops. For as long as he could remember, he had watched the brother, played his games and participated in his missions, hoping to learn something for the future. No matter how much Santiago wanted to believe this was just another game like all the others they shared in Colombia, the screaming and kicking was no longer a joke; it had crossed over into something that made him feel he was one of many chains around the brother's neck, like they were being held here hostage.

"What?" said the brother, suddenly quiet. All the pain over. He sat up with a yawn and linked his arms around his head in a halo. He was determined to make a fool of the world. Not even the mother could stop him. He had been a problem before, but never like this. "Do I have something on my face?"

The mother cleared her throat. "No leaving the apartment. No answering the telephone. But if it's three calls in a row, answer—it's me." What Santiago heard now was not the mother's old power but its poor substitute—whatever she didn't like and could not change, she ignored. "No opening the door. Not for anyone. Leave the thermostat where it's set and turn the lights off after leaving a room. Don't shower for too long. And keep the curtains shut at all times—"

Dropping his arms, the brother snored dramatically.

"This isn't a joke, Manuel."

Santiago tried not to hear her helplessness, or her pain.

"This is serious. No one can know you're here alone."

The mother picked up her purse from the ground and unhooked her lab coat from behind the door—there was work to go to, samples to slide under her microscope—and looking over the room, she sucked a deep breath between her teeth. This was it, Santiago's last chance to tell her everything. *The brother, the walks, the portal.* But it sounded crazy, even in his head. In an instant, he saw everything he should have done that he hadn't; he should have risen when she did, today and every day before that; he should have sat with her in the kitchen, kept her company instead of letting her talk to herself—he should have, but he hadn't.

"Right here," Santiago said, pounding his fists on the mattress. His voice was loud like the father's, which startled them all. "We'll stay perfectly still, right here, until you come back, Doctora."

He spoke so fast he didn't know if he made any sense. But a second later, the mother was back in the bed, telling them how much she loved them, and there were tears starting in her eyes; he'd reminded her of who she was—not Madre, Mamá, or Mami, but la Doctora—the name everyone, from the housemaids to her siblings, called her in Colombia.

"You worry too much," said the brother. "It's not like I'm going to lose him." He threw his blanket over them like a net, and in the dark, he dug his knuckles into her ribs, then Santiago's, until the three of them were laughing, their bodies warm and slightly damp under the covers.

With a shock of pleasure and surprise, Santiago realized this was, in fact, his only family in the world. *Today will be different*, he told himself, beginning to try as best as he could to really believe it would.

One day many years later, the brothers will be at a Latin fusion restaurant on the Long Island City waterfront. After two margaritas, they're undoing their long-unspoken truce of forgetting those first months in America.

With the same persuasion of his fifteen-year-old self, the brother recalls Santiago's fits of sleepwalking, of pissing in random corners of the apartment like an untrained dog, and after a silence he brings up the morning they found the unopened mail, fast-food napkins, and hot sauce packets from the glove box strewn across the empty parking spot—their golden Saturn gone. They even talk about how the mother, for no rational reason, claimed to Santiago she was ten years younger than her true age. They laugh at the strangeness of these stories, and their laughter continues, taking them from the present to the past, from one end of their minds to the rarely visited reaches.

"But there was no portal," says the brother. "You made that up yourself, Santiaguito."

The first day the mother went to work at the lab in Miami, the brother told Santiago about the portal. And even if Santiago was old enough to know such things didn't exist, he listened. What he heard in the brother's voice—that they had to forget the rules, forget everything the mother said, that they had to go, because on the other side of that portal waited the house, the fathers, the friends, everyone they'd ever known—was the promise of their togetherness. That first day the world had still seemed solely their own. He would've said yes to anything.

Now, Santiago kneeled before the bathroom door. He peered at the strip of metal between the carpet and tile, getting the angle and distance right, until the brother came into view on the other side. The brother leaned forward on the toilet, his shorts bunched up around his ankles. Santiago had been watching the brother go to the bathroom for a week, a month—hard to tell, exactly, how long they'd been in America. Despite the betrayals, small and large, despite all the ways the brother had changed beyond recognition, Santiago couldn't stand being alone. This loneliness was the beginning of his voyeurism. *How would he know he wouldn't be forgotten if they suddenly moved again? What if everyone changed without him? What if the mother forgot she was a mother forever?* These questions ran through his head, one after the other, and he was there on the floor for some time—mind fast, world slow—before the toilet flushed. Santiago spied a moment longer. This was his favorite part, when the brother wrapped his hand in a cocoon of toilet paper and, leaning to the side, patted his ass clean with fastidious care. The brother resembled neither Santiago nor the mother; he must have looked like his own father, smooth-haired, cheeks soft with black fuzz, amber-eyed like a jungle animal. Santiago felt intensely alive.

What if we aren't wasting away the summer days? What if there is a portal? I would cross it. His mind raced to fool him. *Where he goes I go.*

The worst part of leaving the apartment was the distance to the sidewalk. From the moment he stepped outside, a mixture of denial and humiliation drove his feet forward. He couldn't shake the thought of an aunt watching them from somewhere in the sky—like Tía Nelcy, with her beady eyes and sharp tongue, was looking down from a cloud with a telescope. The morning light struck their hallway head-on, revealing the silky webs hanging from the ceiling spotted with meaty flies and tiny, translucent red spiders. The building resembled the motels at the edge of town in Ibagué set amid warehouses and discotheques with lavish names like Santorini and Vizcaya, where men rented rooms by the hour to meet their other women. Before he could escape the complex, the wind picked up the stench of trash and smacked it across his face, a smell so hot and dense he didn't let himself breathe until they were past the gate, on the sidewalk, where he heard the brother curse America, curse the mother, his father, the boy's father, everything. The moment filled Santiago with pity for himself and for them all.

"Whose fault is it?" he asked, but the highway at the end of the street, several stories above the sidewalk, tore his words apart before they reached the brother.

They walked along the shoulder of the road, past the border of overgrown trees and loose trash, past the used car dealership, until they reached the mostly empty avenue, where he turned to the right, following the brother's lead.

When he asked the mother why they were here, she told a story of violence. A seven-year-old boy in Cali was kidnapped for no more than a few dollars; the next day a whole school bus somewhere else. Guerrilleros armed with guns entered the very hospital where she worked and took a doctor for three days to treat the muchachos wounded in the mountains. And we had a way out: Abuela had married a Cuban in Miami in the eighties. She had been working on getting them papers for years. But no matter the story, no matter the reason, Santiago didn't want to forget the father. He believed that if he remembered the father often enough, in the right way, whether happy or sad and with a pure heart, he could keep the father alive in his head. His job was to remember, and what he remembered now, and every morning, were the nights they'd spent in front of the muted television while everyone else slept in their rooms. In these private hours, the father told Santiago stories of abductions and gunshots, of men jumping off the bridges they'd built with their own hands. Stories that never ended, that bled into each other in smears of color and feeling. And when it was really late, Santiago drifting into sleep, the father told him of his girlfriends—of the dark, thick women with hair down to their hips who brought him steaks and bottles of whiskey late at night—and by then, all Santiago could think was *That's real life.* The stories made him ashamed of the comfort and order of the house; the father needed more, something he couldn't find here, something neither Santiago nor the mother could provide. No matter how much he listened, or laughed, or sat docile on the father's lap, none of the little tricks he made himself perform had stopped the father from leaving again. He wondered what made the father wander, and why the farthest-out pueblos in Tierra Caliente, as violent and lonely as they sounded, were where the father chose to call home.

Cars whipped past booming radio hits. Gulls cried atop the palm trees. Santiago's thin T-shirt and cargo shorts did almost nothing to save him from the asphalt catching the sun and beaming it back in every direction. The brother walked ahead, his gaze fixed on the ground, inspecting the blackened wads of gum and white-green splatters of bird shit, like they were a map only he could read. Santiago's own senses opened each time the brother lifted his shirt to mop his brow. The hairy centipede scaling the divot of his lower back and patches of coarse, werewolf-like hair sprouting everywhere were a landscape Santiago committed to memory. He knew no body better than the brother's. Not even his own. Yet a part of the brother had always been beyond his reach, distant and unknowable. Now, Santiago counted every new pimple and hair on the brother's back—if he could track every change in the brother, he could contain the distance between them before it grew monumental.

There was no life here. Only cars, stretches of long, strange silence, and the endless yellow stucco walls of gated communities, which he couldn't see into. The cars shooting down the avenue he gave necks and beaks, horns and legs, and just like that, the traffic transformed into a dust-billowing stampede of dinosaurs. Every minute he was getting better at blurring the dimensions of time and space in his mind; he blinked and he was in the centro of Ibagué, surrounded by voices trying to sell him and the brother knockoff jeans and fresh empanadas, voices calling their names and asking after the mother or the fathers or what they had thought of the soccer game last night in short, passing conversations as beautiful to him as music; cousins, uncles, aunts, friends, classmates, teachers, maids, all these people he hadn't known he'd miss leapt forward in his imagination. But at the sound of a skidding tire, he was back on the sidewalk with the brother.

This wasn't the Miami of their visit a year ago, of beaches and sunscreen and ice cream melting down his fingers, of burying the mother beneath piles of sand and seaweed, and of dinners, hours long, on hotel terraces they never wanted to leave. Looking at the palm trees, black with smog and towering over the road, the snarled bushes and patches of yellow grass here and there, he had to ask himself if they hadn't already slipped through an invisible portal.

In the early days after moving to Miami, their expeditions felt enchanted with a sense of discovery: to malls, mostly empty, where the women dressing the mannequins looked at Santiago and the brother indifferently or not at all; to supermarkets, where they picked cereal boxes from the shelves and dropped them off several aisles away like they had changed their minds, looking busy, like they belonged; to parks and playgrounds, where they held their breath to piss in the unlocked bathrooms and filled their mouths with stale warm water from the fountains, avoiding the men on the benches who were smoking, surrounded by sweet but menacing clouds. They found the schools they would attend when summer was over and stared into the windows for hours, imagining other lives, until a white man with a walkie-talkie chased after them in a golf cart. Determined to find a body of water, they got on the bus once and rode for hours. Santiago took everything in: the strange, spiky plants, the way the earth cooked under the sun and gave off a smell, the repetition of buildings and gates and trees and names. Every now and then, when they peeked into restaurants and bakeries, or shops with Colombian flags above their doors, Santiago remembered the portal. They were looking for something. If not a portal, something else that was theirs to find.

But there was no portal. He knew this, and when he lost his patience with the brother, he would ask himself, *What are we really looking for?* The question sat within him, small but always present. On some days it ran wildly inside of him like a creature with many legs.

It felt like hours later when the brother stopped at an intersection. "We're getting hot."

Santiago, wanting to see what the brother saw under the traffic light, leaned over the edge of the sidewalk. Identical beige buildings and billboards of the most saturated reds and blues he'd ever seen curved out toward the end of the world. He couldn't tell where they were. Dazed and unstable on his legs, he stepped onto the road. The asphalt buzzed beneath his feet.

"I have a good feeling," he said to himself, to the brother, to the bus hurtling toward him, and to the man behind the steering wheel, to the gray curls crawling out from the sides of the bus driver's blue denim cap. The brother pulled him back just as the bus thundered past, blasting their faces with tiny rocks and exhaust.

"I'm sorry," said Santiago, not understanding what had held him in place.

The rest of the way he was prisoner to the brother's hand, clammy with sweat as it guided him by the neck toward a strip mall, one they'd never visited. The parking lot, all gleaming metal, was bigger than a soccer field. The brother cut down the middle of a lane toward the stores, and Santiago, freed from his clutch, followed a pace behind. The cars snaked their way from row to row, almost all the parking spots full. Santiago was suddenly aware that what he and the brother were doing wasn't normal, that there was something desperate about two boys wandering strip malls on foot; shame—he'd felt it for weeks, never quite naming it or locating it in himself—bubbled up in his stomach. Just then, a car pulled up behind him. It was clear the driver was trying to pass them; the engine's heat grazed his calves like two solid white hands. The brother must have felt the car creep closer, too, and yet he slowed down even more, unperturbed, dragging his feet. Then the car's horn exploded, so close Santiago's bones shook all the way up his spine through his jaw, and something vibrated deep in his ears. Too afraid to look back, he reached out a hand and found the brother's arm.

"Wait," said the brother, his bicep flexing.

By his voice alone, Santiago knew the brother was wearing his tight, plotting smile. A smile that said this was no accident, no misunderstanding. This was just what he wanted. To make a fire from thin air.

When the car honked again, the brother stopped completely.

Santiago's own limbs froze; he could make no move without the brother.

The driver unrolled the window and out came a man's rough, heavy Spanish: "¡Oye! ¿Pájaros, están buscando una muerte pendeja?"

The words were almost familiar. Like an uncle's or a neighbor's—someone back home shouting at a gaggle of indifferent chickens in the middle of the road—but no, this was only the trick of a tongue shared among strangers.

Before Santiago understood what was happening, the brother swept him into the space between two parked cars; then they were running, fast, away from the *pájaros, pájaros*, shouted at their backs. Ahead of him, the brother stamped his sweaty handprints on every car window, laughing to himself, a madman. This laughter the only thing keeping him together. *What's so funny?* Santiago wanted to shout, even as he recognized that this question was just one more shadow cast by all their new differences, differences laid next to differences, differences stacked atop more differences into the sky. Was the brother losing it, or was he?

"Did you see the face on that comemierda?" said the brother, when they finally crouched in the space between two vans. He was himself again, an expert at forgetting. He put a hand on Santiago, squinting in the brightness. "What's the matter, little man?" For a moment, this was the same brother he'd had in Colombia. The brother who promised him everything was okay when they walked home through the woods, several boys behind them heaving and crying—someone's nose bleeding, someone's shirt torn to pieces. For one delusional moment, Santiago was the boy he was back then, too, the boy who could count on the brother to protect him and take care of his wants and lessen his fears. But the delusion vanished before he could sew himself back together; the brother slapped him across the head, neither hard nor soft. A flat *plap* sound. "This is her fault, you know. It's her fault you're so weird," he said, his gaze flickering over Santiago, a gaze without tenderness, summing him up and moving away, already bored. The brother stood up and the sun burned all expression from his face: a smooth, golden mask in which his brown eyes shone like chips of amber.

"You're right," said Santiago, because he couldn't say anything else. Because nothing else mattered. Because he was thinking about being as far from the brother as possible, but where exactly that would be, he had no clue. A new place. One that didn't yet exist. That he'd have to make himself. Like a portal only he could go through, where everyone on the other side will love him and nothing will ever change.

They reached the strip. The brother ran his hand over the shop windows, flat glass storefronts one after the other, dragging his reflection by the fingertips. They peered into the dim expanses of nail salons, gyms, and bakeries, and moved on. In front of a sea-food restaurant, the brother stopped. He smiled at his reflection like he was his own best friend. All along the edges of the window, there were pink corals and white bubbles drawn in thick, pasty paint, already half washed away by the rain. It looked as though the brother were facing a mirror, trying to see past the dark, scuffed surface of himself, because somewhere here—camouflaged—was his true self.

From the door came a clamor of voices. Mostly men's.

"We're here," said the brother, low and quiet.

"Where?" Santiago looked down at the cigarette butts his foot had swept into a pile and the lizard perched on the white crest of a crumpled receipt.

"The portal."

"Really?" His voice betrayed him, sweeping high.

"Did you doubt me?"

"No. Of course not," he said, though he was all doubt. He stepped toward the door and pulled on the cold black handle, his hands and legs no longer his own.

He wanted to believe the brother. Believe nothing but reason had governed their lives. They'd been looking for a portal, and finally, this was it—the way back. But he already knew that this was something else. There were no fathers, no friends, no family, no other house or country past this door.

He crossed the threshold into the sudden darkness of the restaurant. The familiar smell of fries and shrimp undid the knot of his hunger, a hunger held for hours, a hunger now swelling into his throat. His eyes adjusted slowly to the dim yellow light inside, the outline of faces and bodies emerging, and then he saw everything with startling clarity: the restaurant, the tables swarmed by Americans in unflattering mesh jerseys, faces blue and green with paint; between the tables, in every inch of space, were even more of them, jostling and yapping, passing pitchers of beer overhead. The restaurant was so packed it was impossible to see to the other end. Waitresses in red polos and matching lipstick maneuvered their way to tables balancing trays of food high in the air, their faces drawn in concentration. Plastic fish—some the size of a foot, some longer than Santiago, than the brother—filled the space on the walls between the televisions. He counted eight large televisions, aglow and crisp, all set to the same channel. Tiny men in blue uniforms swarmed the identical green fields and terra-cotta diamonds all around the restaurant. The camera zoomed in on a single man swinging a bat through the air. Then he ran for his life as men lunged to catch the small white ball. The room fell silent, still. A roar cracked through the restaurant. Clapping, cheering. A voice here, then there—Santiago tried to find it—rose above all the others: "YES YES YES!" More voices. More words, ones neither Santiago nor the brother knew, shouted in the awful crunch of English. The celebration stretched out, lasting seconds, minutes— hard to tell, exactly, how long they'd been in America.

When the brother shoved him, Santiago found himself pitching forward—flying—into a pair of khaki trousers. He caught himself on a man's legs and, realizing they were legs, he let go, startled by how much he wished he hadn't.

The man in the khakis lowered his eyes. His face was long and blue, the paint veined white by the skin beneath, his mouth wide and curled, his chin round with a crevice etched in the middle. Santiago stepped back with his hands out at his sides, fingers spread wide, afraid he might fly again. Behind him, the brother was staring across the room, his eyes scrunched like he was reading something far away, his expression offering no explanation. Santiago tried his old tricks, tried convincing himself the brother knew what was happening, that in his head everything was in order. But something was wrong. It wasn't working. Something solid had left him.

He squeezed past the brother, out the door. For the first time he led his own way. He marched down the strip, head high, the heat thick as water, determined to retreat as he'd learned from the brother. The sun had shifted, lower now, bending over the cars, slamming the side of his face. He passed two ladies talking in front of a hair salon, their heads ablaze with wide strips of aluminum reflecting the sun. He stomped forward, unstoppable. The only thing in his mind was a spiteful picture of the brother being sad and alone and groping his way through a pitch-black tunnel. The thought made him feel like he was already distant, so far nothing could touch him.

Santiago stopped in front of a flyspecked display case full of empanadas and pandebonos. A wall-mounted speaker inside the bakery pumped a vallenato out of the open door. Over a guacharaca, an accordion, and a drum, he heard the songs the father loved and the mother hated. The father danced to them at parties clutching his heart with mock sadness for a lost love. But for the mother, these sentimental songs reminded her of where she came from—nowhere—and that nothing was forgotten, not even the first cry she'd belted on the dusty floor of the barn where she was born.

Santiago turned to ask the brother if they could buy an empanada with the five-dollar bill folded in his sock, but the brother wasn't there. Santiago panicked. He didn't know where to go or what to do now. He realized, never having ventured out like this on his own, that he was only a boy. His scalp, his neck, his whole body was complaining, breaking out in a sweat. A fluorescent map of Miami lit up in his head as he imagined walking back to the apartment alone, but a new problem presented itself: The key was also in the brother's sock. And what if someone stopped him to ask why he was alone? They weren't even supposed to leave the apartment. What if they'd moved across the ocean only for him to walk into a stranger's car and be murdered in broad daylight? He didn't even want to go back to the apartment. In truth, he hadn't planned further than stepping out of the restaurant because the brother was supposed to come after him right away; the only plan he'd had when he left was to weaponize his absence—and it had failed.

The two ladies in front of the salon asked if he needed help, and he kept walking, wishing he could fly at them, punch them and make them stop asking questions. He ignored them as if he'd lived on his own all his life.

Pressing his hands to the restaurant's dark glass, he found the brother standing in the same place, waiting—but for what? The glass left Santiago's fingers greasy, and without thinking, he ran his hands down the front of his shirt, shocked by the black smear they left on the fabric. He stepped away from the door and was startled to see himself. The dark glass revealed to him a sweat-drenched shirt sagging down to his elbows, his hair like a bird's nest pointing in every direction. He looked like one of those boys in Ibagué who went from restaurant to restaurant begging for the meat left on bones and the spare change at the bottom of pockets, the street boys the mother called *gamines*, as if they were their own species of pest. Facing his image, he felt how alone he was, how there was no end to this hollowness. There was no one else in Miami. Just this brother, this mother—and both, somehow, were drifting away from him.

"We have to eat," he said to the brother's back, inside of the restaurant.

What went through the brother's mind now, what caused the brother to ignore him, he didn't know. He didn't know anything.

"Please," he said, trying to sound small, helpless, like something you'd never dare hurt. "Please, let's go home."

Glasses clinked. Fists hammered tables. Laughter rumbled above the din.

"Let's look somewhere else, please." He pulled on the hem of the brother's shirt. His throat was heavy and tight, packed with pebbles. He said the last thing left in his mind, knowing as he said it how stupid he sounded, how useless: "I'm going to tell la Doctora."

The brother turned quickly, pushing Santiago against the door, a hairbreadth between their faces. "Where do you think we are now?"

"I don't know." The handle of the door dug deeper into his back. "I'm just hungry."

"You're hungry?" It was theatrical—the way the brother raised Santiago's chin with two fingers, the way the brother glanced at his face to see if he was afraid, as if setting up a scene he'd rehearsed in his head a hundred times. "How hungry are you? Tell me."

"Really hungry."

"Then eat this," said the brother, angry and filled with joy, all at once. With his crotch squeezed in his hand, he pushed his way out of the restaurant.

He bolted out the door, his white T-shirt a sudden blur racing away. Santiago was already outside, sprinting after the brother before he'd even realized it. The brother was making a run for the end of the strip mall. Past the hair salon, past the bakery, Santiago gave chase. They were only messing around; this was just another game whose rules he'd piece together any second now. But then he realized the brother hadn't looked back to see if Santiago was after him. Santiago stopped. He could walk in the opposite direction, get them both lost, but they were far from home and had already walked so long. He decided then that he would leave the brother the way the mother left the father: suddenly. That's how it felt, when she returned from visiting the father in one of the little towns Santiago thought of as Tierra Caliente, when she came through the door with her cheek injured, her dress torn, and the following morning, when the three of them threw the father's closet into the stream behind the house, packed their bags, left. It was more than his mind could bear, to think the mother had planned the move, orchestrated it all without them knowing since the trip to Miami a year ago; there was no other way it had all been possible on such short notice. Before he knew it, he had a plan to leave the brother. Not now, but someday—and he was running again, ready for the next thing to happen, the next act in this drama having nothing and everything to do with him.

At the end of the strip, he caught up with the brother, melting back into his shadow. A shrug, followed by a curt laugh, was the brother's only acknowledgment of their reunion. They turned around the back together, into the long, empty lot behind the stores. A central gutter, garbage bins, cables, the windowless backsides of businesses and restaurants. Cats prowled the dumpsters, guarding the heaps of fishy black bags. A delivery truck spewed heat and smoke at the far end of the alley. The brother, he realized, was talking to him, pointing toward a doorway. "This is it," he said, with a forced grin.

The door was silver, scuffed, bandaged here and there with duct tape. A sheet of ruffled white paper said "Employees Only" in red marker.

"You're going to thank me one day," said the brother. His face was a stranger's—or rather it was filled with such contempt, Santiago wished it were not the brother's, but a stranger's.

On the other side of the door was a kitchen. Large, foaming cauldrons whistled on the stoves. Cooks paced and cussed at their stations, hands piling french fries onto thick white plates and stirring pots full of steaming red shells. Across the kitchen, a man who looked like a bear in an apron inspected the plates and slammed them down on a metal counter. His hairy fists came down on a bell. The sound—shrill, piercing—cut through everything.

A moment later, a waitress in a red polo appeared in the long, narrow window at the end of the kitchen. The sight of her stilled Santiago's heart. What he saw was an apparition. It was the only way he could explain it, because it couldn't be the mother; because she left each morning in a white coat; because she worked at a

laboratory, at a hospital like she did in Colombia; because she was
la Doctora; because in the evenings, when she came home from
work, she threw her lab coat over the arm of the sofa and told him
of the strange specimens under her microscope and the lives she'd
saved because no eyes were as sharp or as patient as hers; and yet
here she was, in the red polo, her short hair pulled through the
clasp of her hat in a puny nub. She picked up one plate, then another, until three plates balanced on her arm. Her other hand
reached for a tray with even more food piled high.

"It can't be her," he said, not looking away. He didn't believe
what he saw, or he didn't know how to explain it, or maybe there
was no difference.

"Don't you realize we eat this same shit every day?" said the
brother, bracing him from behind; Santiago could not run away
this time. The red of the mother's polo shrank until it disappeared
into the dining room, leaving only a color burning in his head.

"Do you get it now? She took us from everything for *this*. She
had no clue what she was doing. And she still doesn't. We're not
leaving that apartment anytime soon. We live here now."

That evening, Santiago waited in the bedroom outside of the
bathroom as the brother washed away the evidence of the day. The
shadows deepened in the corners of the room until the outside
hallway light switched on, the room blue-black like in the morning, before daybreak.

Santiago watched his own hands, their greedy movements, as

they dug a hole in one of the mounds of laundry on the floor. His body knew what it was doing, even if he didn't.

Once he'd carved out a circle, he sat in it and began to cover his legs with clothing and bedsheets and towels, anything he could find. Then he cleared a rectangle for his back and lay down flat, continuing to bury his body. He layered a dress over his face, then a shirt, then trousers, and then he wormed his arms and hands beneath the surface. He could feel himself warming, flushed with excitement. He'd meant only to hide for a moment, but when the brother came out of the shower and called his name, he didn't move. Santiago was so still, so quiet, for so long. The brother checked the other room, paced the kitchen, inspecting the cabinets and even the fridge, and, not finding him inside, opened the front door. Santiago felt nothing when he heard his name again, far away, muffled through walls and clothes, as if it belonged to someone else.

When the mother got back later that night, the brother didn't say anything. She dropped a plastic bag onto the counter, the smell of fries and fish so strong Santiago could smell it from his hiding place.

She went into the room, hit the light. "Santiago?"

She walked to the other side of the bed, drew the blinds shut. "Manuel, where's your brother?"

"How should I know?"

"What do you mean, Manuel? I made you responsible for him."

They checked under the bed, the bathroom, the kitchen, the living room, rummaging through the apartment all over again.

The brother was crying Santiago's name like it would summon him from thin air.

The mother was asking how the brother could let this happen.

Santiago wanted to scratch his legs, but he couldn't get up. He wanted to eat, to pee, to shower, but he couldn't get up. He wanted to tell the mother he loved her, and that even after all this, he belonged to her, they both did, but he couldn't get up. Getting up from under the mound was a test too large for even his powers. Too great for anyone.

The brother is outside in the parking lot now, calling his name.

The mother is on the bed now, shutting out the world with her prayers.

Santiago is only a few feet away, under everything they could fit into six suitcases.

This is how their existence as separate people begins.

II

FOUR

Everyone gathered around Daniel the day he came to school in his Boy Scouts uniform.

"Danny, what's this one for? Danny, tell us about that one." They pointed at the round patches sewn onto the silky sash across his chest.

Daniel was two years older than me but in the same gifted class. We may have all been exceptional, but I knew—we all knew—he was more special than us. He wasn't wearing the navy pants and white polos we all had to wear. The morning bell had already rung, and no one was in their seats, but Mrs. Torres didn't care. Even she was sucked into his orbit.

When my mother picked me up, I told her I wanted to join the Boy Scouts for the summer. I explained to her in Spanish that all the boys in my class went, that you learned to camp and survive on your own in the wild, and I didn't know if it was my worry, or hers, or ours I was speaking to when I made the program sound like a replacement for the father we had left behind in Colombia.

At last, I told her the Boy Scouts was very American, since she never knew what to say to that.

We drove to Our Lady of the Lakes and, a block away from the church, found the store with the Boy Scouts sign I'd noticed before, the way I noticed everything. Inside a small, windowless room not unlike my bedroom, I led her to a wall of green pants and dun-colored shirts. Riffling through the shelves and hangers, I turned the tags on a shirt, then a pair of pants, and, doing the math, felt it all cave in on me when I realized the uniform cost more than anything I'd ever asked for. In front of the till, my mother shot me one last inquiring glance, asking herself, then me, if this was worth it. I pretended I didn't notice her hesitation.

"Marica," Manuel said, blocking the front door as our mother drove off to the second job she worked in the evenings. *Marica* was what he called his friends, his boys; still, I squeezed past him with my new uniform, ignoring him as I'd learned to. Over the sofa cushions, I spread the button-down shirt beside the long shorts the way my mother laid out her clothes in the mornings. I ran my palms from the center of the fabric to the seams, smoothing the wrinkles like she did, rubbing each garment between my thumb and forefinger, nodding, as I convinced myself this was the life I wanted to fill.

Before I knew it, I was touching the uniform to my face. The texture was coarse like the arm of a man, and the grain against my skin made me homesick, the same way I felt when my father entered my thoughts. He called once a week now and always asked me the same question—how was I—and his response no matter what I said was always: *Que bueno.* He only spoke of the bridges he was building—how long they were, what rivers they crossed— never of his life outside of work. I knew from my mother that there was a new woman. He'd apparently bought her a car, an apartment, even a diamond bracelet. That's why, according to my mother, we would never go back to Colombia.

It was too late by the time I noticed Manuel. He'd broken into a sprint, his arms flapping at his sides, hollering like a rooster. I froze, my arms barring my face, thinking I was his target. At the last second, he somersaulted over the sofa and landed on my uni- form before I could pull the shirt and shorts out from under him. He dug his ass into the cushions, his face scrunched up in an ex- pression I knew too well. His farts popped like the sound from the exhaust pipe of a motorcycle.

I didn't cry or struggle. In this apartment we each had our own room. He'd disappear into his in only a moment, call his girl- friend, and I'd only hear the first words he said before the boom box blasted Satan's music. He hated everything and everyone ex- cept the girlfriend he'd met in high school and whom our mother despised, because it was that girl who dressed him this way, in long black T-shirts with logos that dripped across the front like blood. When she came over, when he paraded her through the apartment, when they rolled around on our mother's bed and showered in her bathroom, I kept a stone face. I wanted the pulse of my silence to radiate out and charge the air around me. I hoped that I was secretly a storm.

But as he rolled off the couch now, I could see Manuel suddenly and sharply in focus: He was happy. That was the only thing my silence did for me; it proved how small of an obstacle I was to his happiness. Back in his bedroom, he picked up the phone from his bed and shut the door. His girlfriend was waiting on the other end of the line since I'd gotten home.

Alone, it was my time: I escaped to my mother's closet and stepped into the Boy Scouts uniform. My transformation in the mirror was so complete I almost didn't recognize myself; it didn't even matter that the shirtsleeves fell down to my elbow and the shorts far past my knees. Inspired by the wild summer months ahead of me, I tied all the rags in the kitchen into elaborate, senseless knots. I'd be free—if only for a few hours each day, perhaps even a weekend here and there—from Manuel, from this life and all its reminders that we'd left the one place where we belonged. In the living room I crawled on hands and knees under the trees of an imaginary forest like I would a few weeks from now, with Daniel.

After two years in Miami, I still wasn't used to the introductions. They began my first day of second grade, where I was the youngest student in the room full of ESOL students, the only to skip a grade, then again six months later when I was moved into regular classes, and again just this year, after I was tested in a room away from everyone for no reason that I could discern and led to one of the portables, where the gifted students from every grade were kept. Each time it was the same: a room of faces turning to me as if by command, looks of pity and boredom interrupting whatever was happening before I arrived, and the adult, always with a hand between my shoulders, encouraging me forward with a shove.

Now I stood behind Mr. John and his oversized khakis. The room was cold and brightly lit by rectangular panels in the ceiling.

"We have a new scout today," he said, and before I was ready, his polished black shoes stepped out of the way.

There I was, with my hands behind my back.

And there they were: Daniel, his boys. I could see, in the dark openings of their mouths, their bright teeth and wet tongues frozen mid-speech. My mind clamored with realization. Each and every one of them—Allen, Carter, Brycen—even the ones in different classes—Liston, Henry, Benjamin, Jeremy—I recognized, because there wasn't a white boy in our school I didn't notice. They scoured me with their stares. What a terrible new pain it was to be in a room full of boys and know immediately that I was different.

I walked around their circle toward Daniel, and looking at neither him nor Allen, but at the space pinched between their knees, I asked, "Can I sit here?"

The two of them turned to each other—I'd never been so close to Daniel, and in my proximity to him, I found what I'd been looking for each time I studied him across the portable: He was handsome, but only in the same way as a dog. He was all snout and dark, vacant eyes. A golden retriever's simple appearance. But I kept looking at him. I didn't understand why everyone loved him, or why, even if he looked like a dog, I wanted to be him. I could only see him in that moment; the rest of the boys, including myself, fell into haze and shadow. It wasn't until someone in the circle laughed that I noticed the way Daniel was looking at Allen. In a different time, when my brother and I were allies, we had shared that same mocking look against our mother.

Allen scooted over. I took his place, folding my knees to my chest to fit where there was no room for me. Mr. John told them to get to know me while he said goodbye to my mother, whom I'd forgotten was waiting in the adjoining room. I turned and to my terror, her eyes were closed and her mouth a little open. Somehow, she was asleep, sitting perfectly upright.

Through the open door, we could all see Mr. John approach her and wave his hand in front of her face. In the pale blue scrubs she wore to clean houses, she at least looked like a doctor or nurse. When she didn't move, he wrung his fingers, checked his watch. He was unprepared for this strange woman sleeping in his chair. I had to draw the attention away from her, to myself, and so without thinking, I said to Daniel: "We're in the same gifted class."

There was a long, tired silence. I didn't know who to look at in the circle of towheaded boys. It was May, their faces already freckled by early summer. They all fit perfectly into their uniforms; my mother had said I would grow into mine.

"What's your name?" asked Henry, across the circle. His short, gelled hair sat like a crown on his head.

"Santiago," I said, too quickly.

"What was that?" another perfect boy asked.

My jaw locked itself. I couldn't fathom speaking again for fear that I would become the punch line of another joke.

"What did he say?" someone whispered.

"His name is Sandiego," said Daniel.

They all laughed, except for him. He turned his face toward the sound, followed it around the circle. The joke was lame, really. Not even clever enough to be cruel. When he beamed his smile toward me, it looked like stupidity, like triumph, like boys and harmless fun, like he'd done me some kindness. He couldn't have meant to hurt me. He saw how I looked at him, I knew he did— I'd been staring at him in the lunchroom once when he turned in my direction and winked, and he must have known then, with that little flare of recognition, how deep my devotion was to him.

"What's so funny now?" asked Mr. John. His body guarded the door to the other room.

My mother was gone.

"Nothing," said Daniel. "I was just introducing everyone to Sandiego."

All around the circle the laughter went again, contagious.

For the rest of the evening, I sat there quietly between Daniel and Allen. I didn't correct anyone when they got my name wrong, but I also gave them no reason to call on me. I just smiled at everyone as they answered questions about which berries were edible and which would kill you, and though I understood what they said, I missed most of it because I was no longer in the room. I was in my head, looking for a door out.

Finding excuses to skip Boy Scouts meetings was easy. I had to read and study, I told my mother, because if I started now, I could be the world's best engineer, better even than my father. What I said didn't really matter. She believed anything.

When she stopped asking about the Boy Scouts, I felt like I had triumphed—if you could call it a triumph, defeating your own weak mother.

The store wouldn't take the uniform back, she said one night, holding the hanger out at arm's length.

We returned the uniform to the closet, where it gathered dust, moving day by day behind another hanger, and another, toward the dark end.

I stayed home with Manuel all summer. I practiced silence, perfected disappearing. I didn't say anything when he pushed the living room furniture against the walls and laid down cardboard boxes to breakdance to the music videos on MTV. One moment he was a pinwheel, spinning on his head, and it was impossible to believe he was my brother, and then the next, he was himself again, shouting "What the fuck do you think you're looking at?" over the television. I said nothing when he blasted Korn and did push-ups on the balcony wearing only his gym shorts. When he dipped and his penis kissed the ground, I said nothing. Nothing when we watched *The Real World* on the sofa, our stomachs roiling for more than rice and eggs.

"You're so serious," he said, as if he hadn't made me this way.

After that, I was never quite in the room again, but atop the mountains where I pictured Daniel and his boys, their faces lit by fire. *Bloody Mary, Bloody Mary, Bloody Mary.* I could hear him repeating the words in a dare. His fingers, in my mind, were glazed in chocolate, a dark sweetness touching everything. Sometimes the price seemed small—I could have gone by Sandiego, gone with whatever else they said—to be one of their pack. Sometimes it felt like doing so would have been the end of me. When I snapped out of it, I returned to the commotion of Manuel and his girlfriend moving around me in all their black clothes.

Later that summer I passed Manuel the screws for the shutters. He dragged the ladder from window to window, sealing our apartment in total darkness in preparation for the storm. My mother went out and came back with two gallon jugs of water and a small flashlight that looked like a pen.

"This is all that was left," she said, passing me her purchases.

The first night of the hurricane, we slept in the bathtub, the three of us side by side, because I told them we had to, the lady had said so on the news—and because I barely spoke in those months, they didn't question this. For three days, the lights were out. We crammed every towel we owned into the gap under the front door, but even that wasn't enough—the water crept into our living room.

When school started everyone brought an umbrella or poncho in their bag. The rain fell wild, warm, without warning, from everywhere and nowhere at once.

During the first week, to avoid Daniel and his boys, I tracked their every movement from under my umbrella. The buzz I felt as I memorized their new schedules and the routes they took through the halls and portables rang through me. I had an awareness no one else could see, and it sustained me, even if every now and then I thought back to the Boy Scouts meeting.

After the last bell, I waited for the classroom to clear. I wasn't in any rush. I didn't have friends to meet, and my mother would be late again. Under the portable's awning, to my surprise, was Daniel. He looked alone, even timid, with his backpack clutched between his arms. I passed in front of his dark, vacant eyes, but they looked through me, at the puddles swelling below the stairs. Although I wanted to ask what was wrong, I didn't. Instead, I opened my umbrella and invited him to walk with me if he wanted to. I wasn't even sure if he'd heard me—the rain was deafening—until one of his arms reached around my shoulders.

We descended the steps and took the cement path toward the shelter where everyone else was already waiting for their parents. Headlights and honks scattered in the sizzling white rain. His nails were clean and long, and he didn't notice how they dug into my wrist as he helped me steady the umbrella against the wind. I didn't want to reach the shelter. I didn't want the illusion I had, of him and me at the bottom of all this rain, to end.

The water curved and folded around our shoes, but sometimes the current swept over our laces and I could feel the pressure, almost enough to drag us away. He had forgotten his umbrella. That was the only reason he was with me. I wrapped my arm around his waist, tucked my fist to his side. What luck I had, I held on to.

FIVE

lies rained down on the van. Bottle-black and -green, peanut-sized. Thousands of them hovered over the wiry waves of yellow grass on either side of the road.

The flat expanse outside my window was the Everglades. Almost everyone at school had been here before; I had heard their stories of field trips and birthday parties, airboats and alligators. Now, finally, I was seeing the swamps with my own eyes.

Beside me, my friend Matthew clicked his tongue each time a fly exploded on the windshield. Just as quickly, he resumed biting his nails as he always did in the car.

Talía, his mother, filed her fingernails in the passenger seat, her blue-veined legs sprawled on the dashboard like the wings of a butterfly. Somehow, she kept a magazine open between her toes.

Jack, Matthew's stepfather, drove. I sat behind him, only his neck visible to me. I didn't mind not having room to move my legs. Every few seconds, a whiff of the coconut oil souring on his skin reached the back seats.

Matthew's small, white hand crawled over the middle seat toward my knee as if it had a mind of its own. His eyes were trained on Jack in the rearview; he was about to say something stupid, something to land us in trouble. He leaned into the middle seat, closing the distance between us. "How much was the car wash last week?"

As we left Miami he'd warned Jack about the flies plaguing this route. Once a month Talía put him right behind the Greyhound driver to visit his real father in Clearwater, which was somewhere outside of Naples, where we were headed now in the little green van for a weekend camping trip to celebrate the beginning of summer. So Matthew knew about the flies, but Jack hadn't listened. He wasn't the kind of man who took advice from a child.

Jack, his hands at ten and two, choked the steering wheel. Nothing irritated him more than a wasted dollar, except, maybe, how often Matthew and I touched. The leather squealed; the color drained from his fingers. His eyes didn't leave the road. Not even when Matthew clicked his tongue to echo the hollow thud of another fly splatting into the windshield. Jack had all the deadly patience of an alligator. I waited, with thrill and caution, for him to reach back and wipe the smirk from Matthew's face. A single, solid slap was all it took to fix Matthew's behavior.

This had to be another American thing. Perhaps like Matthew I, too, would one day talk back to my mother, and it wouldn't look bold or foolish but completely normal, absolutely necessary. Another essential part of becoming American.

The gnawed pinky tapped my knee this time.

"The car's gonna look pretty by the time we get there."

"Mateo," Talía said, dropping the nail file into the console between her and Jack. The flies, stuck to the windshield like bloody boogers, mottled the side of her face in a sickly light, and still she was prettier than my mother.

They had met at their Inglés Sin Barreras class one night. Talía, who had worked in restaurants, convinced my mother she could make more money as an empleada. For a while their agency assigned them to clean mansions together on Star Island, then my mother was assigned her own clients: a woman named Sharon and a family on Fisher Island. Talía sometimes let slip brief anecdotes of their time together—how my mother had almost gotten fired for baking a tray of brownies while working, or how once, when a family went to Europe, the two of them had painted their faces with the matron's cosmetics, done their hair, and taken turns trying on her wedding gown. My mother never spoke of those days. Though I wanted to, I held back from asking Talía for more of these stories. I was scared by how little I knew of my mother, by how much she seemed to exist in the world without me. When Talía spoke of these times, I tried as hard as I could to believe her stories belonged to the past—to lifetimes ago—when in reality it had only been a year since my mother had started working for Sharon on her own. When Matthew and I found ourselves in the same school, in the same class, I had never heard of Talía. It embarrassed me how my mother had forgotten her, or had never mentioned her, but it didn't surprise me. My mother was nothing like her. She was always cutting herself—and us—loose from the past, from her story.

"This boy is asking for a whupping," Jack said to Talía, and then to Matthew, "Smart mouth." It was a thing Jack said often. There was no equivalent phrase in Spanish, or at least none that I knew of, so I had first understood it as a sort of compliment: Matthew had a voice and mouth he knew how to use. It was because he was born in America, because he had the green eyes, blond hair, and pale skin of his white father; because instead of going by Mateo, as his mother had named him, in school and at church he was Matthew. I thought, as I had a hundred times before, of the stories Manuel told of our own past in Colombia. In these stories, I hadn't cried when I was born and when it came time to speak, I didn't. "You were this close to being an autistic mongrel," he said one night, sectioning off an inch between his thumb and pointer finger, as if measuring the distance between two planets in the sky.

"Can we turn the AC on?" asked Matthew, a wildness in his eyes.

The ripe, briny rot wafting in hot through the vents materialized again and mixed with the smell of french fries and sweat lifting in the heat from the beige upholstery. Matthew pinched the bridge of his nose all ladylike. He wasn't afraid of anyone, not even Jack. That's what he had really been saying. This was what I loved most, sitting inside a family that wasn't my own, understanding them better than they did themselves.

"Oh wait, right. It's been broken for months."

Jack lifted his hand from the steering wheel. He gripped the knob controlling the fan and stared back at Matthew through the mirror.

Look at what you're making me do, his eyes said as he turned the fan off.

Talía groaned, the magazine fell to the floor. She leaned in closer to the window and touched her forehead to the glass, paying no mind to the exploding flies.

Click!—Matthew tore into his thumb again, the pink flesh sliding in and out of his mouth.

My hand crept over the middle seat toward his thigh. I wanted him to feel how I felt—lucky—even here, in the stench and heat, crossing this no-man's-land to a campsite in a place called Naples. When the tips of my fingers graced the hem of his shorts, I held on, and nobody—not Matthew, not Jack, not Talía—noticed.

We had to spray down the van and unload the chairs and cooler, then set up camp. Jack had delivered these instructions as if permitting us a place to sleep tonight, since nothing was a given when he felt the need to assert his authority.

Only a few seconds after his mom and Jack had gone off into the campgrounds, Matthew started talking: "You shouldn't have come." Like a punch, the words left me breathless and stunned. "I mean, you didn't have to come." Matthew tugged on the hose without undoing the tangle around the wooden post. "I know, I know, I invited you. I couldn't have gone through this weekend alone, I mean it." Matthew always started with the sharpest version of his thoughts, then whittled them down until all the edges were lost. But the bits splintered off in revision were what I kept and held on to. I untangled the hose, feeling small and useful. From one moment to the next, water shot out with the smell of hot rubber. Matthew didn't question it. He dug his thumb into the narrow metal opening of the hose, forcing the water out into a sharp jet. The spray thundered across the windshield, along the hood, down the chrome grille, over the license plate with a black frame and yellow letters saying "United States Army." There was an emptiness in his eyes now, his mind elsewhere. It frightened me how he didn't even have to go anywhere to abandon me. Where he went when he fell silent was a mystery to me, since I never felt more present, more alive and myself than when we were together. Looking at Matthew, I saw who I wasn't and who I could yet become.

"I would go anywhere you go," I finally said, casting my words to Matthew like a rope, even if I knew they wouldn't pull him back to me.

Jack, tall and skeletal, could still be seen across the parking lot. His white tank top was tucked into camo pants. A forest-green explorer hat hung like a target over the back of his neck. He dressed no differently in Miami. At first, I had been struck by how terrifically out of place Jack looked lurching through the aisles of grocery stores and the lobbies of banks. Now I couldn't think of Jack without these clothes. They belonged on his body as the color blue belonged in the sky. He craned his neck sharply. He had eyes in the back of his head or shoulders—eyes everywhere. He swatted the air toward us with his hand, which meant *Get to work.*

I figured there was a reason for all this. The way Jack treated us like men when we were just boys could be nothing less than a father's lesson on love; he was testing how far he could push the two of us to love each other—and how perfect it would be if that were the case, if it were true only love could run deep through a person.

Matthew scraped the last of the flies off the van with the edge of his hand. He snapped his wrist, casting their bodies off. The hose fell to the ground. Without regard for his leather sandals, he stomped through puddles to the back of the van.

I wanted to direct Matthew's attention to the car ride, to every little thing he had said, and say, *Stop doing this to yourself.*

Instead, I picked the hose up from the ground and turned the water off. Then I wound the hose around my arm like a lasso the way my mother did at home. I knew Jack would check to see if we had left things as we had found them, even if the hose had been tangled around its post; the reality of the world didn't matter as much as his vision of it. This gift for anticipating what others wanted was the source of my goodness.

I avoided the pits of water around the van and found Matthew in front of the open trunk with his thumb in his mouth, staring fixedly at the cargo. A cluster of flies was marooned on the pale islands of his feet, and dark, piss-like stains stood out on the front of his shorts.

I climbed into the trunk and handed Matthew two of the folding chairs with great care, imagining I was putting all my love into these heavy bundles. The other two chairs I hauled over my shoulder and slid off the bumper to the ground, almost shyly. The blue cooler with the white lid we carried together, but even as we walked, I held my side higher to lessen the weight Matthew carried. It was what my mother would have done.

Through the opening in the wall of trees, we found sun-bleached picnic tables and prehistoric grills scattered under the dappled shade of tall trees. I had the sense of witnessing something private, as if the walls around each family had vanished in the rooms the palms and shrubs made. It thrilled me to watch and eavesdrop, to glimpse how other people lived when they thought no one was looking.

In one room, a father with his hand wrapped around the neck of a beer danced bachata by a grill. The smoke enveloped him in its hazy light. A mother was putting out paper plates and plastic utensils on the picnic table for the hot dogs blistering over the flames. She noticed flies perched on the bowl of sliced oranges and swatted them away. Two shirtless boys who looked like miniatures of their father ran circles around a tree, swinging branches at each other like in *The Last Samurai*. The girl in a pink sundress must have been around sixteen. She sat with her back to the picnic table and fanned herself with a paper plate folded in half. Her voice was loud and plaintive, cooing *Mami* and *Papi*, as she complained about the sun and her brothers and the hot dogs burning on the grill.

I watched them, spellbound. What would it be like to grow up like this, with both of my parents, with a brother who wasn't many years older than me and from a different marriage? What would it be like if I weren't always the guest?

In one of Manuel's tales, we were at the finca of some relatives for a party. Everyone was drinking, eating, dancing, and so it wasn't until hours later, once they lit the three candles on the cake for me, that they realized I was missing. It was my birthday. They searched for me under every cot and bed, in every cabinet and closet, every bathroom and shed, even in the chicken coop and stables. Melodramas spilled out from the aunties and girl cousins searching the tamarind trees around the house, holding on tightly to their skirts. Perhaps the Guerrilla had stolen me. Or perhaps a snake or spider had stung me. Perhaps I had fallen down a well, into a pool or the river, forever lost. My brother, the narrator of this story, was the hero who found me in the middle of a field across from the house. Somehow, I had gotten past the barbed wire fence and nestled myself beside a sleeping cow, where I, too, slept. Myths like this hovered over the everyday surface of my life; I was always unprepared when they swooped down on me, revealing something of what we had lost since the move.

Because I was only six when we left Colombia, I had no memories of my own there. And since our mother never spoke of the past, I only had Manuel's stories to go off. In our lost kingdom, we'd had maids, the latest clothes and games shipped over from the USA, a second home with a sparkling pool in the lush mountains outside the city where lawyers and doctors lived. My brother remembered a time when he was among the popular kids, when every day after school there were six boys crammed on the couch stuffing their mouths with fries and racing cars on the television. My brother told me all of this in the tiny, hot apartment in Little Havana, where more often than not we found ourselves alone, surrounded by the hum of the window fan and the yellow circle cast by the bulb in the kitchen, like two princes waking up from a long sleep, realizing we were in exile.

My mother and brother never would've spent a weekend camping like this. We would've gone to the outlet mall or a restaurant. To the beach only if I begged, but never in the water. We would come back home, retreat into our separate rooms to watch MTV or call Colombia. But this story was proof: We had known nature; we had known family—we hadn't always been this way. It was clear to me that my mother and brother had chosen the past over real life. They moved through Miami in a willful daze, as if the less they saw of this city, the more alive and fully formed our hometown would remain. It was one or the other, and they had made their choice. This trip to Naples was another choice in a series of choices that set me apart from my mother and brother, and these days that was reason enough to do anything.

"What are you looking at?" shouted the girl in the pink sundress, shooing me away with her paper plate like a stray dog. "This ain't no show."

Jolted by her voice, I almost screamed. I felt visible, as if I suddenly gave off light. I never could tell when I was and wasn't seen.

Without looking at her, I mouthed *sorry* and turned to Matthew like we had something important to discuss. My expression must have shown my fear or embarrassment because Matthew's face shed its seriousness from one moment to the next; he was back at my side, returned from his thoughts. It was like the time-lapse videos we watched in science class. A massive, sudden change.

"You're already making friends," Matthew said, punching my shoulder, knocking any fear out of my body. Laughter spilled from both of our mouths.

The campsites branched out from the dirt path like private rooms. Recessed in the trees were sleek tents catching the sun, camping chairs arranged in circles around ashen pits, and large dogs lapping water from plastic pails. I could have been anyone else, if only the world were different by a degree or an inch, by the distance my brother had caught between his fingers one night not so long ago. I'd almost forgotten where we were going when suddenly Talía and Jack came into view. Matthew dropped his side of the cooler and ran to his mother's arms. I dragged the cooler the rest of the way. The sun lay in a crisp, golden sheet over them and it hit me that I didn't want another life. This family that took me every other weekend when my mother worked back-to-back shifts at the lab. This family that took me now that Manuel wanted nothing to do with me. Who loved me like family. This was all mine.

"Preciosos," Talía said. "Como hermanos."

She waved us together with the black disposable camera in her hand, her bracelets clinking up and down her forearm. I lined my back up with Matthew's, our heads together. Matthew pushed his skull against mine, and I pushed back. I laughed, tasting the salt of my sweat on my lips, smelling the earth already clinging to my body. Then Talía called Jack's name in a whine. When he didn't come, she sucked her lips and pulled him away from the patch of ground he was sweeping clear for the tent. He stood behind us, his arms reaching far beyond our shoulders, thumbs up on both hands. The three of us stared ahead at Talía.

"Whiskey!" she said, snapping the picture.

She had collected the three of us, brought us together and made a family. It was she who was at our center, where I wanted to be, where one day I hoped to find myself, with these men or others. I wondered what it would be like if my mother were more like Talía, who was soft, feminine, smiling—not like a woman trying to be both mother and father, trying to be everything. Talía would never forget she was a mother. Feeling shame and guilt and pity all at once, I wrapped my arms around Matthew's shoulders. Talía noticed and, thinking we were posing for another picture, crouched to get us from a lower angle. Jack dropped his head, his shadow spreading and deepening over us. Talía snapped another picture, and this time we all yelled *Whiskey!*

Not a second later, Jack gripped our shoulders tight.

"Don't get too cozy," he said, shaking us from our ears to our toes. The floor beneath my feet fell away. I heard Talía say, "Are they not adorable?" to herself, to the air, because Jack wasn't the kind of man who found anything adorable. He let go of us, and then Talía flew, hanging over his shoulder, laughing.

"Let those boys get to work, woman," he said, carrying her away like a sack of rice.

I noticed the sweat smeared on my forearms, belonging to either Matthew or Jack, and ran my arms across my face.

The campfire crackled like in the movies. Smoldering flecks rose above the flames but disappeared into the night without getting too far. My skin mesmerized me: the way the oranges deepened into reds, then lightened into yellows. Everyone else, with their heads bowed in prayer, glowed like I did. Around us, the darkness of the forest was boundless and complete, almost solid.

Matthew's family prayed before every meal and before bed every night. The first time I'd stayed with them, I returned from brushing my teeth to find Jack flanked by Matthew and Talía, all three kneeling at the side of the bunk bed in Matthew's room. It took me a moment to realize what they were doing; and then I wasn't sure whether I was supposed to join them or not. I sat at Matthew's right and looked over the curve of his cheeks at Jack with his long, quivering lashes and Talía with her full lips moving silently over private words. I couldn't remember the last time my brother and mother had prayed as a family, or if we ever had. Then, as now, Jack said *Amen*, and Talía and Matthew followed, and without thinking, I said it, too, though I had been watching them the entire time, rather than praying.

We ate the way Jack liked, in silence. Our mouths moved over the aluminum foil pouches unfolded across our laps, the pale pieces of fish surrounded by moats of oily juice. Talía had also prepared roasted yams and sweet plantains before we'd left Miami that morning. Groans came from Jack, from somewhere inside him, sounds of tremendous pleasure and relief. She always cooked his favorite foods, and after every meal she asked if he'd been reminded of Jamaica. She never made arepas or anything Venezuelan.

When a boom box somewhere nearby belted out, Jack flinched. We heard bottles clinking and people laughing, reminding us Jack couldn't control all of the world. I hummed with the music, low enough to feel the rhythm thrumming up and down my throat without anyone hearing me. I stopped just as the song finished, and I started again as a new one played. *That was the last one*, I thought after each song returned me to the crackling fire. Nervous, I looked around: Matthew sat on the ground between his mother's legs, eating the plantains with his fingers; Talía plucked the bones from his portion of fish; and across the fire, sitting by himself, Jack unfolded a second aluminum bundle over his first. The silence each song left behind felt final and bleak. Somewhere out there, in the twitching darkness below the trees, were people having fun. When a new song boomed out, the joy I felt was so vivid I could almost see the music spread through the darkness in a wave of brilliant colors.

"You boys better eat quick and get to bed," Jack said, as he spit a mouthful of bones into the fire. He could parse them from the fish with his tongue, collecting them in his cheek without effort. "Tomorrow will be an early one."

Matthew gathered his legs below him and turned around to face Talía. *But it's Friday night*, his eyes pled. When she said nothing, he stood up and sat back down next to me, smirking as if we already shared a secret plan. I'd noticed before how he moved from me to Talía, from one allegiance to the other. Perhaps our whole friendship was an elaborate means to irritate Jack. But when he let our knees touch, I nodded instinctively, letting myself be recruited to his side.

"This is really good," I said to Jack across the fire. In truth, I hated the fish: I mashed every morsel between my fingers until it was a flaky white mound, imagining a needle lodging in my throat if I wasn't thorough and missed a bone. I was too shy to ask Talía to pluck my fish like she did Matthew's. Instead I found myself saying these things I didn't mean and wishing they came true. Because I wanted Jack to know I loved him no matter how difficult he was as a stepfather to Matthew. And I wanted Matthew to know he was the most perfect, beautiful person I'd ever met. And I wanted Talía to know I wanted a mother just like her. I wouldn't hesitate to say or do anything I could to make this happen.

"At least I have one grateful boy," said Jack. He wiped the grease from his lips with the back of his hand and stood up. He made his way around the fire toward Talía—we all watched him—and awkwardly, as if it were a last-minute decision on the way over, he ran his hand through my hair with a firm, terrifying pressure. I felt each finger rake across my scalp, even after he had moved on to Talía. Matthew looked away at the fire. When he stuck his thumb in his mouth, I knew I was alone again.

Behind us, Jack kissed Talía on the ear, then on the opposite cheek, bending her head from one side to the other, spreading his love evenly. She didn't stop him. She let herself be kissed. Before long, she was arching her head, opening up new regions of her skin to his mouth. At some point my own parents must have been the same: two adults in love kissing in front of a fire, though it was hard to imagine. Manuel always said *Who?* when I asked him to tell me about my father. The one photograph I had of him was wedged into the corner of the corkboard in my bedroom; it showed him and me at my grandfather's house in Gualanday, the pool behind us a sapphire jewel. We sat under the star fruit trees in the courtyard, just the two of us. On his lap, I grinned with all my teeth, a smile I didn't smile anymore. He stared ahead, his eyes large behind his glasses, unaware he would one day be separated from his only son. I remembered my father just as he was in this picture, in front of a pool, frozen in time. It was shocking to me that he had been central to my mother's and brother's stories, but I was ashamed of how little I knew of him, of our story, and how little I wanted to know.

Jack's long black fingers now crawled over Talía's head like spiders. They stumbled down her shoulders, then her arms, kneading circles where they stopped. Her whimpers sounded like they had escaped, as if she meant to hold them in. Jack was showing us that he and Talía shared an allegiance no one could shake. "Go on now," he said to us, lifting his mouth from her neck. "Shower time."

The openness of their love put me in a mood. Walking to the restrooms to wash up before bed, I held on to Matthew's arm near his armpit, a cave of damp heat I wanted to enter.

He wrestled his arm away.

"Not now."

After our showers, we found the tent standing. Inside were two inflatable beds, our backpacks between them. After putting sheets on the beds, we sat in our underwear, sharing a box of raisins and playing a card game Matthew made up as we went.

When Talía asked if I wanted to call my mother before bed, I realized I would've forgotten had she not said something. My mother answered almost immediately, and I stepped out of the tent to tell her about my day. She laughed when she heard about the flies. She said she was in my bed and described the dinner she had eaten by herself since Manuel was God knows where. I wandered away from the camp as she talked. A cool breeze came and went around my ankles. The gravel crunched beneath my bare feet. Crickets and other bugs I didn't know cried out. I could have sworn I'd lived this moment before—in another life, in a dream last week, in Colombia. I kept walking. Hearing footsteps and laughter nearby, I turned to see Talía and Jack with towels slung over their shoulders, on their way to the showers; they went on without seeing me, groping each other in the dark. My mother was talking, and I almost said *sorry* for not listening, but she hadn't noticed. A cousin of mine in Colombia was sick. She was wiring money to transfer him to a private hospital after a nurse at the government clinic had misread his prescription and given him ten times his dose of medicine. He was breaking out in hives all over. "Under his tongue, between his butt cheeks. Even his testi-cles." She paused. "Can you imagine?" I fought the urge to hang up on her and be through with the call. Tomorrow I would not call her. If everyone in Colombia died tonight, I would be happy. She wouldn't have to work as hard. She could spend more time with me and my brother. Thinking this, I wished everyone dead.

Back at the tent, Matthew was splayed on his stomach with his arms circling his head in the way he always slept. I lowered myself slowly onto the air mattress, aware of every part of my body, as if one thoughtless movement could rip the tent in half. We had never slept side by side, since at home Matthew had a bunk bed Jack had gotten from their church on which we slept stacked on top of each other, together but apart. Now, I left a few inches be-tween our bodies, my arm hanging off the mattress and my leg teetering on the seam. The sheets already smelled warm and sweet. I wanted more of the smell, more of the rush and vertigo it gave me, like I was creeping to the edge of myself and staring down a precipice. I could have more. I could close my eyes and roll over. I could touch Matthew with all of myself. It would look perfectly normal, even tender. Talía would think so when she and Jack re-turned from the showers. She might even take our picture.

I pretended to sleep when Talía and Jack returned to the tent. I could hear the floor crinkling like grocery bags as they got dressed. And for a moment I even felt their eyes rest on me and Matthew with something like pride, or love, before the light went out. We hadn't prayed tonight, and now, alone in the dark, I wished I wouldn't fall asleep yet, or ever. My hand probed the distance separating me from Matthew, an inch or two in which I could feel the heat his body gave off. I opened my eyes; everything looked lunar and colossal, in shades of blue-gray. I didn't move under the weight of my body stretching out from me like a landscape, like a world apart from the boy I loved. Falling asleep, I thanked God for Matthew.

A hand was pressed over my mouth. The shadow towering above me assembled itself into Jack's outline in the early morning light. As my breath filled the space between my lips and his hand, I thought of my mother whispering into my ear, "Mi tesoro" and "I would die if anything happened to you," many weekends ago when she let me sleep over at Matthew's house for the first time. I could tell my mother about Jack, about all the mornings he woke us before sunrise with his so-called Boys' Missions. One weekend he'd set up a boot camp in the backyard by moonlight. A barbed wire tunnel we had to crawl through using only our elbows as the first birds sang over our heads. A rope tied between the mango trees we had to cross like monkeys as Jack threatened us with the hose. I could tell her how every Sunday he woke us before sunrise to wash the van until it sparkled brighter than any other in the church parking lot. I could tell her about any other of Jack's Boys' Missions. I could—and made the choice not to.

Jack let me go when he read obedience in my eyes. Almost immediately, I missed the leathery surface of his palm on my mouth with a pressure both frightening and comforting. He woke

Matthew in the same way. When Jack stood, the air mattress jumped like a trampoline; I bounced to the center, finally against Matthew. Even with his neck bent, Jack grazed the top of the tent with his head. He mimed jamming his feet into shoes and tying the laces with swift tugs. In the other bed, Talía was sleeping with her arms crossed over her chest like a mummy. Jack nodded at the world beyond the tent, and something of the gesture told us the clock was ticking. We got up noiselessly, except for the soft rustling of our dressing. Talía, mummified, didn't stir.

The headlights of the waiting van singled out a row of trees. Matthew took the back seat. I crossed the yellow beams on tiptoe. Looking from door to door, I realized I could sit in the back with Matthew or up front with Jack. In the foggy darkness of the window, I saw myself smile at Matthew, weakly, guiltily, and then attempt a false, jaunty wave. Boldly, I took Talía's place with an odd heaving in my rib cage, feeling ridiculous.

"Open up the lunch box at your feet," said Jack. Inside of the blue pouch were two protein bars, two bananas, and a large water bottle. Matthew looked down at the provisions I passed him as if he'd forgotten how to eat. *Just play along*, I tried saying with my eyes, but Matthew looked through me.

"Why isn't Mami coming?" His mouth was still sticky with sleep.

"This is a Boys' Mission," said Jack. He wrapped his arm behind my seat to reverse out of the parking spot. "Now eat."

We left the campgrounds. The digital clock on the dashboard said ten past five. I turned on the radio to Jack's station and adjusted the volume until he was satisfied. We weren't supposed to talk while the radio was on, especially if it was a pastor going on about how God controlled every move we made. My own mother never took us to church. There were no crosses on the walls of our apartment or Bibles at our bedsides. She would be awake by now, heating an arepa over the blue flames of the stove and listening to Caracol on the radio. Jack imposed his vision so ruthlessly, so righteously, it was like a trap we had all fallen into and knew no way out of. I almost looked forward to the unnecessary struggles, the shouted commands, the threats of violence—they were nothing like the passivity of my mother, who would now be dumping the rest of her coffee into the sink and hurrying off to work. Like a chicken without its head, Manuel had said. My mother hadn't been able to hold on to my father, or his, or our homeland, or even Manuel.

A short drive from the campground, Jack pulled over. He parked on the shoulder and we got out of the van, led by the beam of his flashlight. Since there was no obvious path into the woods, we made our own, like a small dispatch of ants burrowing through new soil. My senses sharpened with alarm, fearing how little I could see and how much I could imagine. Around us, animals fled, crushing branches below their feet. Only the birds in the trees held their stations. Past a felled trunk covered in moon-bright mushrooms, the branches came apart, opening onto a dirt road large enough for a small car to drive through. The sky came into view—a pale, silvery blue sheet rippling like water between the canopies.

"Look," Jack whispered. His flashlight shot off into the trees.

We stopped behind his wingspan. An iguana stretched across the dirt road, no more than ten feet away. It looked like it was doing push-ups, though its arms were those of a frail, old man. For a moment this was funny, then I realized the animal was alive and real, and therefore unpredictable. Breaths quivered through the layers of skin hanging around its neck like a bib. Dim yellow spikes along the curve of its head flared up and down. And its eyes flickered wildly. Looking back at the wall of trees, I could no longer see the passage we had taken; all the trees flung their branches in the same dark, identical way. Suddenly, Matthew rushed toward the iguana in a sprint. The iguana ran across the path and disappeared. Jack laughed. Here was Matthew, fearless in the face of an obstacle, bold and stupid. This was something Jack could appreciate.

We turned right, following Jack in a line. There was no way to guess what he saw, what compelled him to bring us here. But I assumed he knew where we were going. This thought comforted me.

The flashlight's beam faded as the world began to light up. Jack pointed out the red triangles nailed to the tree trunks, looking past Matthew at me, as if I were the one who needed to hear his message.

"The triangles stay where they're nailed," said Jack, "because the trees grow upward from their branches, not their trunks. In a year, when we come back, the trees will be taller, but the triangles will be in the same place marking the trail."

In a year, I thought to myself. I couldn't imagine living so long.

The sun cut sharp, dazzling shapes into the canopy. We continued to walk under the trees, bound by silence. I put my hand on Matthew's shoulder blade—*I love you, I love you*—hoping this message would pass through my fingers. I felt a fear I'd had before: I needed the people in my life more than they needed me. This fear made me want to be useful and polite and good so no one would ever tire of me; I had noticed the way some people, like my brother and father, drained those around them. And then I saw the problem from a different angle, in a different light, blinding and new: I had to care less about people. I had to separate myself from others. Let them need and miss me. When I pulled my touch from Matthew, experimentally, the shape of my hand clung to the fabric of his shirt like a ghost. Nothing exhausted me more than trying not to care. It was an effort, always. But it was necessary.

I had no clue how much time had passed when we stopped at a fork in the road. The heat weighed on me, and holding my neck up felt like an enormous feat. It was as if we were underwater.

"So what are we doing, boys? Short or long?"

Jack bent down to the height of the green metal sign staked low to the ground.

Despite reading the signpost—one mile one way, seven the other—I had no clue what these distances meant. The most I could remember walking was the length of the mall with my mother.

With a faint groan, Matthew threw a hasty glance down the two paths, shook his head, and fell silent.

"Long," I said.

Matthew glared at me. But it was the right answer, the only one Jack wanted to hear.

After the fork, the sparse trees became dense. The branches swept my shoulders like waxy feathers. Matthew's neck reddened, his hair all clumped into sweaty spikes. I could have said *stop*, turned back, but I waited. I wanted to prove to myself—and to Jack—that I could work through the fear roiling inside me. Past the thicket came a field strewn with tall yellow grasses, where a small white sign warned us of panthers. The ground below our feet became dry and coppery red. We stopped when we found tracks in the dirt, but after a pause, we kept walking. There was no turning back. I hadn't worked through my fear so much as committed to it. The trail continued into a forest, narrowing again until we came to two large sunken mud pits, one after the other, the canopy above them clear as if God himself had reached through and punched his fists into the ground. Spindly branches clung precariously around the pits' muddy sides; we skirted our way around their perimeters without falling into their depths. Miles and miles later, the path before us ended abruptly at the shore of a swamp. The mangroves, the only tree I knew the name of, stood on their roots above the brown water, their understory streaked with living shadows. Winged insects patrolled the edge of the water. Tadpoles festered in the shallows. I saw none of the red triangles Jack had pointed out earlier.

"Jesus Christ," he said, turning to us. He looked down the narrow path in the trees we had taken. "Wait here."

In the silence, the two of us looked down, then back up again.

"Does he think he's just going to find a boat lying around?" I asked.

The wind fingered the water; Matthew ignored me.

A moment later, Jack returned with a branch almost as long as his legs. He tightened the shoelaces of his boots and, without saying anything else, entered the water. The brown murk flung itself away from his body, then raced back toward his legs.

"This is a Boys' Mission," he shouted, like he had so many times before. "We don't tell anyone about this."

Matthew entered next with his arms out in front of him. The water reached his waist.

My heart stilled as I looked down at the water; there was no telling what lurked below the surface of my own face, reflected.

The water swallowed me next. My shoes sank into the loam of the swamp, sucked in like quicksand, and I hurried my steps, thrashing through the water. My soaked shoes and shorts became impossibly heavy; the water felt warm and thick, as if it were living. Ahead of us, Jack churned the water with his staff, frightening away whatever awaited our next steps. I was ready for something to touch my legs below the surface, for a snake to wrap around my hips and drag me away. Would Jack and Matthew even notice? And if they did, how far would they go to save me? I grabbed the back of Matthew's shirt in my fist. His shoulders rose, then shivered, registering my touch with surprise or disgust. I wouldn't let go. I would drag him with me. There was no end to the water ahead. Matthew turned around. His face was saying, *I'm sorry*, and I realized we really were in danger; we were wet and cold and miles from help. I latched my fingers around Matthew's elbow. My hand squeezed down his forearm until I held his hand underwater. I wanted to protect him from Jack, Jack who was his stepfather, Jack who would, after this weekend, if we made it through this day, continue to be in his life for a long time. By Sunday evening I would be back with my mother and brother in our apartment where we kept the AC at seventy-four and where there were more than ten channels on the television, where Matthew and I would have to exist without each other again.

As the other shore came into view, an unexpected emptiness opened inside of me. My fingers twined with Matthew's, our hands the same color as the water. I no longer wanted to make it to the other side. I wanted to die, just once, just now. Here.

The sun was slumped behind the trees by the time we reached the camp. The smell rising from my shirt was ripe and green; I had never smelled like this before. I didn't care anymore if Jack or Matthew liked me, or if they even thought about me. I was just happy to have survived.

I marched past Talía straight to the bathroom, leaving her swinging her head toward Jack for an explanation. We'd been gone all day. In the shower, the water came out in icy spurts, and I washed my hair with the bar of soap left in the stall by someone before me. My skin tightened and tingled until I felt nothing at all. I would stay here until the weekend was over. I hadn't even brought a towel.

The knock on the door startled me. Below the divider, the two pale feet squirming in their leather sandals were Matthew's. He knocked again. "It's just me." I clenched my fists and dug my knuckles into my thighs without volunteering anything to the silence. Trying to see myself as he might, naked and crying, I felt alien, ugly and frightening, but I didn't want him to leave. I slid the lock open and pushed the door back an inch, giving him permission to come in if he wanted to. I turned my back to the door; I couldn't bear looking at him as he entered. Matthew, to my surprise, removed his shirt, stepped out of his shorts and underwear, and flung his clothes over the door of the stall. His arms circled my waist from behind; mine, reaching up and back, circled his neck. I felt oddly safe now. We stood together, bones trembling.

The next thing I knew, I was on my knees. There was only a soft shock as I cradled the weight of Matthew's penis in my palm, as gently as if cupping a small, injured bird. The spray of the shower surrounded me in a deafening hiss; I felt torn away from Matthew, so far away, even as I held a part of him—the most precious, vital part of him. I wiped my eyes once, twice, trying to take in everything in front of me. Down his stomach and thighs, down the center of his pale penis, each thread of water was as fascinating and beautiful as a river. Finally, when I looked up at him, he smiled. But I could see he didn't want this like I did. His lips quivered with doubt, with pity; he felt bad for me, bad enough that he didn't stop me when I planted a kiss on the head of his penis, then a second on the reddening pouch of his balls. "You don't have to," he said, in a whisper so low his voice all but vanished before he finished speaking. I wanted him to love me, but there wasn't love in his eyes. His face was slack now. "But what if I want to?" I said, pulling his hands to me, kissing his chewed-up nail beds. He was enduring my touch. It hurt to know this, to ignore it anyway.

After the camping trip, we didn't hear from Talía for a week. Matthew wasn't at soccer practice. Our calls went to their machine. A month later, just before school started, Talía called my mother to tell her they were moving to West Virginia. I listened carefully: A church in the mountains had hired Jack to lead troubled teenagers on camping trips, to teach them about responsibility, survival, and God. They were leaving in a week, just like that.

Later, the lights off, my mother whispered my name to the back of my head.

"Are you okay?" I asked her.

"I can't sleep," she said, a problem she'd had for years. "What happened in Naples?"

I turned to face my mother. She looked unsteadily at the space between us, where her hand lay not quite reaching for me. The clock on her nightstand cast a faint red glow behind her head. The faintest sounds came from my brother's room down the hall. What I said next could destroy us.

"Hijo."

"I already told you. We ate fish around a fire the first night. We hiked through mangroves in the morning. Jack went fishing, Talía grilled, Matthew and I played games."

"Are you sure that's all?"

My foot found hers under the covers. "What's wrong?"

"You would tell me if something happened. Right?"

"Of course." I took her hand and kissed it. "I'll always tell you everything."

"Okay. Good night."

"Good night, Mami. Te amo."

"Santiago?"

"Yes?"

"Come here."

I inched back toward her. Her chin playfully prodded my shoulder blades, and she wrapped her arms around me. I didn't have another friend for a long time.

SIX

I sat at one end of the narrow hospital waiting room. The man touching his khaki shorts sat at the other. Halfway between us were a small internal window and the doors my mother had entered what seemed like a long time ago. The outline of a head, sometimes two, passed like a shadow behind the cloudy glass. *Save me*, I called out to the nurses without speaking. Half of me wanted to see the man caught, shamed, punished; the other half, not wanting anything bad to happen to the man, kept still. Was this really happening? The man looked at me head-on, even nodded, squeezing his crotch over the khaki shorts. I was twelve this summer and I had never felt more frightened, never so close to—I didn't know any other word for it—*living*. Nothing stranger had ever happened to me.

An hour earlier, when we'd entered the waiting room, the man had greeted us with a smile. He didn't take his eyes off us. He had the look of someone trying to remember the face of a person he once knew. My mother ignored him, as she did most men, and I remained vaguely aware of him in my periphery. He could've been the father of any one of the white boys I'd gone to school with over the years—the Lukes, the Ryans—and for a moment I imagined he was and wanted him to recognize me. Then my mother's name was called, and she disappeared behind the doors with a nurse.

I didn't know how scared or concerned I should feel. She was there to remove her IUD, a T-shaped rod the size of her thumb, she said. The little anchor had been implanted in her uterus after my birth to ensure I would be the last one. After the move to America and all the work of getting our lives together again, she had forgotten to take it out. Now, the IUD had dug its arms into her uterine wall. If it wasn't surgically removed, it could continue to move through her insides or cause an infection strong enough to end her. It wasn't serious, she said, but if anything happened to her, I should call my brother. She had told me this in the taxi to the hospital, a story I had yet to really absorb. And though I didn't understand why, I knew I wouldn't give up this role for anything. The feeling of occupying a secret world with my mother was everything to me.

Still smiling, still touching himself, the man asked if I wanted to watch television. I nodded as the screen in the waiting room turned on to the Food Network. The volume was so low we had to read the subtitles at the bottom of the screen. Every few seconds the man turned to look at me: He stared fixedly and seemed to be on the verge of speaking, but he only chuckled, as if we were not strangers in a waiting room. His khaki shorts rode slowly up his milk-pale thighs as he fanned his legs open and closed, the keys and coins inside his cargo pockets jingling.

Should I touch myself, too? I had done it before. I'd filled the gap at the bottom of my mother's bathroom door with a towel. I'd washed my hands and laid out another clean towel on the bath mat to sit on. Then, with my legs in a diamond, I would close my eyes. Touching my penis, I imagined someone else's hand touching me in the dark; I thought of boys on the internet until it was hard and suddenly my hand seemed to know what to do.

Now, in the waiting room, I decided against doing anything. I had, in my whole twelve years of life, only perfected the art of staying put.

I sat up straight, crossed my legs beneath the chair. And when he realized I wasn't going anywhere, that I wasn't going to stop him, that *I* wanted him to go on, his expression changed. Suddenly he had a magician's demeanor, playful yet serious, like he was performing an amazing trick for me. Horrified, then thrilled, I slid beneath one big black feeling, then another, and another. This was happening as some few feet away my mother was cut open.

The man squeezed the lump in his khaki shorts. Under the fabric, the log of his penis looked squishy yet dense, like those plastic sleeves filled with jelly and glitter I had played with as a child. The man concealed the outline of his penis, then lifted his hand to reveal it again. He did this over and over. His penis stretched the length of his hand.

I understood this was wrong, so wrong, and yet it was ravishing, this secret, this beginning of a new world. The air rang all around me. The universe was calling me into being.

It was a long time before a nurse called the man, too late to save me. And it only struck me then, as he disappeared through the doors, the puddle below his chair drying into a smear, that he was here for another person. A real person.

The same nurse buzzed me in next. I followed her down a corridor of blue and white curtains, almost all of them closed. When I peered through an opening expecting an empty bed, my heart leapt: The man from the waiting room was sitting on a chair with a woman's hand in his.

The nurse opened the curtain of the room across from the man, where my mother lay in a hospital bed with an IV in the bend of her arm. She stirred when I touched her foot, then her leg. She was still sleepy, dazed. She strained to look at me without lifting her head.

SEVEN

It wasn't unusual for my mother to leave before daybreak and return after dark when she worked at the restaurant or when she was cleaning for the family on Fisher Island, but when Sharon offered her full-time work, paid in cash, there were nights our mother didn't come home at all.

Sharon, a retired doctor from Boston with no children or spouse, had cancer. Sharon was in remission. Sharon was healthy again. Then Sharon was dying again. Her apartment was on the seventeenth floor of a beachfront building in Sunny Isles. Turkish rugs covered the unfinished concrete floors, and Japanese scrolls with hazy mountains and calligraphy hung from the walls. My mother related these details to me, fixating on them as if they revealed something strange and impractical about Sharon. More than anything, though, she loved the apartment's view of the ocean, cruise ships and barges frozen on the horizon, the distance and stillness for miles. Sharon was taken by the fact that my mother had worked as a microbiologist in Colombia; they could talk about science and medicine despite the language barrier and still understand each other. My mother often helped prepare lunch or dinner, which really meant watching Sharon cook and telling her stories about Colombia, since my mother had loathed the kitchen since she was a kid. Sharon taught her about feng shui and Buddhism and took her to synagogue on Friday nights. They explored fancy grocery stores where Sharon bought salmon steaks, artichoke hearts, and bottles of pink-hued wine from France. Sharon took her to watch ballet and plays in the theater downtown that resembled a spaceship, the seats so close to the stage my mother could see the actors breathing. And at night, before she left, my mother gave Sharon all her medicines. *Sharon*, my mother said her name so often I could imagine she was in love, and though I had no clue what she spent all day doing with this woman, it relaxed me to think at least she didn't seem to hate her job anymore.

The truth was, there wasn't enough housework to justify all the time she spent there. I learned this when we went over for Thanksgiving dinner. Sharon had cooked for us: a full turkey, mashed potatoes, and green beans with cranberry sauce. In our matching button-downs and V-neck sweaters, my brother and I sat perfectly upright, knowing we were on display. When asked what we wanted to be, I said the most impressive thing I could think of: "A nuclear engineer." My brother said a business manager, and Sharon made him promise her that he would go to medical school, that he would become a radiologist like her, like his father; she already knew everything about our lives from our mother. When I went to use the bathroom, I was shocked to discover the kitchen mirror was a two-way; I'd never seen anything stranger. On the other side of the opaque blue glass, as if through water, I glimpsed my mother, Manuel, and Sharon across the kitchen in the living room, and the open sky beyond. Sharon rose from her chair and glided to the kitchen in her long, baggy dress. She stood right in front of the mirror, washing a knife, then slicing into a pie on the counter with slow, measured movements. Despite the cancer, Sharon was plump. Her skin shone pale and smooth as marble, and her dark wig trembled down the sides of her face in two flimsy ribbons. I was so mesmerized I had a sudden urge to reach out and touch her, like I still couldn't believe she was real. Before we left, Sharon arranged the three of us on the balcony for a picture, and when my mother was in the bathroom Sharon told us: "You poor boys will have your mother back soon."

In the car, my mother explained Sharon was dying again.

Since we'd moved to Miami, Manuel was the one picking me up from school, taking orders from my mother over the phone, re-heating the meals she left in the fridge, and keeping an eye on me until she did or didn't get back from work, so that even though he was still just a boy, even though he was my brother, I had thought of him as a stand-in for a father. In Colombia, we would chase a soccer ball into the ravine next to our house and bathe in the ice-cold streams only we knew of along the mountain. . . . I staged these moments in my mind over and over and over. I was with Manuel as always, only now he wanted little to do with me, and it frightened me to think that maybe he had always felt I was a burden.

So I learned to take care of myself. I became my mother's confidant, and by the time I was twelve I could stay home alone. But one night took us back many years: Our mother had called from Sharon's, and I heard Manuel ask if she was sure it was legal. He held me off at a distance with his bony, ass-scratching hand. He nodded along like he was memorizing a list of chores or groceries; whatever our mother was saying was important. When the call ended, he crossed the living room to the kitchen and poured a glass of water from the tap in silence. I braced myself for the worst. Handing me the glass on the couch, he broke the news: They were sending me back to Colombia.

Who, I asked, and *why*, and I begged him to do something. To save me, *please*.

He dragged my suitcase out from under the bed, instructed me to start packing. I ran to the phone and stared at the row of digits until they swam. I didn't know how to call her back; I didn't know anything.

"Please," I said, "let me explain myself, let me stay, let me talk to our mother."

"It's too late," said Manuel. "She's already in the sky, on her way back to Ibagué."

For a long time I had wanted nothing more than to go back to Colombia, but now, with my breath caught in my throat, the whole world tipped off its axis and I grabbed the wall.

My brother had told me this story many times until I was numb and disbelieving, but tonight, when he laughed, when he called me gullible, when he said he could still convince me of anything,

I picked the glass up from the table, hurled the water at his face, and smashed it on the ground between us. I ran to the bathroom, locked the door behind me, and hid under the sink for hours.

What I didn't know was, that night, Sharon took her life with the help of our mother.

For years, I would think back to under that sink, to the gooseneck pipe, the bottle of Clorox my mother used to clean everything, the squat tub of my brother's hair gel, my mother's blow-dryer, and all the other shapes I memorized in the dark. I could never forget the smell.

When I turned thirteen, we moved to the gated community north of Miami, where the townhouses were identical and the nearest outside street was a twenty-minute walk away. I'd chosen the house with my mother when it was just a miniature on a map under a glass case in a sales office, and we visited its site once a week, sometimes more often, to watch the beams rise from the ground. We had picked the marble counters for the kitchen and bathrooms, the staircase in a blue-white, almost Grecian tile, and the plot on the edge of a man-made lake.

Our mother didn't let us forget that this house was only possible because of Sharon. Along with helping with the down payment, she'd left my mother a lump of money for us to move, two trusts worth ten thousand dollars for my brother and me to go to college, and the white convertible she hadn't driven in years. I saw Sharon everywhere I looked. Our garage was filled with her silver and china and paintings. They were for me, my mother said, for the day I had my own house. My mother agreed to give Sharon's white convertible to Manuel, the way she did with most things we asked for, like she was paying a debt she had incurred. That debt, though I didn't know it or feel it yet, was inside us.

Every morning, after dropping me off at school, Manuel drove another thirty minutes south, his school even farther than mine from the new house. On this, we were a united front: We would burn the world down before changing schools. Manuel stayed late for swim practice every afternoon. He'd lost years of speed and conditioning, he said, when I found him in the bathroom sitting with his feet in the sink and a razor in hand, for the first time looking small, stunted, a boy who hadn't grown in years. It was all for nothing, he'd said weeks later when he got kicked off the team. My mother let slip brief details about his life that he would never have told me himself: His father had forgotten his birthday; a spelling error on his immigration papers was delaying his residency card.

After school, the public bus dropped me off at a strip mall with the cheap Latin American grocer and the karate dojo where I took lessons until my mother was off in the evenings. Most days our sensei led us through choreographies of kicks and punches and stances until we memorized and perfected the katas for our belt ceremonies. On my favorite nights we put on spongy gloves and helmets that smelled of plastic and sweat and stepped onto the circular mats two at a time to spar. Manuel came to these fights when he could, and the sight of him cheering from the plastic chairs, among the mothers and fathers, made my bones feel hot inside. It both frightened and exhilarated me how easily I forgot all the rules, and swung for faces, groins, piling on punches until I had to be pulled off the boy on the ground. I bloodied several mouths, I broke a nose once. My roundhouse kick brought boys who were older, taller, heavier to their knees. I hated how good it felt to make my brother proud.

My mother now worked at a laboratory again. She'd been studying for her technician licensing exam while taking care of Sharon, toting a large green binder wherever she went. By the time my brother would come home from his girlfriend's house, my mother and I were already in bed watching television. Her favorite talk show was hosted by a Peruvian journalist with swoopy black bangs and thin, wire-rimmed glasses, whose face—resembling mine, boyish yet austere—visited my dreams. My brother, if he popped his head in to say hello, would just as quickly disappear to his room. Even though I had my own room, I slept with my mother for several years, as if each morning she might disappear.

When I was home alone, I kept the living room television on at all hours. I set the volume loud enough to make me feel like I was in a room full of people. I booted up the desktop computer and logged into chat rooms, where I talked to men from all over the world, told them I was seventeen instead of thirteen, learning just what to say to get them to masturbate for me on camera and message me every day saying they were thinking about me, their best boy. After my mother bought me a webcam—for a school project, I insisted—I touched myself the way men told me to, and when I was finished, I closed out of everything, all the pop-up ads, the chat boxes, the squares of tiny, glitching video. I never thought about what I was doing until I needed to do it again.

When Manuel came home and I was alone, he acted more like my brother. He taught me Colombian slang, cataloged all the tits and culos he'd ever touched, and described the difference between cubanas, dominicanas, and venezolanas, delivering these lessons with an air of determination and loyalty, like only he could give me this vital knowledge. I quieted the low hum in the background of my head telling me this was another ploy of his and went along wearily with his familiarity. I never stirred when he snuck out of the house at night. I greeted the girls he brought over when our mother worked as if each one was the first. When his girlfriend visited, I said nothing, and still said nothing when he went to the bathroom and she cornered me with questions about my brother's life. This was the price of doing what I did when I was alone.

This period of peace didn't last long. A few months later, when Manuel got rejected from every university he applied to and had to enroll in community college, he blamed my mother and me. If it wasn't for us, he would be going to medical school in Bogotá, becoming a radiologist like his father. He made himself almost completely absent from then on: We didn't know when he came or went, only that his clothes piled up on his bed, the dishes on his desk, little paper bracelets for concerts and clubs on the floor. The door to his room at the end of the hall was always open. In the drawers below his bed, I found an unopened deck of cards for a sex game and a box of blue Trojans.

Whenever they ran into each other, my mother told him this wasn't a hotel, until one day when he was out she gathered all his clothes—even the ones in the closet, hangers and all—in the center of his bed. She untucked the corners of the fitted sheets and tied the four ends together. The bundle slumped out the window like a body.

The following day, when Manuel came home, he went upstairs without saying hello. As always, I was alone. I stuffed my cum-stained socks beneath the sofa and watched his clothing on the other side of the sliding doors, baking under the sun in the backyard. A single lizard, pale as the skin below my wrists, crawled out from under his Miami Heat jersey, and a bright, cruel joy coursed through me. I was happy I hadn't done anything to bring his clothes inside.

"She's crazy," he said, storming down the stairs. "Do you see this? She's crazy."

He left the house with a backpack full of clothes like he was never coming back, but it wasn't more than a week before he drove the white convertible into a concrete median. I didn't know what deal he worked out with my mother after totaling Sharon's car, but from then on my brother was back at his desk, studying for hours. His room returned to its spotless state. He took to bouncing a blue rubber ball against the wall between his room and mine as he read problem sets aloud, repeating formulas and scientific names to himself. At first he only asked me to keep the television down, he could hear my silly cartoons from his room, but before long, if I let the microwave beep while he was studying, he screamed that I was trying to ruin his life. "I fried eggs for you every morning in Little Havana"—he yelled—"I washed your clothes in the rat-infested basement of that sorry building! Why can't you do a single thing for me?" I learned to shut doors and cabinets slowly, silently. With the grace of a swan, I tiptoed down the stairs so none creaked under my weight.

He'd had a whole life back in Colombia, my mother often said, another brother and sister, his father's children, no less related to him than I was. Best friends, too—el Negro, Camilo. His girlfriend, Luisa. And though my mother meant for me to see how much he had lost in the move, nothing changed the fact that my brother had willed his heart to stop loving us.

Later, I understood how difficult it was to love someone when you were bound together by forces outside your control. Later, I understood how the world our mother had brought us into had been so profoundly inhospitable to him that he couldn't endure it without hardening himself against everything, including me. Later, I understood clearly what my brother never did: We had both lost our history, our youth. There was nothing for us back in Colombia. Nothing for us anywhere.

EIGHT

By fifteen, I was on MySpace enough to know all the gay boys from Doral to West Palm, where they went to high school, who they were dating, and who could be found at which mall—Dolphin, Sawgrass, or Sunset—on a Friday night. There was an intimacy in watching the movements of their lives, their affairs and fights, even as they knew nothing of me. Since Matthew moved away, I had stayed home almost every weekend. I couldn't go anywhere without my mother asking too many questions. I spent hours online looking at boys I never imagined meeting in person. Which was why I was surprised when Leo found me.

We lived only a few miles away from each other. We would've gone to the same school had I transferred after the move. He was seven and his sister eleven when they left Venezuela. There was a faint scar on his cheek from the time he'd broken up a fight between his sister and mother. They had first lived in Jacksonville, but he couldn't remember why. Every few years they moved farther south—Daytona, Sarasota, Fort Myers—while my family moved farther north, albeit shorter distances—Little Havana, Miami Lakes, Pembroke Pines. We messaged for hours. We had never imagined that there could be boys like us. Not anywhere.

We started talking on the phone every night. Leo's father was an Italian businessman who'd mysteriously disappeared right before Chávez was elected. I told him about the boy who'd been kidnapped from a school bus near Ibagué, the last of many straws for my mother. Leo's first crush had been a Cuban boy in elementary school named David. They were best friends until Leo confessed he might be bisexual. I tried talking about Matthew—how he had disappeared from my life without a goodbye. Leo explained how the ancient Greeks imagined lovers were one soul, split long ago into two bodies; I tried to ask, *What about our parents? How had they gotten it so wrong?* but he kept talking. The soft rasp of his voice on the other end of the line was enough to convince me I was alone in a room with him, far removed from the reach of my mother, Manuel, and the ruins of humanity.

In the mornings I awoke with a sense of unreality. At school the feeling grew even stronger. The calls with Leo resembled an illusion, a dream, as if I'd received a message from the stars. A strange kind of emptiness caused me to feel furious at the world and all the forces I suddenly noticed working tirelessly, violently, to keep me from Leo. Days passed in a rage.

After a week of calls, Leo asked me to meet him at the mall in Pembroke Pines.

"I don't know," I said. "My mom's already suspicious about how much I'm on the phone."

"Colombian mothers," Leo said, "every one of them thinks she has a son made of gold."

Leo's mother didn't insist on meeting his friends. She didn't lie awake at night when he or his sister went out, then complain the next day about exhaustion and migraines. As long as he didn't ask her for money, he was free to leave the house and do whatever he pleased.

I dodged the question for another week, until I had a real excuse: The phone bill had arrived for three hundred dollars, and I was grounded. I was only allowed to use my phone after nine, when the calls were free.

Each night I learned more about Leo. His family didn't have meals together. Their mom brought back food from the bar where she worked and left it in the kitchen for them to pick at whenever they felt hungry. She had been bartending for seven years. Leo's living room was nearly empty, the only furniture a wood-laminate table bought from a Goodwill three years ago, where they folded laundry and stored the cases of bottled water that didn't fit in the kitchen. Our house had two living rooms: a formal one in the front full of white-upholstered furniture we were all too afraid to use and one in the back, just off the kitchen where we ate our meals around the marble counter while watching television. I told him about how my mother worked at a restaurant for a while when we first moved here, before she cleaned houses, about how she got lucky with Sharon, who left her enough money for us to buy a house and for my mother to get her laboratory tech license.

Leo sometimes seemed lucky to have a mother who didn't hawk

over him. But also, Leo deserved more love than she gave him. I had already begun to despise her, feeling that she didn't care enough about Leo, and that my mother cared too much.

After a month, we had a nightly routine. I stayed up until I could sneak into the hall and turn the thermostat down to sixty-eight—that way the whole house hummed when I jerked off with Leo.

One of these nights, just after coming, he asked if I had given any more thought to the mall. "I'm tired of waiting," he said, as I reached for the sock on the nightstand. "It's been a month." The phone slid off my pillow and his voice became cartoonishly small in the dark. "How are we supposed to call ourselves boyfriends if we haven't even met in person?" The sock, once peeled open, was still moist from yesterday; my thumb sank in its center. "Fuck. Yes, I'm listening," I said. The phone was too hot to hold against my ear for more than a few seconds. "My mom," I started. "You know how she is."

"Lie to her, Santiaguita."

"She has a sixth sense."

"*She has a sixth sense.*" He parroted my words back to me.

"I hate you," I said lovingly.

By the phone's weak light, I cleaned out my belly button. After a moment, Leo said: "What about your brother? Tell him you're meeting a Venezuelan princess with a fat ass. Technically you wouldn't be lying."

I waited for a Sunday when my mother worked two shifts at the lab. I told my brother I was going to see a movie with a girl from school, and after I begged for ten minutes, he said he'd take me if I shut up. In the car while we were driving, he asked how far I'd gone with this girl. We were taking things slow, because school and all, I said. And we didn't speak for the rest of the ride.

When we entered the mall's parking lot, my brother opened the flaps of his wallet and offered me the shriveled blue condom inside. There was a long silence in which it was impossible to tell if he was serious. I looked at him, then at the condom with shocked, wide-open eyes. This was his way of saying we were two men in a world of women waiting for our cocks, because imagining I was like him, a man, was the only way he knew of loving me.

I reached for the condom, that little square of blue.

He snapped his wallet shut.

"I'm kidding, marica. Mama would kill me." He laughed deliberately, raucously. His fist swung toward me and tapped where the two sides of my rib cage met. "Besides, you're too young for pussy."

It was only once he'd driven away with the radio at full blast that I felt a keen sense of a part of myself pulling away, too.

Under the yellow columns and red arch of the Disney Store, Leo stood, short and slender and dark, dressed in black jeans and a gray long-sleeved T-shirt. Looking at him from across the Piercing Pagoda, I felt a swell in my chest. I blurted out his name. He glanced up nervously, and suddenly I met his eyes; they were black and large, one slightly larger than the other, and even so they seemed to shine from within, beaming a creaturely light.

This is Leo, I told myself when he threw his arms around my neck in front of the store. Looking down the back of his shirt at the floor beneath our feet, I held him tight and took in the force of his arms, the soft heat of his neck against mine, and the smell of Dial and sweat behind his ears. For several moments, we didn't move. The swelling in my chest slowed, but a bird, or something like a bird, still fluttered inside me.

"Imagine," Leo said, as he led me inside the Disney Store. He picked a stuffed doll of the fish from *The Little Mermaid* out of a bin near the entrance. "Forty dollars." He shook his head at the tag. I took the doll from his hands, stared right into its huge plastic eyes: "I could make dinner for a week with you." When we laughed, the woman at the register looked at us like we'd done something wrong; her eyes followed us to the next bin. I wondered what kind of sight we made—Leo and me, with our long hair and delicate faces, picking up dolls and laughing—because she didn't look away. Leo noticed me noticing her and told me not to worry.

At the back of the store, out of sight from the woman, Leo held my hand as he browsed the shelves of marked-down T-shirts. He stood next to one with "Aladdin" across the front; they resembled each other, I had made the comparison on a previous night and regretted it immediately. "Who's hotter?" he asked, teasing me. "Be honest." Leo's left eyelid was red, slightly puffy—a sty. He'd told me over the phone not to look at it. I glanced briefly at his smile, perfectly white but too large for his face. As if I were really considering the question, I ran my hand through his hair—thick, black, shiny—and stopped myself from doing it again.

"You," I said, playing his game.

"Am I your little Aladdin?"

I tried to kiss him then, but he stopped me.

"Let's wait for Macy's," he said, winking.

We sat at the back of the store on a wooden stage covered with books and toys and talked. Below the shelves and racks, I could see shoppers, strollers, bags, and families creeping past the window, unaware of us. Leo spoke of future outings and adventures, and I thought, rather gravely, that I now had a future to fill because of him. The sign behind him said that every Wednesday night Mickey Mouse hosted a reading on this stage. It felt strange to be in a toy store, to be out in the world without my mother or brother. I stacked the picture books around us, gathered the plushies into a neat pile, until he took my hands and placed them on his knee. Love gripped me. He was saying that next time we would go to the Egyptian-themed movie theater by the highway. Next time, he would get dropped off near my house, and we would wander on foot through my neighborhood and its backstreets. Leo spoke without a doubt that we would see each other again, when all I could think about was that we were two boys on a stage surrounded by books and toys. Leo was asking me for more secrets and lies. I tugged at his fingers, rubbed his palms. Every now and then, I brushed his knuckles against my lips. His skin was cool to my touch. "Where else do you want to go?" I asked. Even if escaping my mother and enlisting my brother again seemed impossible, there was a part of me that didn't care what they would say or do.

I followed Leo to Macy's, up the escalator to the second floor, through rows of quinceañera gowns and prom dresses, trains of tulle studded and shining.

"This is it," he said as we snuck behind a closed register. We huddled side by side on the ledge of a large, circular window that looked out on the parking lot and watched the shoppers below us glide through the rippling heat. In the quiet, in the warmth, in the stale air behind the closed register, I finally kissed Leo. We made out for several minutes, but when he reached for my zipper, I stopped him. We were too vulnerable here. "The parking lot," I said. The top floor would be empty at this hour.

We crossed the bridge from Macy's, then ran up the stairwell. We pushed the door open against the wind and squinted at the bright, forbidding sun. I couldn't say why or how, only that all this emptiness, four stories above the ground, lit up everything in me. We stood before the ledge, looking down at the thick band of trees surrounding the mall. Past the green rim were busy four-lane roads with strip malls on every side.

"My apartment is over there," he said, his voice muffled by the wind.

He was pointing to a swarm of beige buildings in the distance, near the hospital where my mother had surgery a couple years ago.

"I live over there," I said, pointing in the opposite direction, where the highway looped and split into smaller roads.

The distance between our homes was a few neighborhoods, five or so miles. I could see the route a car would take to get to him. But the more I looked, the more the strip malls, doctors' offices, parks, and warehouses looked like an infinite city. In order to see each other again, the scheming and lying of today would have to become the rule. I would have to become a good liar—an actor.

These thoughts filled me with a dizzying heat. Looking from one end of the horizon to the other, I felt a stupid, unshakable will to cross any distance to be with Leo.

Between the stairwell and the ledge was a space hidden from view, big enough for two bodies. Leo leaned toward me there. I parted my lips in anticipation, but he looked down at his fingers and clumsily pulled on my zipper. I didn't stop him because it didn't matter whether I was ready or not; I didn't know if or when this would happen again. I covered his brow with kisses, thinking that this was gratitude, this was love, each time my lips met his skin. When he pulled my penis out, the tip was already wet and, seemingly without any thought, Leo tapped the dot of precum and brought it to his mouth.

He made tasting me look easy, necessary. Then, with a sudden movement, Leo jerked away from me. I was scared by the suddenness. He began to apologize; I placed my hands on his waist, gripping him like he might run away. There was nothing he could do to disgust me. If this was what we were, and this was what we wanted, then I was okay with it. As long as we were together, I wanted all the pleasures. Every terrifying one.

"Look," I said, squeezing the head of my penis until a drop of clear liquid pearled out and bringing it to my lips. "Delicious."

"Sucia," he said, sounding like a mother, which made me smile. He raised his lips to mine. "It actually tastes kind of good," he said, and we pushed the bitter taste back and forth until it dispersed. We kissed in wet clicks, finding a rhythm. Every few seconds I stopped to catch my breath. I stole looks at my penis in his hand, the first time anyone had held it. His thumb drawing a circle around the head shot a shiver down my spine. I gripped the back of his neck and found it cold, already covered in sweat. I surprised us both when I pulled his mouth an inch from mine and held him there, apart from me. He looked different—helpless, obedient—and this fascinated me. I dug into the tendons of his neck until they pushed back. A feral part of me was about to force his head down—it was what he wanted—when a car swerved onto the top of the garage.

An image flashed in my head: my poor mother leaving work early to pick me up from a windowless office in the basement of the mall; the moment she saw me and this boy her heart would break.

"Don't move," Leo said. In the corner of my eye, a white van circled the empty garage. "It's just a wannabe cop."

"Did he see us?"

"I can't tell."

"What now?"

Leo bolted from my arms into the stairwell. Before I realized it I was chasing after him. He leapt down a whole flight at a time, his footsteps thundering against the concrete walls. No matter how fast I ran, I didn't catch up to him until we were back inside Macy's. He threw himself on a display bed, his breathlessness giving way to laughter as he rolled around on the beaded duvet, his feet still kicking. I saw the joy on his face and wanted it for myself. He closed his hand around mine in an effort to pull me into the bed, but I stiffened; registering my fear, he let go and I perched at the edge of the mattress, scanning the store. No one was coming to stop us.

"How much do you love me?" His voice strained as he rolled over and planted his chin on his hands; he seemed to look at me in a way he had not before.

"From here to Beijing," I said, borrowing a phrase from my mother.

"Would you do something crazy for me?"

He told me about the mall's nursing room. I had no idea such a thing existed, but he'd seen it before when he'd been here with a family friend who had an infant.

The mall was beginning to crowd as we made our way through the food court. The nursing room was next to the bathrooms, which meant my mother and I had walked this same hallway many times—which meant from now on I would forever think of Leo when I'd pass it.

Across from the bathrooms was a waiting area filled with rows of upholstered wooden chairs like the ones in a church or a doctor's office. Leo plopped us down near the entrance and immediately began to complain about our imaginary mother's bladder, loud enough for the woman fortressed behind shopping bags and a stroller at the other end of the waiting area to hear. She met my eyes, sucking loudly on a pink smoothie the size of a foot, and I stared at her for a few seconds—tentative, thrilled—before I turned back to Leo. Alone or with my mother no one noticed me, but a boy next to a boy, two boys holding hands was a sight to behold. This was how it felt to be perceived, I thought. This was touching someone else's skin, so alive, real, and strange. This was Leo holding my hand, petting it lightly—not in the back of some store, not in some dark corner, but in front of someone. A sense of duty arose in me then. I told myself Leo needed me to be brave; Leo needed this more than I did. I was no stranger to this duty. I was the same way with my brother and mother. I could do it for love.

Before long, the nursing room door opened, and a woman stepped out with a baby swaddled in her arms. The baby, with its tiny open mouth, resembled an old drunk man the way babies sometimes do. Pink smoothie stood up and asked her friend if she had everything.

Leo patted my hand then. When I got up, it felt like we moved faster than possible, the world hurtling toward us.

A wormhole opened up.

We entered.

The door shut behind me. I found the handle and turned the lock. Leo ran his fingers along the walls. Here, a hook for a coat. There, holes where paintings once hung. Along the opposite wall were two crumbling leather chairs, a knee-high table leveled by a wad of McDonald's napkins, and a palm tree–shaped lamp with a buzzing bulb. A mural of puffy white clouds and a yellow sun covered the ceiling. I thought of babies asleep in a field.

"What do you think?"

"It's dingy. I don't even want to sit on those chairs."

"Well, you're just in luck." Leo wrestled his shoe off. His big toe poked through a hole in his sock. "I got us floor seats."

I took a deep breath and nodded.

He left his other shoe on and, without waiting, grabbed for me. After a stuttering dance, he had my back against the wall. My hoodie slid down my arms, every inch of skin buzzing. I closed my eyes after he landed a kiss behind my ear. A bright, bubbly feeling fizzed through me. I held on to his meaty arms, sensing the army of small bumps dotting his skin, the muscles just underneath flexing and softening in my grip. Even with my eyes closed, I felt like I could see everything. Every muscle on his bones. Every living fiber.

Leo stopped to pull his shirt over his head. Then I saw, in the middle of his chest, tugging his nipples and a raisin-shaped birthmark inward, a dimple, a sinkhole, a landmark he hadn't mentioned on the phone. This time, I leaned into him, my mouth to his. I placed my fist on his chest, where a second heart could easily fit, and he held my fist there with both hands, firmly. My free hand dragged down the bones of his back, over his goose bumps, to the small clearing just above his ass, following his moans and quivers as they guided me toward what gave him pleasure.

The leather chair crackled with his weight. Spread on the chair, Leo sat like my father used to sit alone in the mud-caked Jeep taking work calls. His belly arched forward; a shadow filled the dip between his nipples. On my knees, I got rid of his remaining shoe, and then, with a swift tug, his jeans. In the warm light of the palm tree lamp, his briefs glowed a light rosy color, the fabric specked by the black bristly hairs below. I peeled the underwear off, revealing the word *puma* pressed into his soft-skinned navel, and below this, his dark, pulsing erection. A thick vein traversed the shaft. The same vein, if followed, would take me to his heart.

From below, with him in my mouth, I watched Leo watching me with his barely opened eyes sparkling, wet with desire, with fantasy. He smiled at my bobbing head as if my hair were his new best friend. His hands, clasped to my ears, pushed my head down like the men we'd seen in videos until I coughed. Leo stopped, sat up, and asked if I was okay. Two small tears rolled down the side of my face and met at the crest of my lips. Frowning, he lifted my chin with a finger and said sorry.

"Want to try fucking me?" he said.

"Now?"

"We're already here."

Leo lay down on the floor and raised his legs to me with his face turned to the ceiling, a thin frown creasing his forehead. Silently, as if trying not to wake him up, I undressed and got us both wet with my spit. For several moments, I rolled my fingers over his hole, waiting for him to soften, to open like fruit. I waited for him to take the lead, but he kept his hands at his side, his eyes on the ceiling. I had imagined we would become one boy, sharing one movement, one set of muscles, one wetness, one breath, but he didn't stir as I entered him. I said his name to the silence and moved myself into him. Once inside, I tipped clumsily over him, my knees buckling with warmth. He made no sound. After a few thrusts, I stopped. He looked like he was in too much pain. As much as I wanted to say that we'd had sex, I didn't want to hurt him. I pulled out and instead gave him head, which I found I was good at, but after a few minutes my jaw locked. We ended up jerking off and coming together. We had not thought about what to do with our cum. Leo took the napkins that held the side table level, and I rubbed mine into the carpet below the chairs.

We stayed on the floor, naked, not caring that the carpet was dirty. We hadn't considered how we would leave the nursing room. There was so much we hadn't thought about. Both of us stared up at the ceiling in silence. The sky remained bright blue, the clouds frozen in place, the yellow of the sun unchanged.

We would worry about each other. We would hurt each other. We would fail to be good to each other.

"Pectus excavatum," Leo said, bringing my fingers to the dent between his nipples. "If you push down hard enough, you can kill me."

There was no expression on his face. My index finger drew circles around the edge of the dip, spiraling down toward its center, never daring to reach the bottom. He laughed gently at my reluctance, his breath casting a spell through my hair. I felt I had hurt him, but I didn't know how or why. I told myself I'd done what he'd wanted, but the sensation I feared calling *regret* or *guilt* didn't stop growing in me. We didn't say another word.

This was before I knew how far into his life I would sink; before I knew the darkness in his heart, his explosive immigrant rage; before our first breakup; before the years of fucking each other's boyfriends as if for sport; before the clubs and the beaches; before the times between cars and under highways; before I was no stranger to his mother's unfurnished apartment, to her habit of locking herself in her bedroom with Venezuelan calling cards while Leo and I snuck boys, friends, and drugs in through the front door; before the summer I came back from a visit to Colombia with a nose job; before I left Miami and visited to find he had a new best friend every few months; before Leo visited me at college with a new nose of his own, and then in New York City; before I lost him in a bathhouse one night and didn't find him until the next day, all the good parts of him burnt up; before I ended up trying meth with him one night to see why he loved it; and before we only talked about being horny, desperate faggots, too afraid to talk about anything besides the holes in our lives because we both knew that only in our loneliness and want we were still alike.

We were shaken when someone tried the handle of the door and, finding it locked, proceeded to knock loudly. I could hear a baby crying. We could make out a pair of feet strapped into sandals in the rectangle of light below the door. Another knock. The realization that we were here, in a mall, in a nursing room, shocked us. The world had been there all along—it had never disappeared.

The woman was now asking someone to find the janitor. We undid the tangle of clothes and jammed our feet into our pants as silently as possible. We decided that on the count of three, we would throw the door open and run in opposite directions. That way we would be more difficult to catch. Our pupils were large, shining like silver dollars. We would meet across the street from the mall, in another parking lot. Our lips kissed one last time. We were at once giddy and terrified.

"Three.

"Two.

"One."

III

NINE

Soon after Leo and I got together, I met Maria online. She lived in the same gated community as me, but on the other side of the lake from our house, in a single-family house with a pool.

Maria was sixteen, a year older than me. She had gone to Everglades High like the rest of the neighborhood, but her mother transferred her to a private Catholic school run by nuns after she flunked freshman math; she'd had no overlap with Leo. Maria was five when her mother left her in Puerto Rico. And two years passed before her grandmother put her on the plane to Miami. Before long, her mother was pregnant, then busy with the baby brother, and Maria learned to stay out of the way of her new stepfather until the day he finally left them for a younger woman. She told me this like she'd known me all her life. And I told her about Leo, my father, and the chat rooms I visited.

We spoke for weeks online before I finally asked her to meet me halfway between our two homes, where there was a large green electrical box surrounded by a wooden fence. Like with Leo, I stood there quietly shaking inside as if caught in an earthquake when I saw her in front of me, and she turned into a person in my arms. "Look at what Ricky sent me last night—" On the screen of her phone was the thick white cock of the twenty-seven-year-old club promoter she was fucking behind her boyfriend's back. I zoomed in like a mosquito to a lamp. "There's more," she said, waving her hand over the phone. *Sin pena.* I swiped through a blown-out picture of him in an elevator mirror holding his dick out, then one in his car, shirt pulled up, cum dripping down his abs—and before I realized it, I was looking at a picture of Maria holding her small, boyish breasts in her hands.

From a fabric pencil case, she took out her pipe. Small, colored like a candy cane. The bowl already filled. It was broad daylight in the middle of a Sunday, and we sat with our backs to the green metal box and the wooden fence, which hid us from the road. Someone would only see us if they were looking, but anyone walking would smell the smoke. Next to her, I didn't care. She was already my sister.

On Sundays, my mother worked her back-to-back shifts at Quest. My brother stayed at his girlfriend's house in Kendall, across from the mall where they both worked at the Guess. So it was just Abuela and me at home. She had sold her apartment a year or two after we moved to Miami, and was visiting us from Colombia for an indefinite amount of time because the only doctors she trusted were American. The first floor of the house was hers. Pots simmered on the stove all day filled with nothing I ever wanted to eat: oatmeal, rice, lentils, broths, boiled strips of chicken. Abuela sat on the phone for hours yelling over the television, checking in with each of her children and friends back home, making sure they didn't forget she was visiting us in America. We took walks at different times throughout the day. She only went around the cul-de-sac, too scared to stray farther. I walked to the gate and back. Sometimes I rollerbladed to the gas station at the nearest intersection. I hadn't seen Leo again in person, though I was almost always on the computer with him.

When I introduced Leo and Maria, they were instant friends. We smoked in her bedroom taking turns holding her ferret until I was the only one on the bed, Leo and Maria trying on clothes from her closet and deciding what to throw away, placing these into a pile next to me. They were so fun together that I didn't even have to talk, which was a relief, not having to fill the silence between two people you love. Leo and I never went back to the mall again. We were always at Maria's. When her boyfriend came over, they'd go off to her room and we'd claim the guest room.

Once in a while, the three of us walked around the lake to visit my mother and Abuela. They already loved Maria, called her *princesa*, pinched and spanked her butt playfully whenever they saw her; *compórtate*, they said, to her and to me, like she was my sister. Leo, who disguised himself as Maria's friend from school, remained *el Venezolano*, like he was no more than his country of origin.

We never stayed long at my house. At Maria's, Leo and I would hang out in the guest room, watch television, and make missions out of going downstairs to raid the fridge. Maria's little brother didn't mind us—if anything, he thought we were all freaks. He kept his distance. By ten each night, her mother was passed out from drinking in the living room. We always turned the lights off and left the television on. We circled her alcoholism in jokes, but never talked about it head-on. There was an understanding between the three of us: We all had single mothers and father-shaped holes where our hearts should be.

The three of us went to different schools. It was for the better, we agreed; Leo's and Maria's circles might've overlapped, but I would've been too busy—in some office or classroom talking to a teacher, winning favor with so and so, planning a fundraiser—to ever meet them. Which made it all feel more like I was breaking the rules to love Maria and Leo. During the day, I led the kind of life I could talk to my mother and brother about: I got all As, made the honor roll, ran half the clubs in my school. Then, at night, I went to Maria's for a sleepover, which really meant another rave organized by the promoter, or snuck into gay clubs where it didn't matter how old we were; men always asked us if we wanted to make easy money. We were always leaving, passing by, going somewhere else, especially after Maria, then Leo, made enough to buy a car at the sushi restaurant where they both worked.

By the end of high school, I was student council president and valedictorian, going to Yale. My mother told everyone—her younger son was going to Yale, and her older one to medical school. The most important thing was education. "Just look at my siblings," she said, like her brothers and sister, all their children, were the worst a person could be. This was the case she was trying to make: *Why was I friends with Maria and Leo?* They cared nothing about school.

When I went out with them, when we snuck out together—what was I then? What would my mother say?

The differences between us were many: Leo and Maria were both more willing to ask for what they wanted, even if it meant being rude or unlikable, which meant they often got on each other's nerves and bickered. At the restaurant they fought over tables, and then tension only grew when Leo, two years younger than Maria, was promoted to lead server before her. Leo loved to make her think she was getting fat, call out her daddy issues, and generally make her feel stupid. She simmered until her head or stomach hurt; if she had an excuse to lie around, she did so for hours. I stirred the pot, as they say. I talked about each to the other behind their backs, always making sure everyone was on my side and I was never the villain.

At some point, Leo and I weren't dating anymore. When I asked him when we stopped calling ourselves boyfriends, he knew it to the day—we'd been together nine months. Our relationship had been a baby, about to come out into the world—I could be ridiculously precious, knowing nothing I said could push him away. Even though we moved on to other boyfriends, we still slept with each other. Sometimes we didn't speak for weeks or months, Maria hanging out with us separately, relaying messages back and forth, but when we came back together it was like no time had passed.

We were smoking in the backyard one night before I left for college, our legs kicking in the water, when Maria's mother staggered outside and asked us to get her high. In her drunkenness, she confessed to smoking weed while pregnant with Maria; Leo and I laughed, too shocked to believe this was happening. Maria said nothing, glanced around, and lifted the pipe for her mother. I couldn't remember if the candy cane–striped pipe had always been so little. Even though she'd barely gotten any smoke, her mother coughed and coughed violently, almost slapping the pipe out of Maria's hand and into the pool. When she caught her breath, she asked Leo how long we had been together. It was the first time she'd acknowledged our relationship, and who could blame her if she thought we were still dating? So much of our freedom in her house was tied to her and us pretending we didn't notice each other. "Have you done it in my bed?" We had, at least once. Maria as well, many times. We said *of course not*, too shocked to say anything else.

That night I had no clue how I'd gotten where I was, even though only a short walk away around the lake my mother was in bed next to Abuela or in the kitchen, slicing into an apple or drinking a warm cup of milk, trying anything to fall asleep.

Years later, after I'd left for college, Leo would tell me that he and Maria still talked on the phone every day. She'd met an Austrian lawyer at a music festival in the desert. The following year, she finally left her mother and moved to a suburb of Vienna.

TEN

The front door was open. Moths flickered in and out of the dim yellow porch light. But I checked the kitchen first, then the living room. I even opened the hallway closet and lifted the lid of the washing machine like Leo might be only waiting to jump out and scare me.

I'd left for college and was on Christmas break, visiting home for the first time. I was at Leo's new boyfriend's house. But for the last three weeks it had turned out we were still sleeping together, still sharing everything.

Now, I stood in the empty half of the driveway where Leo's car should be. I looked at my reflection in the black-tinted windows of Nasir's small red coupe, still seeing minute vibrations radiating from my eyes like pond rings and patches of startling color flowing and shifting across my cheeks making complex patterns. The acid had started to wind down, but I had no clue how Leo was driving.

Down the street, I reached the guest parking lot. The lampposts stood between every four cars, pouring down a blue-white light.

There had to be another explanation: Leo had gone to the grocery store or gas station to buy something to eat. He'd just forgotten to shut the door. My mind fought the reality it faced, throwing out whatever other scenarios it could to prevent itself from accepting this one: Leo had stranded me miles from home, alone with his boyfriend.

The wind whipped my hair around my face, pulling goose bumps from my arms and back and chest, and I realized I was in my underwear, barefoot in the middle of the street. I didn't even know what time it was. The windows of all the houses were dark. Behind a spotlit dolphin-shaped mailbox, a cat stared me down like I'd stirred him from sleep. I found a bush next to the white metal gate around the community pool. My whole body shuddered when my feet sank into the wet earth. If I disappeared like Leo, who would find me? A single tear ran down my cheek as I pissed. What had Leo had in mind before he put the acid under my tongue? Before the three of us fucked?

I'd been home from school for three weeks and was inseparable from Leo again. I left my mother alone each night; Abuela had gone back to Colombia at the beginning of December, and though my brother had flown down from Ohio with his girlfriend, they were staying deep in Miami at her family's house. After Leo's shifts at Sushi Sake, we smoked weed in his room for hours and talked about the beginning. He remembered everything better than I did. He could recall what I wore that day at the mall and what I had said in those early messages, while I had tried, with some success, to forget everything about being fifteen. Though I hadn't seen him in four months, I had heard the story of Nasir in the chapters Leo texted me late at night, but as he told the whole story now, straight from the beginning, something in me choked up. It was enough to feel like I was losing him. Then we made out while listening to Shakira, and when it was morning in Palestine we Skyped Nasir and talked about everything we would do when he got back from visiting his family. And it all felt like a promise that nothing would change. We would always have a home with each other, no matter where we were or who we were dating. In the middle of the night, Leo and I went to Walmart and shop-lifted brushes, canvases, and paint, like we had in high school, to make Christmas presents for our mothers. He took me to strip-mall bars with his coworkers and to their holiday staff party where I didn't know if I should act like his friend or lover. My mother guilt-tripped me every night when I told her I was going to see Leo instead of watching a movie with her. She had never liked Leo. It was unthinkable to her that he hadn't gone to college; he might as well have slid off the face of the earth. Tonight, keeping things sim-ple, I told her I was staying at Leo's. I didn't mention that Nasir was back in town, or that we would spend the night at his house, that he was almost thirty. It made no sense to her, how Leo and I hung out even when we had other boyfriends, how I still talked to him when I was now a student at Yale and he was still smoking weed and waiting tables. Before I'd left earlier that night, with all her incredible dependency, she reminded me I was her treasure. She stood at the door long after Leo pulled out of the cul-de-sac. My last night in Miami, and I was escaping again with el Venezolano.

Nasir was standing under the yellow porch lights, staring through and beyond, way beyond, the half-empty driveway.

"Where's Leo?"

I walked past him, barely making it inside before I had to support myself against the wall and slide down to the ground, unsure of what to do.

Nasir didn't look at me again. His phone lit a stripe down his cheek, his face shining with sweat and worry. He was already another man I had failed to make love me.

I didn't know how many times the phone rang before Nasir punched the door and ran past me into the living room. He shoved his hand in between the sofa seats and threw the coins he found against the wall; his car keys weren't in his fanny pack or in the laundry still piled inside his luggage. He screamed at the phone in Arabic, his eyes large and watering. He took a pair of shorts out of the dryer and forced both feet into a single hole, almost falling. I didn't tell him the keys had fallen beneath the bed when he was fucking Leo. I let him run upstairs, the phone still ringing.

In the kitchen, I saw what I hadn't before: All the cabinets and drawers were wide open. I checked a row of drawers, but I didn't know what to look for—this wasn't my home. I had no way of knowing if a knife was missing. Then I remembered the singing; Leo had come downstairs to get something to eat. That's what he'd said, I was sure of it. This was all a silly tantrum. If I could convince myself, I could convince Nasir: Leo wasn't stupid enough to really hurt himself. I could go upstairs, curl into his boyfriend's arms, and fall back into the unmade bed. If Nasir couldn't be ours, then he could be mine. At least for a little while. This was what Leo must've seen. This, I thought, looking around the kitchen, was how he proved me wrong. This wasn't about Nasir, but about me, about Leo and me hurting each other in our old, familiar ways.

The phone, now on speaker, was ringing atop the dresser upstairs. Nasir pulled a tank top over his head and sank onto the bed to tie his shoes; he looked older than twenty-nine, the life draining from his face with each second.

All night he had entertained Leo and me with incredible patience while we tripped. He didn't drink or take drugs but didn't mind when Leo did. I understood why Leo had chosen him, because when I felt exhausted from keeping myself alive and safe, Nasir was exactly the kind of man I thought I needed: a man who would let me spin out of control, watch me wreck myself and my surroundings, and be there to collect me afterward.

"Do you think he took them?" Nasir said, sidestepping me out of the room.

I picked the scarf Nasir had given me at the beginning of the night off the floor. The black-and-white checkered fabric breathed in my hands slowly, like something dying or coming to life. I looked at Nasir blankly.

"The keys!" he said, shouting. And after a dead silence, he was done with me: "Forget it."

I let him stomp down the stairs before I picked the keys up from under the far side of the bed. I left the scarf in their place. I gathered the turtleneck and corduroys my mother had given me earlier for Christmas and got dressed.

———

"Hold still, amiga," Leo said at the beginning of the night when he straddled my waist, pinning me to the sofa. I opened wide, *aah-*ing like at the doctor's, and he grabbed my tongue between his thumb and index finger, then placed the tab of acid—a tiny paper square, nothing more—on the floor of my mouth. He told me not to swallow and sealed my mouth with a kiss, the first he'd given me in front of Nasir. I didn't know what permission we had from him, if any, to touch each other like this, but it didn't seem to matter now; Nasir was emptying his suitcase into the washing machine in the hallway, hardly aware of us. It was hard to resist the freedom Leo gave himself to do whatever he wanted. His attention could make you feel like the two of you had passed through some unequivocal experience together, no one more bound to him than you. There was a seduction to how he sat, ate, talked, and laughed—like a mirror making a pair with you. But his focus could shift at a moment's notice if you didn't go along with him. You'd find the darkness of his eyes weighing you coldly from a distance.

Leo turned the TV on and laid out the sushi he'd brought back from work across the coffee table, setting out plates and chopsticks for us, lining everything up like I imagined he did every night with Maria at the restaurant. While I'd gained a bike tire of fat around my waist and a smattering of pimples on my cheeks and chin, Leo had grown undeniably handsome. His cheeks had hollowed, his smile grown larger and whiter, beaming from his skull. He was no longer the meek, round-faced boy of fourteen. Waiting tables five nights a week and going out dancing every weekend had turned him into a thin rope knotted with muscle. His facial hair was filling out, and his features, year after year, had become sharper and more defined, more like those of a man, promising even greater beauty.

After loading the wash, Nasir came into the room with a plastic bag in his hands. With nothing but warmth in his voice, he said: "You two are crazy." Though this was our first meeting in person, Nasir hardly felt like a stranger. I remembered Leo's text in September, not long after I'd left town for college: "Amiga, I found my husband." The picture that followed showed a short, bearded, Middle Eastern man sprinting after a soccer ball. He had long, swooping eyebrows and short, wavy hair that sat tight on his head like a swim cap. In the following weeks, I often woke up to late-night texts from Leo chronicling their relationship—mostly their fights, but sometimes their sex, too—in long, beautiful, aching messages. When Leo remembered to ask about my new life, I made the one-night stands I was having seem substantial, because I didn't know how to explain to him that I had never felt as ugly or insignificant as I did at Yale. Once, he sent me a photo of Nasir's penis laid across his face. Behind the two-toned, circumcised shaft was Leo's largest, highest smile. I jerked off to this picture, imagining myself in Leo's place, then Nasir's, more than once. Of all the messages, the ones I liked most were the ones in which Leo told me of the men he was fucking behind Nasir's back. That was the Leo I knew. I used every haunting detail of what his loneliness made him do to justify my own whoring around.

From the plastic bag, Nasir took out a black-and-white lump of fabric. He opened his arms wide, blocking himself from view with the kaffiyeh. The black lines formed a loose net against the white. Small, ornamental tassels fringed its side. "For you," Nasir said, throwing the scarf over me. Before I knew it, his hands were tousling my hair and digging into my sides over the fabric. "Where's my gift?" I heard Leo ask. I closed my eyes and felt around myself, my tongue wiggling over the tiny paper square as Nasir treated me like a child. A slight metallic taste seeped throughout my mouth. No one knew I was here.

The TV pulsed a slick blue light over us as we ate.

"I love you," Leo said, mouth full of fish. "Both of you."

I didn't say it back. Neither did Nasir.

Leo rested his chopsticks by the remote, put his head on my lap.

Nasir looked straight ahead, gently pulling Leo's toes. He put me at ease. He wasn't stained by the past. He was new. For a moment, I imagined the three of us as a family, the rest of our lives filling the rooms of this house. We were three people in love. Our bodies settled into one another. A nest of heartbeats. I was pure hope.

"Where are you?" asked Nasir, his voice frayed, desperate, the slur of a helpless man met by silence. The seconds ticked away on the phone screen; Leo had finally answered. I dropped into the passenger seat of Nasir's small car, crowding myself into the sadness of his *where are you*s and *tell me*s. I wanted to take the phone from him and hang up. I knew what Leo was doing. The power he had over this fully grown man was the same power he'd had over me.

"Why aren't you speaking?" said Nasir, his eyes locked on the steering wheel. The whole dashboard lit up red. He pulled out of the driveway without looking at the camera. He was a man with a purpose. He couldn't wait around another minute. "Are you home, habibi? We're driving there now."

My roommates at Yale—this was something they would never experience. Moments like these convinced me that everything Leo and I had put each other through had unlocked something special inside of me, a secret vault of human knowledge.

Nasir swerved onto the interstate ramp. We shot several stories into the sky over the Everglades. The moonlight bent long across the water. For a moment I imagined Leo's car in the water, its nose submerged in the reeds, its back wheels spinning slowly above the surface. What could I do to slow the drift of us? I was reeling in my seat. I tried to close my eyes and let the acid take me back to the beginning of the night, but behind my eyes I could only find Leo's face leaning over me. I was asking him how to make my pain so big it spilled over until I no longer had the choice to make myself small. I had tasted, heard, smelled, and felt this fantasy since I was a boy.

Under a blanket, in Nasir's bed, the three of us watched reruns of *Friends*. The television's light jumped around the room, our faces emerging from the dark in flashes. Nasir's arm was wrapped around Leo, Leo held my hand, and my feet petted theirs softly below the blanket. We looked oily and blue. That's how I felt, less person than substance.

Before long my stomach cramped up like I needed to either shit or barf. I tried describing the pain aloud, but as soon as I started to speak, I forgot how to string words into sentences. Leo touched my hand, his fingers soft, cool, damp, the way his touch had always felt. I pushed the pain out of my mind, focused on the television. It didn't matter that I didn't know what was going on in the show. I felt no impatience. I was exactly where I needed to be. I loved how we had taken acid to watch television, how a night could consist of so small and perfect a plan. My vision swam. Tears pressed up behind my eyes. The room moved, slurried and slow. Leo's legs jerked under the blanket restlessly, mindlessly. My fingers, when I held them up to the light of the television, melted down my palms like candles.

"I didn't say it earlier, but I love you, Leo. I love you so much." I kissed his mouth gently, then I reached over him and stroked Nasir's beard. "I know we barely know each other, but I love you, too."

"I feel alive," said Leo, cupping Nasir's other cheek.

"You two are so high." Nasir laughed, amused by our gentle helplessness.

We held his beard in place, the hairs twitching ever so slightly across our palms. He moved his tongue around, and it was like we were holding not just his cheeks or beard but his slithering heart.

I didn't know how we had gotten here, and I didn't care one bit to retrace my steps. I was just happy we had arrived: I was watching

Nasir fuck Leo from behind. I sat back against the headboard, a stack of pillows behind me. I touched Leo's lips with my fingers as I stroked my dick. His face bloomed with pain and pleasure, his mind flickering in and out of the room. His head dropped to my chest. His breath wrapped around my skin. The cold light of the television settled on his shoulder blades, so that their glow as they pushed against his skin seemed to come from within, aching to rise and go out against the dimness of the room. I held his head against my stomach firmly; he bit down on the skin above my belly button. Nasir smiled at me from behind Leo. If he could read my mind, he'd know I wanted to touch him. There was no past, no future, only the hot desperation of being alive.

For years, Leo and I had claimed the day in the nursing room as our first. It didn't even matter that we'd barely had sex. We told the story to everyone. But the truth was ours: I'd barely made it inside him that day at the mall before the pain on his face had stopped me.

We had been together for five months when I cheated on Leo. A blond guy named Eric was leaving flirty comments under all his pictures on MySpace, and Leo kept making casual mentions of wanting to fuck him. So I messaged Eric. He was a twenty-two-year-old shot boy at a gay bar in Wilton Manors. Eric picked me up on a Sunday when I was home alone with Abuela. We drove down the street to the pool house and parked between two vans, facing a wall of ferns. I sucked him off and swallowed his cum in a hurry. In person, he looked like Frankenstein's monster, with a tall forehead and a too-square jaw. He smelled of cigarettes and sweat, like the shirt he was wearing had still been wet when he took it out of the dryer. I didn't like him. But knowing Leo wanted this boy made me want him, too. That night, Leo didn't call me the way he usually did. A week later I'd forgotten all about Eric when Leo told me Eric had picked him up from school and fucked him in his car; we could call it even. It was ridiculous to look back at how we tried to hurt each other even if it meant hurting ourselves. I was fifteen, he was fourteen. Years later, when I lived in New York, Leo left me a voicemail asking if I remembered Eric. He said he'd been out at the Manor the night before when he ran into Andreas, a boy who used to throw underwear parties at his house during the months his parents lived in Argentina. Andreas asked Leo if he'd ever met up with a guy named Clifton when we were teenagers. *El escándalo*, Leo said: Clifton was Eric's real name. He hadn't been twenty-two but thirty-two when he'd met us.

Our first threesome was in high school. I had a new boyfriend then, a premed student who was twenty and looked like an older, paler, taller version of me. I convinced him to fuck Leo and me. The three of us piled into the back seat of his car, our bodies tangled and damp. I made the mistake of coming first. Their pleasure was no longer mine. I sank my nails into my boyfriend's milk-white thighs. When he didn't stop, I pressed down harder, as hard as I could. I wanted to break skin. He must've thought they were Leo's nails because he fucked Leo harder. I crawled over the cup holders to the copilot seat, watched the windshield fog over and the light dim. I stayed with that boyfriend right up until I left for college. Years later Leo told me they had continued fucking every few months after that night.

I slumped down until I was between Leo and the mattress. My eyes moved slowly over Leo's clavicle, a vast meadow of brown skin and moles ringed by stiff, black hairs, each one an argument for his loveliness, then below this meadow, the pit between his nipples, where a second heart could fit. Trapped under his weight, I raised my head, kissed his cratered chest, but even this took great effort. The force of Nasir's thrusts pressed down on us. I filled my lungs with the smell of spit and shit and sweat; it was in the bed, the sheets, all around me. I had wondered how I would leave him, this person who had held me for so long, and if the shape of who we were would be lost. I felt proud of the boys we had been and still were. Sometimes, it seemed, we were boys trying to become the kind of women who'd stolen our fathers from us, or at least the women we imagined them to be. We were boys who fucked each other's boyfriends. Boys who snuck into clubs and threw drinks across dance floors. Boys who put out cigarettes on the arms of our enemies. We were unafraid of everything we could destroy. We were daring to create ourselves out of love and loss, and we were thinking of our mothers and everything they didn't know about us, and we were dreaming, always, that nowhere in the world were there other boys like us.

After coming between my legs, Leo flung the covers off the bed and crossed swiftly into the bathroom without finishing Nasir off. The yellow light spilled out from the open door and over the bed. We heard the shower run, and shortly after, Leo began singing. He hit a high note, loud and dramatic. Nasir stared at me without expression, deciding if he should apologize for Leo, but this was nothing new for me. With a small movement I raised my hands toward his face. At last, we were alone. We could look at each other the way we were meant to.

Nasir fucked me on my back, touching his forehead to mine. Each thrust pressed my skull deeper into the pillow. I couldn't hear what he said, his words smothered before they reached me. I wrapped my legs around him, surprised by how far my feet stretched—just short of his neck. I locked my feet around him, drawing him deeper into me. The more animal I was, the more human I felt. He refused to kiss me, but I was still saying *I love you* softly to the space between our lips, though I couldn't be sure I was saying the words loud enough for him to hear.

Leo abruptly quieted when we entered the bathroom. He spread his arms wide as if to hide a person behind him. A long, cheap mirror, the kind I'd seen in dorm rooms, was propped up against the shower wall. Then, all at once, he laughed. His laughter struck me as faintly hysterical. I laughed, too, matching his energy. I assumed the worst: Leo was mad. I was justified, of course, in letting Nasir fuck me. After all, Leo had left us alone. If it was a problem, I decided, it was Nasir's problem, not mine.

Nasir got in the shower first. I wiped up my cum and checked my ass for blood or shit to give them a moment alone together. Nasir's cum I would hold until I had the bathroom to myself. I looked at my reflection over the sink, then away, frightened by how my face moved, expanding and contracting, more alive than a face should be. Meanwhile, Leo held his arms straight up for Nasir to wash his pits. Their tenderness softened all the arguments I was building in my head. Not long after I joined them, Nasir said he was tired. Our pleading didn't make him stay. A shower was just a shower to him; he wasn't high like us. He wasn't like us at all. He was a good, dependable man who wasn't suspicious of love. A moment later, he popped in to leave two clean towels on the toilet seat.

Leo and I sat on the floor. The shower cried pearls over us.

"So how was it?" Meaning Nasir.

"Good," I said. "How are you feeling?"

Leo kept his lips together, wanting me to say more. When I outlasted his silence, he said, "I'm still coming in and out, but I peaked when we were in bed."

"How much longer are we going to be tripping?"

"Once the ball starts rolling," Leo said, "it doesn't stop." He was talking about the acid, but I imagined he was talking about us and the rest of our lives. I didn't notice Leo's hand reaching behind me. Suddenly the water went as hot as it would go. I reached for the handle, but he sat on my lap and pinned my hands down. I bit his lip until I got used to the pain. We kissed without talking. Steam billowed up from the floor, up our waists in majestic mounds. I felt light-headed, each breath shallower than the last. His head was on my shoulder for what felt like a long time before he said the words *Nasir* and *gonorrhea*.

"What?" I asked, thinking I'd heard wrong.

"Nasir has gonorrhea. I gave it to him," Leo said. "But he left to see his family before I could tell him."

He saw the look on my face. I was confused. My heart sank with fear, and then a moment later I felt a scalding anger and hatred.

"I'm fine," he said. "I got treated."

"Why didn't you say anything?" I itched all over. I saw one, then two, then many tiny bugs scuttling on my forearms, weaving in and out of my skin. A hallucination.

"It's no big deal, amiga. We can go to the clinic in the morning. They'll just give us all horse pills."

I looked straight ahead into the fog. I couldn't decide what to do with my anger. I hated how suddenly unsafe I felt, like a switch flipped on and off, slowly draining the life from the bulb. Leo palmed the fog from the mirror. He was taller, skinnier, a long brown stain next to the blur of a smaller, lighter me. He told me I was beautiful and then kissed me again. Before long, the fog subsumed our reflections. I laid my head on Leo's clavicle, listening for a heartbeat in his bones. We weren't scared, we weren't delicate. We were covered in bruises and burns. We had survived the past and so much was still possible.

The highway lights made the landscape of my childhood pale, ghostly. Gated communities replaced the Everglades. The parking lot of the Egyptian-themed movie theater where Leo and I had sucked each other off was empty. Fenced-in backyards. Identical townhouses. Artificial lakes spewing jets of water into the night air.

How did Nasir feel so far from me when just a leather gearshift and a soggy cup of flat soda separated us? He hadn't looked at or touched me since we'd gotten in the car, as if Leo had eyes even in here. Deep down, Nasir must have known he was losing Leo to his dark impulses. He was a fool if he didn't.

The problem with Leo was that he still thought we were fifteen. Still thought he'd be abandoned for some prettier thing. I remembered when he walked five miles to my house in the middle of summer. He'd stood on the doormat sweating through his sweater and jeans, wearing them just to torture himself. After nine months, I had finally broken up with him for making out with one of our friends at the movie theater. My mother drove him home. I sat up front next to her while Leo sat in the back. A year later, she found him—the boy who had walked five miles for her son—fucking me in the living room.

We weren't far from his apartment now.

"Why do you put up with this?" I couldn't tell if I was asking Nasir or myself.

"What?"

I didn't respond.

"He needs us right now," said Nasir.

"What about us?" I felt evil. Like I was trying to convict my own flesh.

"He talks about you all the time. He tells me you ignore his messages. You don't answer his calls. He still loves you. It's the only reason I agreed to tonight."

"You don't know yet how hard it is loving him." I said this out loud for the first time.

Nasir looked forward. The road filled his eye like saucers, reminding me I was still high.

"Who else if not us? What if something happened to him? How would you feel then?"

"Why didn't he just stay with us?" I said to Nasir, resisting the urge to call him *babe*. "Don't you want something simple?"

Nasir hung his head. I looked at him, and continued to look at him. He swept his bald patch with his hand. "I don't know what else to tell you if you feel like this."

We drove silently. I wished I wasn't high anymore. I felt hot and loud, then cold and silent, like I was moving through weather systems. The ball kept rolling.

"Do you have his mother's phone number?"

"No."

"His sister's?"

"I said no."

When Leo went downstairs to make us food, I nestled myself into Nasir and pulled his arms around me. We were lying on top of our towels on the bare mattress, the sheets half off the bed, oily and stained. The room—drawn curtains, small piles of our shed clothes, *Friends*.

I watched the television light move over the dense layer of

stubble across his stomach. I touched his dick, which was soft, and made it stand in the light.

"Hey," I said in a low pitch, wiggling the shaft from side to side, like it was talking. "You come here often?"

There was a silence where the two of us looked down at my hand, then back up again.

"Leo doesn't like this," he said, pointing at himself, then at me.

"What do you mean?"

"This." He pointed again.

"But this," I say, pointing between us, "was his idea."

Leo, downstairs, was closing and opening drawers in the kitchen and singing. He was cheating on Nasir, going to the bathhouse in Fort Lauderdale almost every weekend, fucking every white boy he could at the Manor. All I needed to say was that he'd given us gonorrhea.

"Let's just enjoy ourselves." I bent down to kiss his dick. He didn't move, didn't say anything, didn't even get hard.

"You're right." I stopped. Got up. I didn't look at him.

This was a game for Leo. Nasir and I, pieces.

We found Leo's car in the parking lot of his apartment complex.

"I told you he'd be okay." The words coursed through me as if from the earth.

Nasir got out, but I didn't think I could leave the car.

"What's the matter?"

"I want to go home."

"Let me go up and check on him first," he said, his face as flat as a sheet. "I'll be right back."

I waited—waited until I had to call the waiting what it was: foolishness.

I slammed the car door hoping they'd hear me. Staring at the black curtains of Leo's bedroom, I smelled the first vapors of rain. I could walk upstairs. I knew the front door would be unlocked. A space in the bed would open for me.

I crossed the parking lot, first at a jog, then running.

Months later, during another visit to Miami, Nasir and I would meet in his car, in another parking lot. I'd see Leo afterward, and he'd tell me to suck his dick like I used to.

I reached the next building. Down a corridor humming with a hundred ACs, I came upon a wall of bushes and trees, dark as night. For just a moment, I looked at my phone hoping I'd somehow missed their call. I slithered through the thick brush, the sounds of the building receding to a hush. The one thing I could take from Leo was myself. I didn't need someone to chase me. I already had a life elsewhere. At the road's edge, the wind, an angry hand, pushed me into the bushes' limbs and needles. Peals and peals of thunder swept the horizon. The first cold drops fell from the sky. I called Maria from a bus stop shelter. When she didn't answer, I called my mother. She told me to wait where I was. Her sleepy voice pressed the sharp edge of reality upon me. She would rather I be a simpler animal. Or like my brother, half of a pair. The two of them were not, in fact, simpler, but they had better ways to be lonely.

ELEVEN

I made it through college without killing myself.

TWELVE

On the night my best friend Anais and I moved into our own apartment in Brooklyn, a cop pulled over next to our U-Haul. This was a hot block, he said, looking over at the Black men two doors down from our house, who were drinking and playing music from one of the parked cars: "Are you lost?" It took us two more hours to finish unloading the van. No one helped us. We kept on asking each other: *Are you lost?* We almost ditched my bed frame on the street. By the time we got home from dropping the van off in Park Slope, our new neighbors had gone to sleep.

A railroad apartment, the realtor had called it—heavy, sliding doors connected all the rooms. I could imagine how the layout must have worked for the families before us, but now it was proving impossible to find a stranger we trusted—and who trusted us—to walk through both our bedrooms to rent the last room. The living room had a built-in bookshelf, stained-glass windows, and parquet floors, but these beautiful details were overshadowed by everything else. In the hallway and kitchen, the linoleum tiles curled away where the floor met the walls. Layers and layers of paint coated the light fixtures, frames, and doors. And even before you got inside, trash and shattered glass littered the street, and a police tower on the corner blasted a blinding white light every night. In the first two months I hadn't invited anyone over. On the phone with my mother and brother, I described the living room, the cheap rent. I withheld all the rest, especially the fear I felt at night planning which side of the street I would walk down the moment I got off the train, how I would evade the men wearing red and white and shouting at each other, sometimes shouting at me to call me faggot, to ask if Anais—whom they called *Chun-Li*—was home. Even under the covers of my bed, I was tense. I asked myself why, why was I here.

All I wanted was enough money to live. After working through the summer at the university art gallery, I had eight hundred dollars in the bank. If I knew anything from visiting Anais in the city while I was still in school, it was that my savings would get me through a month—maybe two—if I didn't go out at all. But by my third week in New York, I had run through half the money, and I was no closer to finding a real job at a gallery or nonprofit, the only two places I felt qualified for with my anthropology degree. "Para atrás ni para impulso," my mother said, not understanding where I'd gone wrong; it wasn't too late for me to finish a science degree, to go to medical school, to keep being the best, the most successful, but she still hadn't realized I'd given that up halfway through college. I reminded her that Anais worked at a sex-toy shop and wrote freelance for several magazines, and she'd also gone to Yale; that there was precedent for my decision to not take a real job. My mother liked Anais because her parents were doctors. But it still made no sense to her why I was sending out applications for barista and server positions. I wasn't trying hard enough, she said, and she was right; I wanted to stop time for a bit, to just work and live in the city taking my life less seriously than I ever had. I had options, I told her. But first I wanted to try things out my way.

When I couldn't even get a job at a restaurant, I turned to Craigslist and with Anais's help found a part-time artist's assistant gig so I wouldn't have to ask my mother for money again. Bill claimed to be a retired art history professor turned photographer, but I couldn't find him on any college website. After a short email conversation, he invited me over for an interview at his apartment near Columbus Circle without so much as asking me about my experience or references.

I didn't tell my mother. She would be skeptical, and if something happened to me, if I got murdered in a stranger's apartment, I would rather it be my secret.

Bill was about as tall as me—a small, neat man. He shook my hand, pulled me in for a hug, then kissed both my cheeks and smiled big like we were old friends. He was bald, his head as shiny as the polished floors beneath his bony legs; both his nose and his ears were large and sprouting hair.

His spare living room consisted of a glass table the shape of a bean and a white leather sofa that faced floor-to-ceiling windows. The dining room was tucked into a narrow space just to the side of it, and the dining table was covered in piles of curling photographs separated by white paper towels, which I noticed gave off a musty smell that would've made my mother complain of a headache.

Bill patted the spot next to him on the couch. I realized with some embarrassment that I was looking around like I had never seen an apartment as nice as this before.

I asked him what kinds of things he needed from an assistant, but he ignored me.

"So, Sandiego. What a beautiful name," he said, mispronouncing my name the way most older white men did. He surveyed me from head to toe and hummed. "And from Miami. Let me guess . . . Puerto Rican? Or Cuban?"

"Neither?" I said, playing along—Cuban was the worst thing you could call my mother. "Do I look Cuban to you?"

I was used to men trying to guess where I was from. Until I spoke my name, I could be from anywhere—*Is that boy Arabian?*—I'd gotten it all from men, and I wasn't offended so much as I was bored by this game. "I'm Colombian."

"*Colombiano!* That was my next guess." He smiled as if we shared a secret—as if he already knew me—and leaned back on the couch so that I could see up his nostrils. "I love Colombian men."

"I'd love to see your photographs, Bill."

He bent forward again and put a finger on my knee with the faintest pressure. "We have all afternoon," he said, lowering his voice, his finger now pressing firmly on my knee. "You can talk to this old man for a few minutes, right?"

That first afternoon Bill showed me the studio at the end of the hallway, but not before he pointed to the door next to it—his bedroom—and shook his finger in my face.

The studio was sunny, bright. I was sweating within minutes. A long, empty wooden table ran down the middle of the room. Its surface was fastidiously clean, which was peculiar since the shelves along the sides of the room were in complete disarray with photographs like the ones in the dining room—but these ones looked luminous, almost wet. Bill had stretched them around sheets of glass and wood and a third material he called *mother-of-pearl*. The pictures were of men, all of them white, young, and lean. There could've been three different faces or thirty—I couldn't say. These men had stripped off their shirts—in exchange for money, I guessed—and posed for Bill in fields of tall grass and on derelict piers. One boy stood under the doorway of an abandoned church with both arms behind his back so that they looked lopped off at the elbows. A window outside of the frame cast a grid over his body, dividing his skin into quadrants. I imagined Bill tracing those black lines with his tongue. He watched me closely over the top of his glasses. I paced slowly around the table as I looked up at the shelves, moving farther away from him. The only thing I could think about was how Bill had been in the same room as these men—they had breathed the same air. I felt a chill; I felt ugly. These images were a catalog of beauty neither Bill nor I possessed.

My job would be to paint the paper photographs with glue, evenly covering the surfaces. The following day, once the glue had dried, I would paint on a second coat perpendicular to the first. By the third day, if I had done everything right, the glue would have pulled the ink from the paper, transferring the image. I would soak the photographs in hot water and carefully peel the glue from the paper. If I was good and patient, the glue would come away intact like the skin of a delicate fruit. That was it. I would come back the next week and do it all over again for fifteen dollars an hour.

"Let me see," Bill said, his eyes traveling down my arms to my hands. He took them, turning them over in his. "We'll see if they'll do."

He placed a paintbrush and a small plastic pail of glue in front of me, then laid out six photographs of dancers in what looked like Central Park, the prints large enough to cover half the table. After a moment, I realized it was the same lean, muscular boy wearing a black Speedo in all the pictures. In one image, he was balancing on one leg, the other drawn back like a bow; his arm stretched out from his head like an arrow. In the center of an open field, the colors all muted by Bill on Photoshop until only a green-blue tint remained, the boy resembled a statue. My eyes went to his bulge, to the tan line above the mouth of his briefs. As he leaned forward, the smooth paleness of his hairless armpits emitted a faint glow.

After Bill closed the door, I tried my best to coat the pictures, working the brush slowly across the paper. A few minutes in, the AC shut off, and the silence was stifling. The air felt heavy, as if it were souring and clotting into clumps. I wanted to open the windows—the summer light outside was alive, singing—but I was afraid to touch anything.

Bill came back into the room with a cup of water no larger than a shot glass. He set it down on the other end of the table and we exchanged places.

"This is no good," he said. "Come here. Hold it up to the light. Look here. And here." He stood behind me, pointing to the places where my strokes didn't meet, all the spots where I'd started and stopped. "There, too."

He made me pick up the brush and show him how I used it.

"Bad hand." He tapped my knuckles gently, then held my wrist up like a soiled rag. "You can't listen to her." He laughed, a whiff of fish on his breath. Then he shook my wrist and said, "You must ignore her."

I pretended I understood.

The following day, Bill took me to the bathroom in the back of the apartment. We stood close together as the tub filled with hot water.

"What does paper do in water?"

I looked at him and realized this was a real question.

"Paper soaks up water. And why do we want that?" He grabbed my elbow impatiently and gave my arm a shake as if to wake me. "Because we want to get the glue off." I didn't like the way he was talking to me, hesitation and concern in his eyes, the way white men talked to my mother when they assumed she didn't speak English. "To start, you let the print soak a little. Then you peel the glue from the corners of the paper, slowly working toward the center. Then, if you're gentle with those hands and haven't torn the glue, the image will float free."

I said nothing. The steam was rising around us, so thick and soft I could reach out and stroke it.

After the first print, Bill left me to do the rest. I plunged my hands into the steaming water. The initial shock made my eyes tear up; Bill hadn't even flinched. It surprised me how quickly my hands went numb.

The torture was worth it: The first image I pulled looked like nothing I'd ever seen. The glue was intact, malleable, skin-like as it floated to the surface. The inky blues and mottled greens glowed against the overhead light. It was like I had peeled the top layer of scum off an ancient pond. But my heart skipped when I looked at the time: It had taken me fifteen minutes to do a single print; Bill had said no more than ten. I started on the next one. I worked faster. I wondered if he had given me an impossible task. The paper wasn't coming off clean this time; it was sticking to the glue in fuzzy, white streaks—Bill had warned me this could happen. Afraid of what he would say, that I would be fired, I took my shirt off.

When he returned, he let out a little scream. "Sandiego, you've gotten naked!"

He surveyed my happy trail and small, pale pecs.

"It's just so hot in here," I said, facing the unfinished prints floating in the water.

By the third week, I had abandoned all work with the prints. I sat between silent strangers on the train three days a week on my way to Bill's, enjoying having a reason to leave the apartment and, at the same time, a reason not to look for another job. Whenever Anais or my mother asked about work, I kept the details to a minimum. I was embarrassed of my routine with Bill. As soon as I walked through the door, I took my shirt off and listened to him explain the arbitrary tasks he had invented to occupy me for the day.

Tuesday, I organized his filing cabinets; Wednesday, I painted his bathroom baby blue. I picked up a task and did it until I grew bored of it, or until five hours had passed, whichever came first. We stopped pretending it mattered what I did or how I did it. We never spoke of his photographs again. Every moment, I waited for him to make his advance—part of me wanted to see what would happen, what I would do—but instead of relieved, I felt ugly when he didn't.

Thursday, I sanded a wall in the hallway for a mural he wanted to paint. He stood behind me, his toes crinkling the plastic covering I'd laid on the floor. He was wearing a tank top, and for the first time I saw his bare shoulders, his small potbelly and hairy pits; it was odd seeing him so exposed. I could almost picture how he might've been attractive in his youth.

"Do you ever go to the galleries?"

I wiped the wall with a rag to show him my progress. "None of them hired me, Bill. Remember?"

"I should take you with me. Show them what they missed out on. You'll be a hit."

I sat back on my heels, my abs flexed. White dust powdered my skin.

"Sometimes I just sit in my studio thinking about how I have this poor boy in the other room slaving away." The way he said it made me think he actually quite enjoyed this fact. "What about tonight? The galleries. You and me."

"Sure, Bill." I brought the sanding sheet back to the wall; he'd been too cheap to let me rent an electric sander from the hardware store. I was straight-faced, scrubbing away at the wall again, thinking surely he was going to leave, when he said: "Here. Hold still a moment."

I froze with my hand still on the wall. I heard him tiptoe across the plastic covering and crouch down. He was writing with his fingertip across the dust on my shoulder blade.

"What is it?" I asked.

"My name."

I swung my head like a dog, and he sank into himself with a little giggle as I tried and failed to see what he'd written.

There was so much dust that I spent the next hour cleaning. When I finished, I showered in the spare bathroom. Bill offered me one of his T-shirts and a pair of shorts as if they were gifts from a fancy boutique. His clothes swallowed me. I looked like a son who'd raided his father's closet. For dinner, Bill cooked cod,

brown rice, and broccolini. We ate at the dining table surrounded
by stacks of drying pictures. He told me about his ex-wife and
daughter, his Paris years. I looked for the right time to tell him I
needed more money if I was going to keep working for him. We
could drop the pretense. I clearly wasn't here because of the quality of my work. For the right price, he could fuck me. My hand lay
next to my fork, palm up. I couldn't eat. I was hoping, hoping,
hoping he would just offer me a new life, my resolve weakening
the longer I kept silent.

He startled me then. "Sandiego, do you know how lucky you are?"
He looked into my face.

"If only you could see yourself," he said. "You're so beautiful. Do
you know that?" He wasn't the first man to tell me I was beautiful
as if he had discovered my beauty himself, found it, laid it bare all
on his own. He knew about wasted time and spoke like he could
solve me. "Tell me. How many hearts have you broken?"

I pulled my hand away and asked, "Bill, are you paying me for
these hours?"

We rode the train downtown. Exhausted, I took a seat, and Bill
stood, holding on to the steel post above my head and touching his
knees to mine. Even if no one was staring, I couldn't stop thinking
about how we looked.

We came up to the street in SoHo, surrounded by crowds of
young people in light jackets ducking out of bars and into cabs. I
felt like I had in college, like everywhere I looked people were

playing a different game than I was, the rules all hidden from me. I had no way of knowing how not to lose.

He was taking me to a gallery where he would have a show the following year. I vaguely hoped that while I was there, someone would offer me a job.

The gallery was on a corner. I followed Bill through the crowded entrance that smelled of fresh paint and expensive perfume. Circles of older men and women stood drinking plastic cups of red wine, every one of them dressed in black, white-haired, and clearly moneyed. I was conspicuous in Bill's shorts and T-shirt, an outfit which I began to think he'd fashioned for my suffering. I cradled my tote bag, which was bloated with my own dusty clothes, to my chest. I felt out of place, but he introduced me to people he knew, his friends, and I found myself happy to be near him. For a few moments, he basked in the looks his friends gave him when I told them that I was Colombian and had gone to Yale, and I imagined repeating these same two facts about myself at galleries and parties at Bill's side for the rest of my life. When their conversations turned to people they knew, memories they shared, I slipped away unnoticed.

I got a cup of the red wine everyone was holding. When I tried to pay, the bartender explained that it was free, and I tipped him ten dollars like it was nothing to me. The wine went down my throat warm. With that heat in my belly, I walked around the gallery. All the photographs, on all of the white walls, were of dogs. Their bodies were small and their heads cartoonishly large, distorted by a fish-eye lens to look like bobbleheads. I sipped my wine as I stood in front of each photo, counted to twenty, and moved on to the next. I hoped someone was watching me. No one was. I finished my wine and got another. I cut across the circles of men and women in black, feeling like I alone had the perspective to see how this was all bullshit and pretense, but even so, I wanted to be part of it. I wanted my photos hanging from the walls. I felt drunk, angry; I couldn't help it—I was.

"So do you always hire boys straight out of college?" I said to Bill. He opened his eyes wide. He shot a glance at his friend, a man in a blazer and blue jeans with a deep widow's peak, who he'd been talking to.

"Now, now. Sandiego, how many wines have you had?"

"Are we easier to take advantage of? Is that it?"

He pulled me outside. My head was spinning, but from what I could make out of the spiral of light and sound, he preferred to hire young gay artists who needed work. It was his way of helping out *the community*; I hated how he used the word. He'd hired another Yale boy a few years ago. He'd said his name, but I couldn't make it out. "I've behaved myself," Bill said, "I've been nothing but nice to you. Don't you agree?"

"You turn the AC off when I get there. You give me the smallest cup of water in your whole kitchen when I say I'm thirsty. You make me do the most inane, useless tasks—"

He dabbed my chin and I flinched.

"A drop of wine," he explained, teasing, but his voice was kind. He polished his fingers off on his pants, beaming his white smile at me, then at the crowds behind me on the street. He was concealing everything—his anger at my distress and accusations, my lack of discretion.

There was nothing I could say to truly hurt him.

"You're different, Sandiego. I've fired boys with more skill than you after only a day. Like this one Wesleyan boy. He was beautiful and so talented. But unlike you, he could barely hold a conversation. It was a true shame."

It was stupid that this comment made me feel special.

The following Tuesday, we fell back into our routine. Bill brought me the tiny water glass and watched me prepare the hallway for another sanding, and I pretended he wasn't there. We didn't talk about the argument at the gallery, but there was a new sour, impatient look on his face. He disappeared into his studio without a word. Dust floated down from the walls. It stuck to my damp skin and the black hairs on my arms and thighs, capped my knees, and filled the creases in the plastic sheet on the floor. When one arm went numb, I switched to the other. Bill turned on the radio inside his studio to the classical station. Every few seconds the music seemed to grow louder, as if to drown me out. I scrubbed harder. I sanded with one arm, shaking the fire out in the other; I wanted him to hear me.

Soon this will all be over. Soon, very soon, I was telling myself when I heard my name over the music. I stepped both feet onto a rag per his instructions, so as not to track any dust on his clean floors, and shuffled to the studio.

The swell of violins made me feel dizzy, like a whole flock of birds was in the air, rising over and around me, battering the walls with their wings. The photographs were out of the filing cabinets and spread across the worktable.

Bill, at the other end of the table, was holding a pose. His elbows were firmly planted on the tabletop, his hands delicately folded below his chin.

"I want you to have one," he said. I looked out over the flashing surfaces of the boys. In the middle of the table was the dancer in Central Park from my first day, now stretched over a sheet of glass, catching diamonds of light in the gaps between my brushstrokes.

The music encircled us.

"This isn't working out." He took his glasses off, pinched the red ovals on the sides of his nose, and there, again, were his intelligent eyes.

"Are you breaking up with me?" I said, jokingly.

He put two twenties on the table and clasped his wallet shut in front of him. With his head bowed, he stole another—one last—look at the trail of dust-frosted hair dividing my stomach. "I liked you. I liked talking to you."

"Is that it, Bill? You like me and my conversation?" There was a meanness in my voice I'd learned from my brother. Bill didn't move even as I stepped forward, closing the gap between us. I felt nothing for him—he was weak, pathetic, hideous, a monster, a coward, a starved old faggot. I grabbed his hand; he let me move it to my chest. I cupped my breast in his hand and squeezed hard. I willed myself not to look away. "Is this what you've been waiting for?"

"What? No, not at all . . . how could you think that?" He blinked several times like there was something in his eyes. I could tell he didn't know what to do with me. He wanted this to be something else, not what it was. Even I was scared to see what I was becoming.

"Please, just stay for dinner. Let's have dinner again. Let's talk."

"Do you really think we're going to be boyfriends, Bill? You really think I'm here to hang out with you?"

He frowned at his hand on my chest. He was like any white man. He thought he could see me and understand me because there was never anything in front of him that was outside of his understanding. But what he couldn't see was himself; and he wouldn't be able to, I thought, not until he could see the way I saw him—something he would never be able to do. He was telling himself he wanted to take care of me. That he was a good man for wanting to love me. It made me miss my mother; it made me want to hurt him.

I ignored his hesitation and lowered his hand to the waistband of my shorts. I shoved our hands inside. I grasped at my pubes between his fingers. When his fingers curled into my skin, I pretended they were mine.

I needed more than two twenties. And I needed so much more I didn't know how to ask for.

Two weeks after moving into our place in Flatbush, the fashion student renting our third room had a mental breakdown. He threatened to kill us when we asked him to clean up the dye stains in the bathtub. Anais and I kept to my room for a week. We slept with all the knives in the house under my bed until the student finally packed up and left.

When people at the laundromat or bodega asked, Anais and I said we were married. We held hands everywhere we went. The cashier at Popeyes, when I asked for honey, always said I had all the honey I needed right next to me. I loved the protection this love afforded us. I kept telling myself: *She's reason enough to be in New York.* I had no job, no plan, no other options.

In Miami, my mother was living at her new boyfriend's house, where the television played Fox News and westerns every night. My brother and his wife were in Ohio, trying for their first baby now that he'd finished medical school.

My father was still sending me three hundred dollars a month when we moved in, but after his split with my stepmother, I had to call and endure conversations in which he pretended he hadn't hurt anyone before he would wire the money. I couldn't do it anymore. He was too much of a coward to tell me he was cutting me off when he did. He left the mess for my mother to clean up.

After Bill, I went to an open call for a hotel restaurant. The manager was amused by the fact that I'd gone to Yale and offered me a job in the café instead, since I had no experience. I got up at five in the morning, rode the train into Chelsea—the lights off in all the galleries that had rejected me—and served breakfast at the hotel. I cleaned spilled coffee and swept up cold bits of hardened egg from under booths. I pulled a double espresso for the same man in a camel coat every Friday before he met his Russian escort. In the afternoons and on weekends, I got drunk by myself or with Anais and her writer friends, always ashamed to say what I was doing for work and having to leave early. Home alone in the evenings, I cooked small, easy meals that I ate in bed, listening to the men outside party and argue.

When Anais finally got home, clomping up the staircase in her boots, missing the keyhole several times, I would flinch awake in bed. I always left the doors between our rooms slightly open so I could hear that she'd made it back safely, but always, I kept my eyes closed. I listened to her piss and sit on the toilet for much too long on her phone, and then collide with her desk on the way to her nightstand lamp, before finally saying *I love you* to the dark of my room and shutting the doors between us. I felt immense longing. Longing for a life that shared its rhythms with the lives of others.

I watched television and browsed Grindr for hours because I was lonely, had been lonely for weeks, and I couldn't afford to meet up with anyone for drinks or dinner. I listed my race on the app as Latino, my gender as nonbinary, and wrote witty summaries of my life; then the next day, I would erase everything, leaving behind only the vaguest outline of myself. I couldn't help feeling giddy, stupid hope every time my phone went off with a notification. I was living for the messages of strangers.

It didn't take long for me to know every single profile in the neighborhood and to give up the hope that any one of these men would run through my life and change everything. There was the bisexual NYU film student who lived above a bar on Flatbush who always tried too hard to be funny and smart, but never wanted to meet up unless I had a third. There was the guy with the headless gym selfie who always took two days to respond, but who messaged me question marks when I didn't reply right away, and who never, no matter how many times I asked, showed me his face. Other guys were vulnerable and tender, which I found equally suspicious. There was one Puerto Rican boy farther down on Cortelyou, an opera singer also named Santiago, who offered to bring me Gatorade and soup the week I was sick. And despite all these boys, I was still alone. We were all within a few hundred feet of each other, in our beds, on our phones, reaching out to strangers, all bound by this same fate, and yet I felt like there wasn't another soul for years and miles.

When I was young, I had written my mother's eHarmony profile. I translated the messages American men sent her, and I made her as funny and as eloquent in English as I knew her to be in Spanish. In these hours we had to ourselves, I got to know her better than anyone. For her pictures, I chose a long black dress from her closet, painted her nails red, clasped a fake gold necklace around her neck, and sat her on the staircase of the old house. Peering through the thirty-five-millimeter camera she'd brought from Colombia, I watched my mother until her smile widened, grew bigger, and just as it turned to laughter, I snapped the picture. Nothing ever came of the dating site. She was alone for more than fifteen years, an unfathomable magnitude of loneliness. It was enough to think about her, alone for all those years, to know that I was okay. That I'd only been in the city a few months. That my life could yet change.

Sometimes I spent entire afternoons looking back at photos of my graduation: one of the happiest and saddest moments of my life. My mother, brother, sister-in-law, cousin, father, and step-mother had all come to New Haven. It was the first time my mother and brother had seen my father since we left. My mother and stepmother didn't, in fact, look alike the way I'd sometimes imagined because of their shared name—Luz. At night we went to the tapas restaurant I had wanted to try all my four years at Yale. My father toasted my brother and me with his Coca-Cola. We would always be his sons, he said, turning to my brother and recalling those years before I was born, when it was just him, my mother, and Manuel; he put his soda down and reached his hands out across the table to fist-bump us. I had never had so much family together at once, not in America. Looking around the table, I felt a rare sense of being at home in this country, at this school I had barely survived. I cherished the feeling, knowing it would last only a weekend.

After graduation, we all took the train into New York, where we left our bags at a locker station, and before we had to be at the airport, I led them through what I knew of the city from my visits to Anais. I stopped at all the crosswalks and waved a little imaginary flag, wrangling them like a tour guide on the way to Rocke-feller Center. Soon we were all pretending to be tour guides, all shouting *Rockafella, Rockafella*. We flew to Miami, and the next morning my father, stepmother, and I drove to Orlando to see my

Tía Tata. Everyone reminded me I'd never reached out to her all these years.

We were eating breakfast the next day when my father called out from the front door. He was going to get a taxi; we should just meet him at the theme park, he said, as if we were taking too long.

I turned to my aunt and stepmother. Around me, my father was usually careful to only be happy and pleasant, never knowing when he'd see me again, so this side of him surprised me.

They were sharing a look that said, *Let him exhaust himself.*

So I didn't worry much. We were in the suburbs; there were no taxis. He would only walk around the neighborhood, get some fresh air, and come back to the house. In a better mood, I hoped.

We found him just down the street twenty minutes later. In a bizarre scene, he sat alone on the stone marquee of the subdivision's entrance like a little boy waiting for his mother's car. When we pulled up, he got in and began to complain about his phone. He was expecting an important work call from one of his engineers today and needed a new SIM card before we went to the park; my aunt, a force of nature, vetoed the idea. She said we had to get to the park right when it opened. Otherwise we would be stuck in lines for hours. My father didn't challenge her when she said we would find him a SIM at Walmart when she picked us up in the evening.

At the park, my father disappeared every half hour to find Wi-Fi to call his engineers, telling us to go on ahead and enjoy the rides without him. He'd find us after he cleared up an issue at one of his construction sites. It's hard to say now when I realized something was off. I want to believe I had more foresight, that I wasn't blind-sided, but in truth I was too deep in my own happy story to realize what was happening. In line for a ride that afternoon, alone with my stepmother again, I was already reminiscing about how great this trip had been and telling her how I couldn't wait to visit them soon in Colombia, when suddenly she let out a wail. She was leaving my father, she said, her face distorted with pain. She stum-bled into my arms and told me my father was still seeing the same moza, a word conjuring rot, gnats, decay—another woman—that she'd warned me about when I was seventeen. My stepmother had tried to change him, then to ignore it, but she couldn't anymore. Those weren't work calls he was taking. It was *her*. It's hard to know what to say when a woman you love is in your arms crying because your father has hurt her, hard not to think this is how your own mother must've felt when it was happening to her, when you were too young to remember and too young to hold her. My stepmother's tears dampened my shirt. The line behind us zig-zagged without end; people were staring, touching their compan-ions' shoulders, telling them to turn and look. I didn't know what to do, whether I should get her out of the line or stay; both options seemed like an ordeal. A part of me still wanted to get on the ride, to scream my lungs out until this moment meant nothing and I felt nothing; another part of me wanted to get back to my aunt's house right away, to get back to Miami, back to New Haven, to my life as far away from my family as possible, as soon as possible. My stepmother gripped my back tightly, squeezing handles out of my skin. She had no idea she was hurting me. I kept my face smooth for everyone around us, like her emotional collapse was nothing new for me. I didn't show anything of the storm inside of me. I didn't ask her not to leave him; I didn't beg her to stay. I comforted her like I would my mother, because in that moment, sobbing into the soft cotton of my shirt, that's what she was. My mother. My Luz.

We stayed in line. She regained some control of herself, but her eyes were red and her cheeks smudged with mascara. As we were about to get on the ride, she decided to sit it out, and the attendant put me in the front row with strangers. When the safety harness came down on either side of my head, I began to cry. On the other side, I found my father and stepmother next to a snack kiosk, and there was something so disgraceful about how he stood next to her like he didn't know her, oblivious to her tearstained face. I slowly waded through my shame and the crowd, and when I reached them I hugged him instead of her.

Even as a young man, my father was a bacán: gregarious, daring, untamable, hungry for a good time. He was generous to a fault, often crass and too friendly. He had a heart of gold, my mother loved to say, explaining to me how he built roads where there were none, in jungles and valleys where danger always lurked. He'd liked to laugh and eat more than anything those summer days we spent together in Colombia. He wasn't a bad man. More than anyone, I understood the stupid things loneliness could make you do. I tried to understand that it was hard for him to avoid these affairs when he only saw us, his family—and then her, my stepmother—once a month. But when my stepmother decided to leave him, and he decided to let her leave, what I felt most powerfully was this: My father had done it again, chosen himself above everyone.

Even with my job at the hotel, I was still desperate for money. I updated my Grindr bio to say I was looking for gen men only and changed my profile name to a dollar sign and a money bag, like I'd seen other boys do. This thing I'd never considered doing—fucking someone for money, hooking—seemed not only exciting but also, after my father cut me off, necessary.

Jordan messaged me every day for a week on Grindr. I didn't respond because he didn't have a picture, until one night, feeling combative, I finally asked him what the fuck he wanted. He responded with a picture of himself as if it explained his persistence. I wasn't surprised when he didn't look like me or any of the other fresh-out-of-college twentysomethings gentrifying the neighborhood. He reminded me of the man in Paris during my semester abroad who kissed me at a bar only to mug me on the walk to his place; he reminded me of Nasir, who had lost all contact with Leo to find a wife. Jordan said we had to meet. That I was very beautiful, very feminine. He wrote in short, incomplete sentences, often misspelling words, omitting prepositions, conjugating verbs bizarrely—a broken language I found primal, arousing. I imagined his rough, overworked hands touching me, hands that knew long hours and days; I imagined Anais seeing him come out of my room with a hard look on his face, or the girls in the downstairs unit watching him exit the front door, everyone asking themselves why I had let this man into our house. I responded to Jordan, not on the day he showed me his face, but eventually. Over several weeks I got him to show me his body, his cock, and then more photos of his face. I toyed with the idea of meeting him but left him on read whenever he asked to come over until the day he wrote to me: "$100."

I wiped away the ring of pink mold in the sink and toilet, imagining he would need to piss before or after he fucked me. In case he peeked his head into the kitchen and living room, I organized the bananas and onions and stacks of books until they looked like a spread from a magazine. I closed the sliding doors between my room and Anais's, then piled up all my belongings and threw them into the closet. Finally, I douched in the bathtub so that even my asshole gave the impression of happiness and order.

I looked up and down the street from my second-floor window. The wind had swept the last yellow leaves underneath the parked cars and against the metal gates around the porches. I almost didn't recognize Jordan when I saw him. He glanced nervously from his phone to the houses, checking the numbers above the mailboxes. He stopped next to the trash cans in front of my house and wrote to say he thought he was here. In my life, I had met many men, hundreds; I believed I could spot the potential for violence in one with only a look. All I saw by the trash cans was an ordinary man, the type of man my life in college had separated me from for the last four years. He tucked his hands in his pockets, shivering. His forgettable face comforted me, grounded me in the bashful fizz of doing this for the first time. I opened the door with the peripheral sense that he wouldn't hurt me, knowing very well he could.

He was shorter than me, his face jowly, ashen. He flicked his head at me in recognition. His hair was freshly cut, short on the sides, spiked with gel on the top. At a bar I wouldn't have looked twice at him. He was the first man ever paying me for sex. I wouldn't be the same afterward, and I was okay with that. This was life with its necessary threats and jolts of excitement. Leading him up the stairs, I was still convincing myself this was what I truly wanted. His cold, eager hands slithered up the tiny running shorts I'd stolen from Anais, squeezing my ass hard. "Anyone home?" he asked. I shook my head *no*, stopping between the two floors. Yellow light poured down from the window above the staircase, casting a glow over the dusty steps and pile of shoes I'd forgotten to put away. There was a satisfied look on his golden face. He knew he could fuck me right there on the stairs if he wanted to. His jacket collapsed into a stiff, crinkling layer when he pulled me into him. We stood so close together his eyes melted into a single white puddle. He smelled like cold skin with the hint of a cigarette. He spread my ass cheeks, one in each hand. My hole swallowed his thumb, no resistance. "Damn," he said, an inch from my face. "That pussy is already open." I stiffened in my underwear, and I was sure he could feel it, too. I was that obvious.

In my bedroom, Jordan made a space between us where he took

off his Nets beanie and began to work on the zipper of his knock-off Eddie Bauer jacket. He stared at the photograph on the wall between the two windows, in which my mother's face was super-imposed over mine, our eyes and cheekbones perfectly aligned, only our chins and hair a bit off-kilter. The photograph was almost four feet long, printed on metallic paper that made the unmatched edges of our features bright, ghostly. At first glance, most people thought it was just me.

"It's my mom and me," I said to Jordan, pointing to my book-shelf, at the original photograph of my mother as a senior in high school that Tía Nelcy had given to me one summer. Then I pointed to the opposite wall beside the door, at the small portrait of my mother with an orchid draped over half her face like a veil. She loved orchids above all other flowers. In a perfect world, it would just be her and her flowers.

Jordan's eyes darted to the pictures, falling on everything be-tween them. It was almost too many, the number of photographs of my mother in this room, or it was and I didn't care. They were the most beautiful things I'd ever made. Sometimes, I dreamed she was inside of my skin, peering out from my eyes, astonished by how vastly different our worlds were.

I had let men buy me meals and drinks and gifts before. They were always older, more masculine; it seemed natural for them to pay. I expected men to treat me like a woman, as I had learned to see myself as one in their eyes. I always thought of my mother tell-ing me about my brother's father when I'd asked her about her past. He was in his midthirties when she had started dating him, which meant that in Ibagué he was old and nobody turned an eye to him. He wasn't giving her what she wanted; he was always busy with work, so when he rescheduled their dates, she acted like she didn't give a shit, like it was a relief to have the night free, even though inside she wanted nothing more than to see him. *Reverse psychology*, she said to me, *sometimes us women have to do crazy things*. This last sentence was what stuck with me. I wondered how much sense my mother had when she said it, if she'd also known I wasn't quite a woman or man, that she and this world had made me something else, though I could not quite say what yet.

He took my shirt off, then my shorts. You had to demand the money first. Everyone knew that. But I was afraid I would not be able to go through with this if I stopped now. I was suddenly not thinking about when he would pay me or if this was wrong, but instead that I could do this, I could do it again even. He wasn't bad looking. Neither was his cock. Giving my body to someone for money wasn't breaking me. Hooking was another way to be in the world that was available to me, another possible future. I wasn't out of options. There had to be a point to this, a purpose, a reason. I had sentenced myself to a life without my mother for friends I sometimes envied and sometimes loved more fiercely than blood; for men I accommodated and served until I'd made myself so small that I would run away and try again with another. I no longer remembered how or why I'd gotten here. But I could leave this city whenever I liked. I wasn't from here. Eventually I would leave. We all would.

"Mami, this pussy is so good." I looked into his eyes, burrowing my stare into him, my lips clamped between his fingers like a second cunt. "Fuck, mami, you're so beautiful." He kept saying it like he couldn't believe his luck at having me, over and over again, like I was his woman. I found myself relaxing. And when I nodded *yes*, I really meant it. I wanted more. "You like it, mami. Yes you do."

As soon as he came, he backed away from me, swiftly pulling the condom off and throwing it on the ground for me to pick up. He stood over his backpack and crumpled jacket. The condom was milky, clean. The floorboards creaked as he looked around. He fingered the papers on my desk and peeked at the street through the curtain. I watched his ribs expand as he caught his breath. Three lines of sweat ran down his pecs. I wanted him to lie beside me and hold me in his arms and kiss the back of my neck again. I hadn't come, but he had. His dick was still glistening. I was not prepared for when it disappeared behind his briefs. Once he was dressed, he reached into his little drawstring backpack and pulled his wallet out. He held it close to his pelvis. "How much did we say?"

"You said one hundred."

He took out several bills from his wallet, counted them twice, folded them in half, and set them on the desk with a grin—the whole thing took longer than it should have—and with a single finger he pushed the money an inch away from him.

"I only brought eighty." He was innocent, unconcerned. "I'll give you the rest next time."

I didn't say anything. I stood to count the money in disbelief.

Eighty dollars wasn't anything; I couldn't believe I'd agreed to only a hundred. I didn't want to appear angry or sad or scared, even though I was all of these things. I feared upsetting him, and I didn't know him or how he would react. I had already made myself entirely powerless.

At the door downstairs, he patted the pockets of his jacket, making sure he had everything. And as he scowled at the cold street, at the men already drinking in front of the house two doors down, I forced a kiss on his cheek. When he left, I couldn't bear how stupid I felt for showing him any tenderness.

Upstairs, I wrapped the condom in toilet paper and threw it out in the bathroom trash. I cracked open the sliding doors between my room and Anais's, letting a sliver of light cut across her rug. My sadness multiplied at the sight of her empty bed, her nightstand and books shrouded in darkness. I pushed the doors completely open and let the light pour in over everything. All afternoon I sat on her bed feeling listless, as tired as if I hadn't slept in days. I was on Grindr again. So was Jordan. Despite the shame I felt at having been used I told him I was already looking forward to seeing him again. Whiffs of musk kept rising to my nose when I least expected it. He was somehow still on my skin, coming off in pieces; I knew I should shower but didn't. There was a dull ache in my ass. My hole pulsed, still wet, still hot. I would feel it at dawn as I speed walked through the chilly streets of Flatbush to the train and put on a smile for the guests at the hotel.

I watched my bed in the other room. The sheets had risen up

the sides of the mattress and bunched up in the center; there were greasy lube stains everywhere. I yelled out to my bed—*Fuck you*—feeling childish, unreasonable. I laughed. His handprints shone above my pillow. I said it again and again.

In the kitchen, I turned the burner on under the pot from last night, singing a Colombian song, one that played so loud at parties you forgot it was about a master and his slave. I sang aloud with the full length of my lungs. I poured a coin of olive oil into the pot. After a moment, I added a spoonful of chopped garlic and a cup of rice. The pan hissed and smoked. I couldn't help laughing at myself, at the impossibility of my life, how funny it was that Jordan called me *mami*, how funny that I enjoyed it. *I guess we both have mommy issues.* And when I laughed at my own joke, I felt like my father, singing and chuckling to himself as I imagined he did in those little towns in Colombia where he disappeared. I fried the rice with garlic before boiling it, like he used to in our kitchen. My father spilled out of me in song. The smell filling the kitchen was delicious and familiar. I set the wooden spoon down on the counter. Above the stove, in the dim, incriminating light, I could see my childhood.

THIRTEEN

Leo stretched his arms out over the vinyl table in the Chinese restaurant.

"This thick one here was the first," he said to Anais, pointing to his wrist.

Anais's lower lip hung puffy and peeling under a glint of white teeth; she was focused, just like when she wrote her sex column cocooned in blankets on the couch.

"The flesh went white along the edges, almost frothy, like a frog's skin."

His arms disappeared under the table, stroking his thighs in long sweeps.

"There's some here, too," he said, looking at me. "The ones I did after you cheated on me for the first time."

Anais had never been a cutter—I waited for her reaction, for her face to suffer some change. I wanted her to see where my story began. Leo's skin, fifteen, Miami.

After dinner Anais went back to our apartment, taking the left-overs. Leo and I walked to the Boiler Room, where I'd been going after my shifts at the hotel. The Scottish bartender who knew me wasn't there tonight, so we paid for our drinks and sat on a cracked leather couch in the back under a pink light, talking and holding hands.

"Amiga," he said, "the saga I have for you."

For nearly an hour, he filled me in on his latest attempts to find Nasir. He told me about his sister finally coming out as a lesbian and the next day moving to Rhode Island for someone she'd met online. He was managing a new location of the sushi restaurant by the beach. He told me about his trips to the bathhouse in Fort Lauderdale and his stint go-go dancing at LeBoy. He had a new boyfriend—nineteen, Colombian, uncut—named Camilo. He showed me a picture of a skinny, pale boy with acne scars across his cheeks. He already hates you, Leo said, when I asked if we were going to have a threesome with him, too. He hadn't told Camilo he was visiting me. Technically, he was just passing through on the way to visit his sister—news to me. Leo showed me the bright red pin on his phone indicating Camilo's location; they had been tracking each other since the beginning.

I was captivated—as always—by how he talked: his turns into the tawdry and the sentimental, his humor and mania, his sudden dryness and gravity. What he had was charm and talent, a way of seeing the world that I'd always loved, so that when he did ask me about la Chinita, the name he'd annoyingly given Anais, I had no clue what I wanted to say except that she was an immigrant like us.

"But we're not chinitos. You know that, right?" I rolled my eyes, but he kept going: "Let me guess, her parents are doctors?"

"Only her mother." I laughed. "Her father is a medical engineer."

He snorted. "So she's nothing like us."

It annoyed me how quick he was to dismiss her, but I also knew what he meant: Anais had gone to a Montessori, then private school, then Yale; her life had always been on the right track, both her parents guiding her toward the success they had already found in America. This was the difference between us I tried to ignore, because it was easier to focus on how we were similar, to get closer to her, to become her family. That was exactly how she loved me, like family, I said to Leo, feeling like I was drawing some line in the ground between him and Anais. I had come to depend on being in proximity of a life that seemed, at least from the outside, a little easier than mine. College had taught me to do that.

We'd met in the back of a chemistry lecture hall like two little rats, I told Leo. I didn't see her again until a Halloween party where she was dressed as Natalie Portman in *Black Swan*, but it took us another year to become inseparable. *The wandering pair*, I said, repeating what a mutual friend had called us. I told him about her sex column, how random people on the train stopped her to say hello, how people had even come up to me at parties just to say they recognized me from her Instagram. I showed him pictures of the model she'd fucked while in Cartagena for my brother's wedding. I told Leo everything about Anais in an attempt to make our love, however platonic, sound as urgent and important as his life in Miami, and for a moment I wondered if I was trying to make him jealous, if what I was really saying was, *You're no longer the center of my world*, but he hadn't been, not for a long time. We were different people, and I hadn't been this attached to another person since him, but only he could still make me this anxious and tongue-tied.

The next morning when I left the house for work, the curdled gray sky stretched all the way down Church Avenue where it cut in between the two- and three-story buildings. Everything was blue in the soft dark of morning. Each breath of cold air sliced my lungs. The zipper of my jacket counted my steps on my chin. It was March. It was Leo's second day in New York.

I still talk to Leo after all these years, I thought as I pulled my sweater off and tucked it onto a shelf behind the counter at work, *for a reason that might break me open if put into words.*

Leo and Anais spent the day at home together. Between customers, I snuck peeks at my phone to read her texts. They'd gotten coffee and walked to the ice rink in Prospect Park. She liked him, she said. It was nice letting her darkness rub up against his, not having to hide or pretend how she felt. I told her: "I know, right?"

On the third night, there was drinking, drinking, drinking. We stumbled into a jockstrap party in the East Village. All the guys in the bar were hairy, tall, white. Dancing in place, they looked like one mass, almost motionless. "It's like they all know each other," I told Leo at the edge of the crowd, holding my folded coat close to my chest, unwilling to pay for coat check. "Like they come from the same place." We took our clothes off, and I was thankful I'd put on cute underwear that morning, then upset when I noticed the cuts on Leo's thighs, the thin ones he had talked about over dinner, glowing pale pink in the neon bar light, as if freshly done. I tried counting them, like tally marks. Then tried to read them, like letters. I didn't know what they were telling me.

In between drinks, I checked Grindr. There was nothing more depressing than being on the grid, according to Leo. "It's like advertising your loneliness." But I still kept scrolling through the columns of men. Waiting. What was more depressing to me was that after four years, Leo was still torn up about Nasir.

I was both surprised and unsurprised that he still missed Nasir. Leo had been the same after our breakup, except this time was longer, except I had no part in this. At the bar we had the same conversation about Nasir; he had left to find a wife, have children, and make a life his family in Palestine would accept. No mention of how Leo cheated and hooked through the whole relationship. Or how Nasir slept with me each time I came back to Miami.

The way Leo talked about his cuts, how he remembered the dates, the places, like he was happy and proud of them, that was why Nasir finally left him and why I never really did. I felt some vague responsibility toward Leo; there might not be another person in the world who could keep up with him.

After four drinks, we ran out of cash. We were drunk, and it still wasn't enough. He had texted me days before his flight to say he wasn't the same kid anymore. I wanted to say I wasn't either, though sometimes I wished I were, like now.

Leo pushed through the crowd toward the door. I wasn't thinking when I followed. An elbow dug into my side. A drink splashed my shoulder. I stumbled forward like we were at a concert, like we needed to reach the stage, like our favorite song in the world was playing. I found his hand, willing to follow him as long as we didn't get separated. Then I remembered it was winter: We were leaving the bar without our clothes. The doorman was talking to someone, waving a flashlight over a license, but when he saw Leo reach for the door, he grabbed his forearms and pulled him in with one tug.

Leo's body drew a long, lazy arc in the air.

"Do you want to die, kid?"

Everyone was watching. I made him put his pants on and wrapped my scarf around my waist because my pants were missing.

We withdrew cash from the pizza shop at the corner and bought a Four Loko from a bodega. It was already three months into the year. It had been nine months since I'd graduated. Five years since we'd drunk one of these together.

We headed to the West Village for another gay bar, and before I knew it we'd been walking for close to an hour. Leo had lost his credit card, we had found it, we had lost it again. We were fighting and then we weren't. It was like we were in a play and nothing we said truly mattered. That's how we ended up in front of a closed restaurant, drinking from another brown bag and deciding to go to the West Side Club. He wanted my first time at a bathhouse to be with him. In the locker room, he stripped down and wished me luck. It was only then that I realized we weren't doing this *together* together.

I was alone, my towel slung over my shoulder, walking through corridor after corridor of little black doors. An anonymous ass in the air. Two guys sniffing a bottle of poppers in a corner. A guy stretched out on a tiny cot stroking a beastly cock the size of a fist. Little black doors and little black doors. Leo's name slid around my tongue like acid, and as I turned a corner, through an open door, I saw him—there—in a dark room, a guy pressing his face into a pillow, the bang of meat against bone. Leo's smile when he turned to me was as radiant as a bolt of lightning in the dark.

I left without him. It was eleven the next morning when I got a text saying: "Hola, amiga, I'm still alive. Leaving soon." He'd spent the night, what was left of it, at the bathhouse. Somehow I was jealous of him, the way he was able to fling himself at the world without fear, even if I'd decided long ago that I didn't need to live like him; I had a mother who pushed me to study, a brother who was now a doctor, a father waiting for me to forgive him. My longing, unlike Leo's, was fastened to concrete people and places on this earth. Sometimes I forgot we weren't the same person anymore, and perhaps we never had been. Now, I was so close to Anais that I sometimes forgot we weren't the same person, too. My yearnings were more intense than hers, more painful, the absence I was trying to fill larger. We had learned to joke about the time I put a cigarette out on my wrist, or the time I came home threatening to chug rubbing alcohol from the bathroom. Below the circle of ruined skin on my wrist was the faint scar of a cut, flat and lighter in shade, the only one I had ever made—and I remembered how the summer after my sophomore year, before I'd gotten close with Anais, I called Leo whenever I was suicidal because some boy hadn't tried to fuck me after a date, or because some other boy had fucked me too hard, spit on my face, slapped me, and sent me out the door, cum dripping out of my ass and soaking my underwear, gluing it to my skin by the time I woke up the following morning in my dorm room. Or because I'd gone back to the same boy for more. I didn't know if I'd gotten better at taking care of myself since then or if I'd only made my life smaller out of protection. Was there even a difference? I watched Anais sleeping next to me, aware that I kept making the same mistake.

Two hours passed. I called Leo again, but his phone was off. He should've been home by now. After Anais left for a meeting, I smoked some weed, cleaned my room, and folded Leo's clothing to keep my hands busy. His suitcase on top of my desk was already open. I poked my fingers through his balled-up socks, his rolled jeans, not ready to full-on snoop through his belongings, but still curious. The only item of interest was a silver lighter—a torch, really.

Three more hours passed. A column of light moved across the living room, passing over the black Ikea table, then the bookshelf resembling a cage, then the couch without legs Anais had brought from her last apartment. Light chased the dark into the empty room in the center of our apartment. Then it was dark out. In another hour I planned to walk around the West Village, stapling missing person signs with Leo's face on trees, handing them to strangers, going back to the bathhouse and asking if anyone had seen him. But for now, I went on Grindr and found a distraction to fuck me while I waited for Leo, who was possibly dead. My distraction, thirty-two, had a long-term partner who didn't know he was here. "Can you keep it DL? Is that cool? Are we terrible people?" I wrapped my legs around him, pulled him in, told him: "No one's ever fucked me this good."

I let Leo in at seven. He didn't say a word, simply went upstairs, stripped off his clothes in a corner of my room, and locked himself in the bathroom. I knocked on the door and asked him if I could pee. He let me in, dead silent. When nothing came out of my dick, I sat on the toilet intent on waiting out the silence. He lay flat in the bathtub, the shower pouring. I thought of the Plath poem he quoted all throughout our youth: *A million soldiers run, Redcoats, every one.* The steam gathered between us. He didn't need to speak for me to know the small metal ball was spinning, the one I'd heard in his chest when I was fifteen, the one that'd always been there, going faster and faster, clearing space for the pain of last night where it will be buried along with the pain of every other night, because this is the only way he knows how to deal with living.

I left the bathroom and scrolled through more distractions on my phone until Leo entered my room with a limp. He pulled the mirror off the wall and laid it on the rug, then crouched over it and examined the underside of his thigh with two careful hands.

On the sixth day, I returned to work at the café. Around noon, Anais texted me to say she had cleaned Leo's wounds. He didn't remember how he'd gotten them—the six, inch-long lacerations in rows like train tracks on his legs, like he had sat down on a radiator, like—she couldn't imagine what would leave such a mark, or what it meant. She couldn't wait for me to get home; Leo's darkness was too much, pitch-black, sucking her in. She was tired, she said. So was I.

That night I tried to get the three of us to sleep in the same bed like we did the first night, but Leo was restless. He kept turning and turning in the blanket I'd brought out for him because he didn't like the smell of Anais's. Eventually, he got up with a sigh and slammed every door on his way to the bathroom. I listened for his cries and whispers, his inarticulate animal sounds, through the walls. I left Anais in bed, knowing she'd understand.

One of the wounds was infected. White pus, green lint. He still hadn't told me anything about what had happened at the bathhouse. I soaked up the pus with toilet paper, applied antibiotic cream, and bandaged his leg. I closed the sliding doors between my room and Anais's and laid Leo down on my bed, where he pretended, still turning, gasping for breath, to sleep while I stayed standing. I paced the room. From the TV stand, I picked up a business card I had not seen before. A real estate agent in his fifties stared at me. How could Leo be against Grindr and be okay with this? The strangers. The little black doors. The dark. I slipped the business card under the bed like doing so could erase this man from Leo's life. I lay down next to him. The seconds passed, each one longer and more brazen than the last. He wrapped my arm around him, wrapped me around his need. His body finally relaxed. The warmth of him spread out in the dark. I kept holding him, wishing I were being held, wishing my pain were the kind someone wanted to hold.

The next time I visited Florida, I waited for my mother and her boyfriend, Mark, to go to sleep before I drove to Leo's. *Hola, mi vida*, I said to the Shakira spilling onto the bushes outside his open window. At the door, Leo looked unsteadily at me as if through a haze. I kissed him on the lips, slipping past him, noticing the jugs of water on the floor, the bags of cat food, the cardboard boxes full of recycling.

"Flaca," I said, because every muscle and bone on his body stuck out from his skin. "You're so skinny. Did you finally get AIDS and not tell me? Or did you start doing meth?"

He led me down the hall by the hand, acting like he hadn't heard me. The living room furniture was all pressed up against the walls and covered with laundry. His mother's door was closed, his sister's room empty.

In his room, he looked at me straight on: "How did you know?"

"About what?" I sat at the edge of his mattress, remembering the torch lighter in his bag when he had visited last year, how he'd disappeared for almost an entire day after the bathhouse and come home with the strange wounds on the underside of his thigh.

Leo turned into Shakira then, shaking his hips and lip-synching into his fist as I pieced it together. He spun, and sure enough, the scars were there, smaller now. He swung his invisible ponytail around the room. Skinny, like when we were fifteen.

"You guys were so worried about my leg. I really did sit on a radiator. I was high and getting face-fucked, hardly realized what was happening. We all make sacrifices."

"You were already using when you visited?"

"Yeah, girl. I even picked up near your house," he said, sliding the back of his hand down my cheek, singing to me. "You really didn't know?"

One night, when he's cutting himself again, I text Leo: *Just don't die*. He responds that if he gets into an accident, I shouldn't call an ambulance.

One night, when my mother asks how el Venezolano is doing, I decide to tell her the truth. That he's smoking and selling meth. I know I won't see him again, not for a long time. My mother would put a chain around my balls before she let me. She's heartbroken, then relieved that it had been Leo, and not me, who'd turned out this way.

One night, he texts me: "I wrote out a whole . . . what's the opposite of an apology? A complaint? I wrote out a whole complaint. To tell you I won't forgive you and you were shitty. But it didn't feel genuine, so I didn't send it. Now I don't know what I feel. Do you want to read it anyway? Can you proofread it? Okay, here goes: You gave up on me. You abandoned me. When I needed you most, you disappeared. You were a coward. I was destroying myself and you walked away. Because it was scary. Because you didn't know how to handle it. You couldn't learn? You went to Yale but you couldn't figure this out? I thought that when I got sober I would be able to understand or be able to sympathize. I don't and

I won't. None of that was love. None of that was friendship. You were a selfish coward who left me for dead." *You gave up on me. You abandoned me. You disappeared.* He wounds me precisely; for weeks I wonder privately if I did to Leo what my mother did to my father, my father to her, my brother to all of us; one long tremor noiselessly, steadily, shaking through the world. When I finally show Anais the message, she reminds me I can't blame myself for letting him go, I couldn't have saved him if I tried. *All of us, including you, Santi, have the right to self-preservation.*

But in his room tonight, I asked Leo to light the pipe for me. I promised myself I would only do it this one time, to know what it was like. Maybe I would understand what was taking him away from me.

I took two hits. We fucked for a little while, licking each other's faces. Both of us wanted to be the bottom but neither of us could stay hard long. Even with my hand fitted into the dip between his nipples, I felt cold and sad and distant in his presence, as if the ghosts of our younger selves were in the dark air in front of us.

The bed was empty when I woke up in the middle of the night to pee. Leo was up, smoking again, offering me the pipe. The art and pictures from his walls surrounded him on the floor: Maria's melted crayon paintings, the canvas Leo had covered in broken glass.

"Redecorating," he said, like it was the most normal thing in the world.

He held up a small square painting of a red boy seated next to a window. A beam of orange light emanated from his skull, reaching straight into the sky.

"It's you," he said. "You made this."

But I was sure the painting was his creation.

Two days later Leo invited me to smoke again. I was at the zoo, pushing the empty stroller next to my brother and his daughter. My mother and his wife, both afraid of getting sun, were walking ahead to buy hats from the gift shop. I texted Leo back saying I couldn't see him, not while he was using. *Like at all or only while we're hanging out?* I don't know, I responded, I can't think about this right now. I'm with family. My phone buzzed: Leo was calling. I had no clue how or when he had started to make me feel the same way my father did. I silenced my phone. Several animal habitats were closed for maintenance. Every few minutes my two-year-old niece asked for ice cream. The lions, her favorite, hid behind the farthest bush from the crowd. I glanced at the words *please don't leave me* sitting atop the stack of unopened messages and switched my phone to airplane mode. At an empty enclosure, my brother asked: "What's this one supposed to be?" "A wild ass," I said, reading the display. Then, taking a risk, I repeated to my niece—*wild ass, wild ass*—but she was still too young to say it back to my brother, still too young to remember me. After lunch, at the playground, I crawled around on all fours and roared like a lion for her in front of everyone.

FOURTEEN

$100
how r u mami
u remember me?
from grindr
what u doing
i wanna see u
hey
u know
want ur pussy now
mami

I hadn't hooked in over a year when Jordan texted me on Christmas Day. We had slept together six or seven times the year I worked at the hotel—the closest I ever came to a regular. Every time he left I deleted his texts and told myself I would never see him again.

He managed an Italian restaurant, a bodega, a CVS—a different place every time I asked. The same went for his name—Jordan, Jonathan, Jacob. There was only one thing clear between us: We didn't want to know each other. Each time we met felt like the first. That's exactly why I invited him over on Christmas Day.

I lit the candles jammed into the mouths of the wine bottles scattered around the living room. Anais had flown back to Portland a week earlier to see her parents and little brother for the holiday and wouldn't be back until New Year's. Our other roommate had taken the morning train out to Long Island the day before. I'd cleaned the countertops so well that the living room was reflected in the spotless black stone, and I could see myself there, spectral, waiting, in the penumbrae around the flames. Sometimes I wanted to live a small life like this. I didn't care how meaningful anything was, or even what it meant, so long as every detail could be considered. That's what I wanted, to be aware in every moment of who I was and what was around me. Life could be simply beautiful if I could live it like this, I thought, sitting in my kitchen waiting for Jordan, the first trail of wax beginning to drip.

Last fall, when I had last seen Jordan, I had been waiting tables at a buzzy new restaurant. I had a boyfriend who took me on vacations to Puerto Rico and New Orleans. I didn't need the money anymore, though it had never really been just about the money. I liked having a secret. Aside from Jordan, I had hooked with a dozen other guys, mostly middle-aged men with hotel rooms on the streets around Times Square, with brunch plans in Hell's Kitchen, with orchestra seats in the evening, men who'd just left their wives, men at the beginning of new gay lives. Hooking, for that period, had helped me make sense of my life in ways I hadn't foreseen and couldn't articulate. The harvest, was how I thought of it—of all the places and people that had mysteriously made me who I was. Every frayed bit of my life weaved into a perfect ribbon.

For the first time I wasn't returning to Miami or Colombia for the holidays. My brother, his wife, and my niece had flown to Peru, and I didn't want to spend another Christmas with my mother and Mark, just the three of us. My mother had made me promise I'd find other plans, for her sake. What was another little lie? To comfort her, to prevent her from worrying, I said I was spending Christmas with a coworker and her partner. How could I explain to her that life felt cluttered and loud? That there was just too much of life and I was just so tired. *Was it just winter?* Asking myself this question every day, at every moment, led me to break up with the three men I had been seeing. And now I hadn't gotten out of bed before noon in days, which was strange, not a good sign, since I usually woke up by ten to brew coffee and read on a bench in the park, even in winter. I also wasn't eating. At around three each day I took the train into Manhattan, my stomach empty, every cell in my body buzzing. My first and only meal was at the restaurant, where the cooks prepped large batches of pasta and salad every night for the crew. I'd moved up the ranks quickly: busser, cocktail server, then working brunch shifts and eventually weekend nights. I'd worked so many hours that I finally had savings. Five thousand, then six. Just last night I had made four hundred dollars during our Christmas Eve dinner service. This money gave me the freedom to cut off all communication with my father. I even talked less to my mother now that I worked nights and woke up every morning with nothing new or good to tell her. I had learned this from her, how to hide my real emotions for other people's comfort, to be palatable, to present a neat, easy image of a life as I disappeared.

My phone said it was only six but outside the streets were empty. The crushed salt across the road gave the blackness a blue tinge. Loud Caribbean music played from every direction. All around me, the twenty or so families on the block were gathered in celebration.

What I wanted tonight was another body. It didn't matter whose, it didn't matter if we didn't particularly like or know each other as long as we could be entangled in bed, pretending to be lovers. Sometimes this was all I wanted—to perform love. The performance was, to me, almost more exciting than the thing itself. After a performance, the curtains closed. You were free.

I hit the switch. A single light—my reading lamp—illuminated a circle over my bed. I prepared the little stage, laying out a towel and remembering how after our first meeting I'd found Jordan's handprints in the greasy lube he liked pressed onto the wall above the pillows. No one ever noticed them except for me. Once they'd dried, the hands were only visible from opposite the window, when the sun pierced through the room at a sharp angle—which only happened in winter, around sunset—this trace of him remained locked in the space and time of its creation. Out of the corner of one eye, at a sudden turn, unexpectedly, his hands would greet from the wall. And I'd think, *Thank God for art.*

After Jordan left, I locked the door and blew the candles out. In my room, I pulled the drawer out from under the bed where I kept vials of medicine from the last seven years, all of them expired, and the tangles of chargers and cables for electronics I no longer owned but was still hesitant to get rid of—there, at the center of the drawer, atop a hair comb, sat the five twenties. A hundred dollars was nothing to me now. And yet the feeling inside of me when I looked at the bills was intense, total, like I was spinning out of my body, leaving myself. I never wanted to see Jordan again.

My mother picked up on the third ring. Mark, in the background, asked if it was me. They were watching his favorite Christmas movie. My mother summarized the plot: A policeman tries to rescue his wife when her holiday office party is taken hostage by criminals. There was no snow. Too much *poom poom.* "You're going to laugh when you see what he got you." The movie made it sound like she was in the middle of a battlefield: bullet shells showering the ground, bodies crashing through glass. "He ordered you power tools. A lot of power tools." We laughed, happy that Mark was so dependably himself. After a moment, she asked about my father the way she always did: "Don't get mad, but I have to know. How's your father?" I told her he was with Pilar in Cartagena, or at least he had posted a Facebook album of photos with her there. But no, he hadn't called. She knew not to push it and said nothing more about him. "I love you." She paused. "There are so many people in this world who love you, Santiago." Before I could ask her if it got easier, being alive, being alone, she said: "Hijito, Nelcy is calling. The mariachis I got for Abuela must've just arrived." "Sure," I told her, "you can call me back," knowing she wouldn't, knowing she'd already hung up.

IV

FIFTEEN

In Duane Reade, facing a wall of dandruff shampoos, I could only manage to half listen as my mother told me again that it was possibly her last chance to see Abuela. For years I'd called her several times a day, whenever I was walking, but we were lucky if we talked twice a week now. She was either fighting with Mark about where to retire or calling me about Abuela. At ten in the morning I was already too stoned to keep my mind from wandering as she spoke. Her visits to Colombia were regular now, every two or three months, whenever there was any change in Abuela's health, while I hadn't left the city in a year. A whole year shackled to the restaurant, to my little apartment. I had worked through my mother's sixty-second birthday, the baptism of Manuel's daughter, Thanksgiving, Christmas, New Year's, my family never far from my mind. I thought of them while I recited the wine list to myself on the subway to the Upper East Side, while I crossed the restaurant's dimly lit dining room with plates of caviar and bluefin crudos in hand, while I dozed off on the train back to Flatbush and woke up at the last stop on Coney Island. I thought about how everyone—from my mother and brother to Leo and Anais—was growing without me into their own vital beings, while my own life resembled a holding pattern.

My job during these calls about Abuela was simple: convince my mother it was okay to take more time off work, to leave Mark alone at home again, to buy another last-minute ticket to Colombia. I never thought too much about what I wanted or what was best. That had always been my brother's job.

Leaving the store empty-handed, I told her not to worry. I would send her the money for the flight. My Christmas present, since I hadn't mailed her anything. I wasn't even thinking when I told her I wanted to come this time.

I hadn't seen Abuela since before the stroke. Nor had I called her, even though my mother asked and asked. My brother, at least, had a wife and daughter to justify his seeing Abuela as a character in our mother's story, a separate part of her life that could never really touch us. Or maybe it was only me who saw her this way.

When my mother replied, she erupted in a rush that reminded me she was my life's true love. She and I both knew I'd had to be the one to suggest this trip, the two of us together, since something about our relationship had changed years ago around the time I left for college, something that forbade her, even as she became more dependent on my help, from demanding anything outright of me.

She asked if I was serious, and when I reassured her, *every word*, she said: "One day I will die happy because of you."

It felt like a turning point, then, to get home and coordinate the flights, to book the hotel, to take care of everything. To really make myself part of her story again. I'd forgotten how good it felt to bring her joy. We would visit Abuela in the morning, stay with her until she fell back asleep, and afterward, whatever was left of the day would be for my mother and me to do what we wanted.

I flew from LaGuardia to Fort Lauderdale. From there, I boarded the plane to Bogotá with my mother. We skipped the forty-minute flight to Ibagué for the scenic bus route—for the novelty, for the sake of doing something we would never have done alone. An hour later, we were only at the edge of Bogotá, passing the crowd of gray cement buildings that was Soacha. My mother asked if I had talked to my stepmother about the apartment she and my father had bought here as an investment, before their separation. I hadn't, I'd wanted to be left out of it. The money didn't matter to me, much less owning something so ugly and small on the outskirts of Bogotá—to my mother, all I said was *no*. "The last time I called her," she went on, "all she wanted to talk about was your father. Crying over the same man after three years. I can't stand women like her." It had always been my mother's tendency to make an enemy where there was none. "She just wants to hold on to the title so she has a reason to talk to you and your father." I, too, was stubborn and cautious like my mother; I only responded to every other one of my stepmother's messages on Facebook. *Mi hijo*, she'd written, *you will always have another mother in*

Colombia. I had no plans to see her this trip and hadn't even told her I was coming.

The rest of the journey was cold and haunted. Five hours later, weak with hunger, I awoke as if from a portal at the bus station in Ibagué.

"Take care of your madrecita," said the taxista outside of Hotel Ambalá. This was his first time addressing me since picking us up from the bus station. "Pilas," he said, tapping the side of his skull—keep your batteries on, stay alert. After we lifted the suitcases out of the trunk, he threw his shoulders back with a sharp nod and clapped me on the back. Another man trying to teach me to be a man.

I hadn't spoken the whole ride, leaving it to my mother, who had gotten him to tell us his life story with an alacrity and a willingness I'd found startling. Now, as if to pardon my silence as a problem of language, I hid behind my English and said *thank you.*

I carried our luggage up the hotel stairs while my mother paid the taxista. Instead of staying with one of my aunts or at Abuela's, where we would have to sleep on a sofa or a colchón on the floor, I'd insisted on a room at the hotel she'd mentioned once or twice before in her childhood stories, the best in the city, hosting beauty pageants and banquets for dignitaries. This scrap of conversation had woven itself into my fiction of her life; she'd never climbed these stairs as a girl, never gotten past the invisible border of the street, the voice in her head saying she didn't belong. I was giving my mother a second chance at childhood.

But now, walking across the patio, I found the chairs stacked in pillars, bound by chains snaked through their slotted seats, and the tables corralled to one side, covered by thick black tarps spattered with bird shit. It came to me quite suddenly, in a kind of tidal shift, everything I'd ignored online, from the outdated, pixelated pictures to the plainness of the HTML website: The hotel as it was in my mother's time, or even a decade ago, no longer existed. In a few months, we would laugh when Hotel Ambalá closed its doors, but for now, all I felt was that I'd made a terrible mistake; we should've gone straight to Abuela's, not wasted a single minute apart from her—that's what my mother would've done—but I had brought us here. I breathed, swallowed, closed my eyes and opened them, as overwhelmed as I was at the restaurant when several tables were sat in my section at the same time. The slow slip of everything from my grasp.

I looked down from the hotel patio and found my mother on the street below, singled out by a streetlamp in a cone of orange light. She was talking to the driver through the passenger window, like friends. She had chatted with almost every stranger we'd met. She was just like Abuela in this respect, indiscriminately making friends while ignoring you at her side. Aside from her question about the Soacha apartment, we had only spoken to each other to point out the views through the windows of the plane, bus, and taxi, to say we needed to pee or eat, as if to conserve a limited source of energy. But with a waitress at the airport, it was *mi gente* this, *mi gente* that, pounding a fist against her heart, with a sense of nationalism I hadn't seen in her before. She tipped the woman a whole day's wage, which was only ten or twenty dollars—nothing to my mother, to us. She was like another person, possessing the kindness and generosity she could only have here, in her homeland, free from the worries strapping her into a smaller life. I hadn't anticipated how quickly and easily she would fall into her old life. Or rather, what I didn't expect was for her to count on me to be charming, to have her open and light spirit, to be transformed in the same way she was. She didn't know I had always been treated differently those summers I'd visited Colombia as a teenager, like I radiated some aura I couldn't control. Here, I was no different than in America: quiet and reserved, mindful of how everything I did was read and interpreted as a sign of my foreignness. Here, I was the same person my mother did and didn't know.

Now, after looking left, then right, my mother dug out the envelope of pesos tucked into the waistband of her panties. *No one thinks to touch una viejita down there.* I took a picture of her with the camera I'd brought.

P<small>AST</small> the hotel doors, down a long corridor and recessed in a pool of amber light, stood the lobby.

The circular galleries of each floor tunneled skyward, the white walls framing a circle of navy sky, such that, as had been my experience with several buildings in Colombia, we were at once inside and outside.

Behind the front desk, a girl in a maroon vest and black bow tie, who'd been smiling, erect, and ready since we'd come in through the doors, greeted us.

"Mi tesoro," said my mother, whispering it like a secret while the girl searched for our room key on the hooks covering the cork wall behind the desk. I drew her into me then, wrapping my hand around her shoulder, finding the button of skin where she'd been vaccinated as a child; when the girl turned around, I was covering the top of my mother's head in kisses.

"My colleague will guide you to your room," the girl said, practicing the little English she knew. She held her palm out to the side.

Below the counter, out of view, sat a teenager on a plastic stool low to the ground. He held his phone in both hands over his crotch, so focused on the screen he didn't notice us looking at him. In his oversized tan workman's suit and black military boots, he gave the impression of a boy dressed in his father's work clothes.

"Armando." The girl kicked his shin and he looked up, startled and innocent, as if we'd broken into his bedroom in the middle of the night.

In the elevator, Armando scanned us from head to toe. He stood several inches over our heads and reeked of the same blue aquatic cologne my brother still wore. When the cabin shook and started, he asked what brought us to Ibagué.

We were from here, my mother said, we'd left in the late nineties and moved to Miami.

The floor numbers lit up over the door with the chime of a recorded bell.

Her firstborn was a doctor now and this one was her artist, she said, gripping my elbow.

This piece of information changed the boy's face; perhaps he was surprised to find out I wasn't a student, that I was older than I looked, and for the first time he met my eyes straight on.

They waited for me to speak, but when I didn't, they shared a complicit smile, like I was an eccentric relative they had no choice but to tolerate.

She repeated the phrase I heard on the phone every few months: "It might be our last chance to see his abuela."

My mother continued to tell him about how Abuela had had a stroke two years ago, and how the doctors hadn't let her fly back to Miami. And now, as she spoke, the realization swept over me: We had planned nothing else for this trip. Not because we were people who went with the flow. Not because there was so much to do in our hometown. But because we were here for Abuela.

My heart was racing when we stepped out of the elevator at what would be our floor for the week. Standing at the waist-high railing over the atrium, I looked down on the lobby, which glowed like a penny at the bottom of a well. "I'm going to take a picture," I said, but my mother and the boy didn't even hear me. They carried on with their conversation down the corridor, the overhead sensor lights turning on one by one. From this distance they resembled a mother and son. I couldn't say, as I stood there looking at them through the camera, to what extent I had grafted myself onto my mother's trip, but it occurred to me now: I wasn't here for Abuela or for my mother, but to escape my life in the city. The thought of going back brought physical pain, like a tiny nail pushed into my sternum. I focused on Armando and my mother through the viewfinder. They were my second picture.

Now that we only saw each other twice a year, it took us longer and longer to find our past selves and settle into being together. I watched my mother inside the hotel room from outside on the dark balcony, as if from behind a two-way mirror.

The large room had a desk, a dresser, a television. Between the two identical beds, one for la Doctora and one for the muchacho, was a nightstand with a phone and a lamp. The lamp multiplied my mother's shadow across the room's walls. Her silhouettes moved with her like an army as she inspected the sheets, the mattresses, the pillows, the carpet, the closet, the nightstand, and each corner of the room. Even out here on the balcony, the smell of cheap hotel was faint but perceptible.

I connected my phone to the Wi-Fi in an instant, but when I opened Grindr, then Instagram, then Gmail, nothing loaded. I switched in and out of airplane mode. I tried again. I opened the email I'd sent last minute to the restaurant. I was telling myself I wanted to get in trouble, as I'd done with so many lovers as soon as I began to feel trapped; but I was getting too old to just disappear, to not care. In the end, I'd lied to my manager and said Abuela died. That I was the only one who could help my mother.

No matter what I tried, the internet wouldn't work. I only wanted to see who around me was online and looking. For a moment, I held the phone out past the balcony, over the narrow downhill road, thinking if only I could let it go, if only, but I was holding on with as tight a grip as I could.

When I looked again, my mother was hoisting her suitcase onto the bed farther from the balcony. She didn't glance up once, not when she stripped to her panties, or when she bared her breasts, or when she stepped into her pajama bottoms and pulled an old fuchsia tank top over her head; she acted as if she were alone. She hung her dresses and blouses in the closet, filed her bras and panties in the drawers, lined up her lotions and perfumes—from shortest to tallest—on the desk next to the television, all with the satisfaction she got out of finding a place for everything. On the nightstand, next to the telephone, she set a small, dark blue box with a thick silver bow that glittered in the lamplight. Finally, she sat on the bed next to her empty luggage. Her reading glasses slid down her nose as she looked at her phone, the small white light in her lap. I didn't register that she was on a video call until I heard the laugh she only used with Mark; the humiliatingly boisterous pitch was, after all these years, still new to me.

They had met on a website for older singles the summer I'd graduated and moved to New York. I'd heard her tell the story many times: Mark saw her in front of the Starbucks, said she was too beautiful for him to just buy her a coffee, and took her across the street to an Italian restaurant where she'd always wanted to eat.

My brother, who was doing a year of residency in Orlando, met him before I did. "Your stepdad," he texted me, "had us making pizzas from scratch. So random, bro." Other than pictures of his daughter, he only texted me with complaints about our mother, trying to get me to see her as bizarre and impulsive, the old madwoman of our youth. Sometimes I went along with him for the sense of camaraderie and to see just how wicked he could be.

When I visited Mark and my mother for the first time, I was struck by how little they understood each other. Mark often responded to questions my mother hadn't asked. My mother, whose English was always improving, often asked the meaning of words he'd said, even simple ones I was sure she knew. I, too, spoke in English when we were with him, which meant speaking slowly, almost unnaturally, enunciating each syllable or she wouldn't understand me, would just stare at me, too shy to ask me to repeat myself. If I felt limited in how I could express myself, I couldn't imagine how she felt, having been trapped in this tongue all these years. The endless translation between her and Mark made me doubt her happiness. Sometimes I loved him, and sometimes I told myself she wasn't really happy with him. She was simply doing what she'd done all her life, driving all her unhappiness underground, which she took great care not to admit to herself in order to be able to live. And yet sometimes I questioned why it was so important for me to think of her as unhappy and trapped. Why did I need her life to mirror my own? I was envious, insatiable, as I had been my whole life, to be her only confidant.

Besides, I told myself, whatever ill will crept up in me was nothing like the solid, inevitable stone sitting inside of my brother. I was, at least, more present in her life than him.

"Santiago wants to say hello," my mother said, waving the phone in my direction as I stepped inside. From behind the screen, she gave me a helpless look that meant *salúdalo por mí*.

Of course the Wi-Fi was working for her. I let her look distressed—for a moment, I told myself, let her think you won't.

On the screen, Mark's jowly face, cast in the spinning blue-white light of the television, seemed to float forward from the darkness of the living room.

I told him what he wanted to hear. We were safe and sound inside the hotel. He only knew our country from Netflix shows about narcotraffickers and worried each time my mother traveled back; he'd never joined her and she'd never asked.

Without thinking, I added: "We haven't been abducted. Not yet at least. If we do, you'll pay our ransom. Right?"

Mark did his best to fish out a laugh for me. I was, of all the children—both his and hers—the only one who visited them with any regularity. My mother's hurt face bored into me—*compórtate*.

I turned the phone around to her, said I was going downstairs to write, the same excuse I had used for years whenever I wanted space from her. Still, I tugged her toes as I passed. I left the room before I changed my mind, already regretting the way I'd looked at her, the way I'd talked to Mark.

The lights in the corridor flickered on, filling the hallway with a low, droning buzz. I headed to the elevator, seeking the sound of other guests through the doors, but the buzz, impenetrable and uniform, confirmed what I'd already sensed: We were Hotel Ambalá's only guests.

———

The lobby seemed dark and deserted, even more so than earlier. My eyes went to Armando behind the desk. The girl was gone, and he was watching something on his phone as he had been earlier. I cleared my throat, and he kept looking at his phone like I wasn't there at all, standing right across the desk from him. The screen's pale white light frosted the tip of his nose, which was long and equine, with fine, red veins on either side like the mesh of a net. Only when I knocked on the counter did he look up, furrowing the thick black slabs of his brows: "¿Todo bien, don Santiago?"

Hoping to catch a glimpse of his life that I could turn into small talk—a text exchange, a background picture—I looked down at his phone between us and found, to my surprise, a video of a man fucking a woman. The camera was zoomed in on the woman's face, the pink smear of her mouth. Her eyes fluttered open for seconds at a time before she shut them in a kind of pain I knew and craved.

"¿Sí?" asked Armando, letting the video play. I didn't know what to say as he met my eyes. I wasn't shy. I talked to strangers every night. I squeezed my phone in my hands like he might steal it. He repeated himself in English. "Yes?"

I felt a great desire to run away and, at the same time, to remain there. My hair was past my shoulders, my body lean from working at the restaurant and eating only the scraps I could during my shifts. I was the most beautiful I had ever been. Then I noticed the premature hardness of his face, like he'd been working for years, like he needed someone to listen to him, to care for him. That someone could be me. He would let me watch him masturbate, maybe even suck him off, while he watched videos on his phone. I wasn't above offering him money to discover what else might happen. No one else was in the hotel. We were alone. This could be my secret—my reward—for sitting through a week with Abuela.

Instead, I found myself asking if there was Wi-Fi in the lobby. It wasn't working in our room. "Could you get it fixed as soon as possible?"

He clicked the button on the side of his phone, blacking out the screen. Like nothing had happened.

"There have been problems with the internet," he said.

"But it's working for my mother?"

"I'll get someone to come look at it tomorrow." He pulled a business card from below the desk and scribbled the password for the lobby Wi-Fi along the margins.

The paper was so thin I could see my fingertips on the other side.

I suddenly felt far away from him. He was still young, with his full black hair, his khaki uniform too large for him. He gave me an absorbed, rather cold look, his hands worrying something below the desk. All men, when observed rather closely, had that air of being hard, hostile, and solitary, and that troubled me. Men, all of them, were very dangerous.

Thanking him, I apologized for the bother and turned away, both wanting and not wanting to return to my life.

There were two black futons in the lobby. I sat on the one that wasn't covered in loose newspaper sheets. When I looked back, Armando wasn't visible anymore. I felt exhausted, in the grips of a great impulse to laugh and at the same time cry. "How young he is, how young! A baby!" I said in English, laughing to myself. "And not even good-looking, just plain!"

Even before opening Grindr, I knew I wouldn't leave the lobby. I was too afraid to go out into the city at night. I lacked the abandon of only a few years ago, when I had put myself in the way of any risk for pleasure.

An hour flew by as I scrolled up and down the grid, each box a nearby man I wouldn't meet.

In the room, my mother was fast asleep, snoring lightly—which she always denied, as if embarrassed she wasn't in control of her body at all times. I threw my clothes onto my bed and snuck into hers, the sheets warm and smelling of the violet perfume she'd worn for years. She didn't stir when my leg touched hers, when I wove my fingers through hers and, in a whisper, said, "Te amo."

In the morning, the curtains heaved out into the balcony, past the railing, where the world vanished altogether in the fog. My mother was in the bathroom, already out of bed; the covers stripped from her side were tangled around my legs. Laid out over the other bed were pieces of her wardrobe: the paisley blouse and the top with tiny mirrors along the hem I recognized, while other garments were new. She would say she didn't know what to wear today and tell me to dress her because I knew her best. I would yield to her

request, be funny and kind, energetic. I was more and more familiar with this pattern on my visits, and yet, knowing how it governed me, all of its predictable turbulences, did nothing to free me
from its hold.

Which was why I was surprised when she came out of the bathroom fully dressed and told me I didn't have to come.

In the same plaintive voice, she repeated my excuse from last
night, telling me she understood if I had to stay and write. The
smell of burnt hair trailed her across the room. She put away the
blow-dryer and took her makeup bag out of her suitcase. I couldn't
sense whether there was spite in this repetition or if she only
wanted to unburden me of a responsibility she sensed I didn't
want. Or worse: She wanted to be alone with Abuela, without the
burden of me.

"Are you kidding?" I said, smiling like my dumb joy could in-
fect her.

I jumped out of bed, picked out clothes. The shower ran cold
over my trembling hand with no sign of warming. I resigned myself to scooping handfuls of water over my head, splashing my
armpits, my cock, my ass.

When I rejoined her after a few minutes, she was sitting on the
bed closer to the windows, with her back to me, staring out past
the balcony. The ends of her straightened hair trembled and lifted
a little in the cool breeze. Though I couldn't see her face, I sensed
her mind was elsewhere, curling privately into itself.

"Let's go," I said, with a jolt of energy, like we were right on schedule, knowing she would've been at Abuela's by now if it weren't for me. "Abuela is waiting for us."

She turned then and held out a small blue box to me. I took it from her with some surprise, having thought little of it last night when she'd set it on the nightstand.

"This is for Abuela," she said, her eyes tearful. Inside, two earrings with pea-sized pearls and thin golden clasps were wedged into a slit in the center of a silver cushion. "Tell her you found them for her in New York."

"They're beautiful," I said.

I hadn't until this moment thought about presents for anyone, and I felt like a child, the child I still was in my mother's head, the child who couldn't keep up with the economies of a family life.

I tucked the earring box into the inside breast pocket of my jacket where it would be impossible to steal.

"¿Y por qué estás llorando?" I asked, laughing like nothing could be so serious.

She closed her eyes and shook her head, unable to speak.

Around her feet were several plastic bags.

"What's all this?"

"Gifts," she said. Her old Dell laptop, brand-new pajamas from American Eagle, two bags of miniature Hershey's bars, clothes she no longer wore, and some documents Tía Nelcy needed. The other bags were errands for later today. Ill-fitting dresses, worn shoes, a pair of broken reading glasses. La modista, el zapatero, and el joyero were all in the same bazaar.

"Don't make that face," she said, still blinking away tiny tears.

"What face?" My smile cracked the way it did when she sounded ridiculous. It pained and delighted me that this was my mother.

In the elevator, I asked her if it was safe walking around town with so many bags. But she wanted to walk. So we would walk, I said. I let her carry only the smallest, lightest bag. I was her hombrecito.

Downstairs, Armando echoed my concern and offered to call us a taxi—there were usually one or two at the corner—but she said *for what?* She was still a señorita. As we drew away from the desk laughing, I winked at Armando, feeling as shamelessly charming as my mother.

We were halfway across the plaza when my mother pointed at the new Dunkin' Donuts: "That's it! I saw your abuelo there for the last time!"

"What was it before?" I couldn't help asking. She loved telling this story as much as I loved hearing it.

"A cafeteria for the businessmen and bureaucrats of the centro. Mamá didn't know I had started smoking cigarettes in Manizales, so when I visited home from college, I would sneak off to smoke there. I'd sit for hours sipping tinto and listening to the men talk about politics and the economy—all the serious things my siblings never cared to understand. I couldn't believe my eyes when one day I saw my father going from table to table asking for a cigarette. We hadn't seen each other in three years, since I was seventeen. He'd been traveling from town to town repairing cameras, estranged from all of us. We smoked through a whole pack that afternoon, talking like two adults, like equals. When I told him I was leaving the following day, we made plans to see each other again the next time I was back from school. So I called him before Semana Santa and made a plan: We'd meet at our table at sunset. *Just like my father*, I thought, when he never showed up. The next day, my boyfriend drove down from Manizales and we took my entire family to a farm outside of the city for a cookout. When we got back to Mamá's apartment, there was a woman at the door we didn't know. Papá had died the night before in the hospital."

Every few months my mother would tell me the story of how she lost touch with her father and how, right when they planned to reconnect, he passed away. That is, she would tell me some version of the story, every few months there were fewer gaps and more coincidences. She liked to say the past was coming back to her. She remembered more and more of her life as a complete picture thanks to me asking her so many questions—being so understood was a blessing. Although it seemed she was also signaling me to learn from her mistakes.

We crossed the street onto the white stone promenade above Parque Centenario, where the fog still wreathed the tops of the trees and a denser, thicker gray pooled ominously in the clearing at the center of the park.

"Don't get mad," said my mother, in the plaintive tone I'd trained her to use when asking about him. "Have you talked to your father?"

It had been a year since I'd last called my father. The handful of times we talked after he left my stepmother, we had run out of things to say within minutes. I'd told myself I was waiting for bigger things to happen in my life: going back to school, another graduation, or even the holidays. But when his mother died and four more months passed without a call, I realized this marked a new depth of cruelty for us. Even I was ashamed. He was likely still grieving.

"Sinvergüenza," my mother said, laughing. "Your face tells me everything." For a moment she cast a blanket of comfort over us, which she pulled back just as soon. "You're his only son. You at least have to let him know you're here."

"Too bad," I said, barely thinking of the words that followed, "because I hate him."

She stopped walking. "That's not who you are, Santiago."

We were blocking the sidewalk. I tried to budge her out of the way, but she wouldn't move. "I'm kidding," I said. "He's living with Pilar outside of Medellín. What's the point of telling him I'm here? He's hours away!" I was lying; I didn't know where he was, but I couldn't stand to see her with her head bowed and arms crossed, not during our special trip. But she had been the one who'd created the sea between me and my father. I reached for her, wanting her to recognize me again, but she pulled away as if my hands were stained with ink. I laughed, trying to ease her. She had no clue I hadn't called him after my grandmother died; telling her now would break her. "I'm just kidding." My hand lingered mid-air, lacking the courage to either touch her or fall down empty. "I promise I'm only kidding."

There was so much my father had said to me that she didn't know about. Like when he told me I shouldn't return to Colombia because I slept with men, as if a man hadn't touched me on this land while on a trip with him when I was seventeen. He'd said I should be like a bird and fly away—using that word, *pájaro*, which also meant faggot—that I didn't need this place. As if he suddenly cared when, for years after my mother told him I was gay, he'd continued to ask if I had a girlfriend. I'd withheld the most damning parts of these conversations from my mother to protect her, or him, or perhaps, in some way, myself. There was no use in adding to her pain if I could hold it myself. I couldn't ever explain to her that I felt my father had taken something from me, something precious and mysterious, something as private as my own happiness, and which I knew was further than ever from me, because of him, because of her, because of the life I had only imagined in our homeland. But in her eyes, my behavior had only one explanation, the simplest one: I was being a bad son.

"Do you see me?" She dropped her bags on the pavement, then held her arms out like featherless wings. "What are you waiting for?"

I tried to touch her shoulder again, to ground her, but she batted my fingers away.

"He's not getting any younger either."

"I'll call him," I said, offering her my pinkie. "I promise."

We turned a block later onto the road to Abuela's apartment. The lines of cars in traffic brimmed with light all the way downhill. I noticed it before my mother: the horse, blacker than tar, at the bottom of the hill. It reared up on its hind legs like a battle horse, and then fell, its hooves clapping and scraping beneath the traffic lights. Several feet away was an older man in a poncho and straw hat—the leather reins were wound around his hands, turning them purple—getting jostled from side to side like he was nothing more than a scarecrow. My mother clutched my arm. For a moment, when the horse's feet caught the ground and its belly lifted, the animal seemed to rise, before its thin legs buckled, folded; the horse collapsed again with a lowing sound, louder now, as if dispossessing itself. A gasp flew up from the crowd. We were all witnesses. The men leaning out of their cars, the maids on the roofs with laundry bunched in their hands, and the guards behind the bulletproof glass lobbies. None of us could look away.

Tía Nelcy pulled us into Abuela's apartment as if we were running from thieves. She slammed the door, secured the three different locks, hooked the rusty chain, and peered through the tiny metal peephole before even saying hello. She called to mind a witch, with her tightly wound black hair and loose purple frock made of cheap, pilled fabric. There was even a darkness about her, hovering around her like a smell that would not dissipate—I remembered this from all those years ago. Even as a boy I had recognized that she was my uncle's wife, not my blood. And I was grateful that whatever was inside of her did not run in me. Nevertheless, under the care of this lugubrious woman, Abuela had lived long past what the doctor had predicted.

"Can't you see your cousin and aunt are here?" Tía Nelcy said—

when my cousin Valentina, half asleep, slid out of the kitchen dragging a pale blue blanket—as if her granddaughter's poor manners revealed something unpleasant about her abilities as a grandmother.

Valentina was twenty now. But as she hugged my mother and then clung to my arm, sucking her thumb like a pacifier, she seemed like a baby. The last time I'd seen her she had been thirteen, stealing sips of my beer, snorting and giggling when I told her about the boy I'd kissed on the farm in Gualanday next to my grandfather's. There was a history between us, a shared past, but I couldn't find my way to its comfort today.

I now knew she had a pituitary issue; that's why Valentina had grown sideburns and started her period late. I knew too much about her through my mother.

"Is this normal?" my mother asked, pressing the back of her hand against Valentina's forehead. The change was almost imperceptible—certainly Tía Nelcy or Valentina didn't notice—but I saw my mother shift just a degree outside of herself. Mean, curt. It embarrassed me that she wasn't very kind to them. "What's the matter with her? She doesn't feel sick. Am I paying her tuition for her to stay at home and keep you company?" My mother cut across the room to retie the golden curtain tassels and push the window open. "No wonder the girl is depressed."

As a breeze swept through the room, I noticed the smell. Subtle at first—foul, stale, warm. And I remembered my brother's word for our hometown, *moridero*: a place where people went to die, where people didn't even know they were dying. My mother smelled it, too. She checked the closet behind the sofa, sniffing the air like a hound after its prey. She inspected under the couch, be-hind the TV. There was a fruit bowl on the dining table, and she turned each orange in her hand. The smell was so distinct my mother said nothing of the red ribbons trimming the window, the enormous bow on the coffee table, and the snowman figurines, one on almost every surface, still out in late February.

While Valentina was left to mop the living room, I followed my mother and Tía Nelcy down the hall. I held on to my camera and pressed my fingers against the edges of the earring box in my breast pocket. My mother, followed by Tía Nelcy, entered the small, bright-lit room, but I stopped at the threshold; I didn't know why I had expected anything other than what I already knew: Abuela was in a hospital bed. Her face was turned to the side, her mouth open. Blankets covered her to the waist and the fabric lay flat over her legs. She had always been small, solid, and thick, but looking at her now, I couldn't imagine she weighed more than seventy pounds. I could have lifted her above my head if I'd wanted to. That's how thin she looked, that much like noth-ing. But it wasn't just her size that disturbed me. There was some-thing that I could only name now that it was gone. A light, her aura. How had I failed to see it when she was still herself? How had I failed to see how bright she had shone?

"She was asking for you all morning," said Tía Nelcy, smoothing the blanket over Abuela's legs, asking us again why we'd decided to stay at a hotel.

My mother lowered the metal bar on the side of the bed, ignor-ing Tía Nelcy and her questions.

I looked at Abuela, at her toothless gray-pink gums, hoping her thin, trembling lips would form a word, any word. Weeks ago, according to my mother, Abuela had said my name on the phone. But I knew she hardly spoke, and when she did, it was in impossible-to-decipher moans and groans.

My mother curled her arm around Abuela and rested her head on her mother's stomach like a child. Looking up, she brushed aside a wisp of silver hair on Abuela's forehead. She was repenting for the years in Miami, just after we'd arrived, when she pretended Abuela didn't live in the same city. "I brought you a very special visitor all the way from New York." My mother turned to me at the foot of the bed. "Tell her something."

Honks and shouts erupted from the street below. Men arguing about the horse.

"He's scared," said Tía Nelcy, like I was a little boy without language.

My mother stroked the top of Abuela's head, showing me how I, too, could touch her.

I patted the length of her leg, unsure if she could hear or feel me. And I felt very much like a child, suddenly powerless, unprepared. Though I had been through much, in worlds neither Tía Nelcy nor my mother could imagine, I had not seen this before.

"They wanted to take her nurse away," said Tía Nelcy. Her fingers played idly with the button of her pants. As they talked about money, pensions, accounts, I stared behind the bed at the ledge of the recessed wall, where a floral etched vase, a Christmas candle under a bell jar, and a porcelain angel kneeling in prayer were set evenly apart. And I realized I'd seen these before; the objects on the ledge behind the bed were our own holiday decorations, the ones I'd grown up with in Miami. *They're here*, I said to myself, surprised, then skeptical, like I wasn't entirely sure of where I was, whether I was hallucinating, whether these were doubles. My mother, for as long as I could remember, had sent boxes of our old belongings back to Colombia, and I must have thought she had pushed them through a black hole, because it hadn't clicked until now that these items lived here. Silently, I panicked. I knew by the equal spacing between the three objects that my mother had placed them there herself. My mother suddenly seemed a whole country away. Without much effort, I could see the future, in which it was my mother in this bed and my turn to make the pilgrimage.

"Don't worry, mi princesa. No one is taking anything from you," said my mother, cradling Abuela's face in her hands, looking at her deeply. Tía Nelcy was saying something now about a new treatment the doctor had recommended, then she listed aloud the supplies we were low on and complained about the price of adult diapers; all the while my mother wasn't listening. She was alone with Abuela, surrounded by what I imagined as a powerful, invisible force field. I was sure she could still see Abuela's light. Perhaps it wasn't all gone. Perhaps I, too, could find it if I looked at her long enough.

Until I was eight or nine, Abuela lived in Miami. For several weekends in a row, and then never again, I asked my mother if I could spend Saturday nights at Abuela's. The two of them were not very close. My mother never met the man who took Abuela to

Miami—she referred to him only as the Cuban pilot—and didn't know how or when he had died, only that through him, Abuela—and now we—had papers. After years in America, Abuela's life didn't amount to much: She lived off her widow's pension, government handouts, and church donations; she never learned English, never got a driver's license, never worked. My mother, if she'd come here with no kids and a decade younger, would've moved mountains. Abuela embarrassed my mother, took her back to times she'd rather forget. But Abuela captivated me. Our sleepovers consisted of watching *Sábado Gigante* until the very end, crayoning sea reefs and dolphins on old newspapers, mixing and matching the colorful suits in her closet into whimsical outfits. I fell asleep next to her, looking at the photo on her nightstand, a perfect photograph of her in a black-and-white swimsuit and deep red lipstick, posing on the beach behind a hotel like a movie star. But I could only see these memories from outside of myself now, like I'd made them up, in the way that all the memories of my youth seemed counterfeit. All I remembered, truly remembered, was that for a brief moment in my life I had wanted to be with Abuela. Then I grew older. By the time I was sixteen and she moved in with us for half the year, I'd noticed how she always needed something from my mother. There was always a headache or pain in her throat. There was always something essential like eggs or milk to buy at the grocery store for her. I grew to resent her like I did everyone who kept my mother on the phone at night. Those pleading souls who wanted the little time and attention my mother had for me.

"Nelcy, se ve flaca." My mother was back in the room. "How much does she weigh?"

Tía Nelcy opened the top drawer of the closet and gathered a large plastic syringe and tub of formula from the shelf in silence.

As the time to leave neared, I found myself alone in the room with Abuela, clutching my camera in front of her hospital bed. I wouldn't be able to take her picture if my mother or Tía Nelcy stepped back into the room. Not that they would stop me. But it would look wrong, wanting to capture Abuela in this state, and I would stop myself. Standing there, I suffered the faint uneasiness of taking a photograph of someone I loved without them knowing that these images weren't just for me. The abrupt, mechanical clicks of the shutter release broke through the silence. I didn't meter the light, focus the lens, or look through the viewfinder. I was painfully aware of the possibility of being caught. After the first few shots, I rotated the focus ring a few degrees at a time. One, at least, had to turn out sharp. Though I knew I needed to bring the camera to my eye to make sure there wasn't too much or too little light, I couldn't, I didn't want to look at what I was capturing. As much as I wanted to make this image, this was as considerate and intentional as I could be.

"I got you these in New York," I said after I'd finished, dangling the pearl earrings in front of her eyes. I climbed into bed with her the way my mother had. But I didn't know what to do now, whether I should put the earrings on her or back in the box. I tried talking to her like my mother did, but I felt like someone was listening through the walls and filling out a scorecard. I fell silent when I placed the box on her stomach and waited for her to get up, to put them on herself. Her lungs couldn't even lift the box.

I waited until the sound of the gunshot came from outside. She didn't even flinch. Her eyes were locked on a thin bar of light shimmering on the wall.

When I looked out the window, the old campesino stood over the horse with a smoking pistol in his hand. I couldn't look at the horse. The blood. People leaned out from the buildings on either side of the road, and it was almost a shock to look to my right and, in the living room window, recognize my mother.

The next morning, the doors to the banquet hall on the second floor of the hotel were open, but there were no waiters, no other guests, not another living soul in sight. My mother wanted to have breakfast at the hotel before going to see Abuela. I told her the restaurant didn't look open, but she entered anyway. The hall was unexpectedly large, large enough to hold hundreds, and the tables were set with elaborate bouquets of artificial flowers, as well as bottles of cheap wine and aguardiente, as if we'd arrived too early for a party. We squeezed through the narrow gaps between the chairs toward a table with a view of Plaza Bolívar. She had put on a peacock-blue dress that reached down to her ankles, although we had nothing special planned for today. I pulled out the chair facing the windows for her, and she sat with her hands under her chin like a cherub. The diamond ring from Mark freckled her bottom lip with tiny dots of light.

The fog had been impenetrable from our room upstairs, but down here it was sheer enough to see the Renaults and motorcycles as they revved their engines. The names of fruits and appliances echoed from megaphones attached to wooden carts heaped with produce. Men in suits filed into the government offices across the street in fuzzy, dark bands.

"¿Qué piensas, hermosa?" I said, finally turning to look at her.

She reached out to squeeze my nose between her fingers the way she knew I hated; I shook my head in mock resistance. For a few seconds, I felt the magic of playing to our script, but the moment faded, as always, into silence, until we were like actors who'd forgotten their lines.

My mother noticed him first: the bellboy peering through the kitchen-door window.

"Armando," I said, reminding her of his name.

He came out the swivel door a moment later, patting his hands dry on his pants. As he crossed the room, squeezing himself between the packed chairs, he straightened his posture, fixed his freshly wet hair, and adjusted his smile like I did at the restaurant, until he found the right one—neither eager nor meek—like he simply lived to serve us. With this face, he was unrecognizable from the boy of the first night.

She pointed her lips toward him. "Your eyes could swallow him whole."

"¡Mami!" I laughed, shaking my head. "He's too young." Then, after a moment: "You know I like my men older." I peeled my eyes open with playful accusation. "I wonder who I inherited that from."

"Manuel!" She laughed so hard she didn't notice she'd called me by my brother's name, so hard the artificial flowers in the center of the table shook, so hard I even worried Armando would think we were laughing at him.

Armando reached our table. My mother sat up straight, like the teacher's pet in another life where we were classmates. I followed her lead.

He had bad news for us: They weren't serving breakfast anymore, or any meals for that matter—the kitchen staff had been cut—only catering for preplanned weddings and corporate events from now on. He paused like he was reluctant to crush our hearts into fine dust—but, he said, he could order us whatever we wanted from a restaurant down the street.

Before I could tell my mother we should just go there, she asked for huevos fritos and an arepa. Then she asked for fresh-cut fruit, for empanadas and pandebonos. What about tamales? She rubbed her hands together, making an excited squeal. Each time Armando said yes, she came up with another dish. Perhaps she was delaying our visit this morning, or perhaps it was that she was with me and she thought this was what I wanted—the hunger of my father.

She became chatty as we waited. She asked after the man I'd dated in New York for over a year. I rolled my eyes when she reminded me he'd texted her on Christmas Day. She was convinced

I was supposed to be with him. *What happened?* she asked again, like I hadn't already told her about his problem getting hard. For months he consulted doctors but found no solution. It was psychological; he was scared of losing me if he couldn't fuck me, and the fear kept him from getting hard, which meant he was losing me and making his fear come true—until sex turned into a disappointing maze where we could never really find each other. Or like I hadn't told her I'd felt stifled by him, how he treated me like a child, working his way into every part of my life like he knew what was best for me. Or how he didn't challenge me intellectually or artistically or socially. And sure, it had looked like he treated me like a king; and sure, he was the only boyfriend my brother and his wife had met; and sure, they still asked my mother about him—my mother was saying something now about how crazy I was as a teenager and in college and whenever I was single. "I'm praying to the universe," she said, lowering her voice, "that you find another quality man."

"So I'm a trainwreck on my own?"

"Santiago," she said. "Please, no seas tan dramático. Let's just say when you were young you could be"—she paused—"you could be a little bit of a puta."

"¡Mami!"

"Fine. I won't ask anymore," she said, both of us knowing she wouldn't keep her word.

I looked at her. I looked at her face, her dyed hair, her long blue dress, her thin fingers turning the diamond ring in circles. I didn't know what else to say. She was looking at me with pity, looking at me like she was remembering something from long ago. We had become mother and son again. Her lips arched into her cheeks, and though it looked like something heavy and painful were flickering behind her eyes, I realized she was smiling, or at least attempting to smile.

Our phones buzzed at the same time. I opened the video from Manuel, knowing it would stop my mother from trying to fix my life this morning.

We continued to watch the video until Armando returned, my mother holding her heart and repeating *la dulzura* every time my brother sneezed and his daughter said, *Salu, salu.* We agreed, like we always did, that he and his wife were doing the right thing by teaching my niece Spanish first, as if it mattered what we thought.

Armando poured our coffee, and then, two plates at a time, brought out our feast from the kitchen. My mother pushed aside the place settings next to ours, stacking them in the center of the table under the dusty artificial bouquets and bottles of booze. She leaned her phone against an empty water glass and wedged it in place with a set of utensils.

"Watch this, Armando. La dulzura en crema." My mother slipped a tip into his palm as he crouched beside her. And the video started again.

After breakfast, we went back up to the room. We decided to rest with the television on for just a few minutes. I was like a baby; if I didn't nap after I ate I became a tyrant. My mother had made this joke off and on for years.

She lay on her half of the mattress, flat on her back and on top of the sheets, with her wedges still strapped to her feet. We had shared a bed the first night, then the second—we would share a bed every single night this week.

I slipped out of my shoes and curled up on my side facing her. She didn't look frightened, exactly, but alert—*pilas*, like the taxista had said—ready to run at all times. Her rib cage rose with loud, deliberate breaths. I wanted to press my thumb to her brow, to soften those creased twin lines, the same ones beginning to appear on my own face. She was always going through more than she let on. Like when I was a boy and the wives whose houses she cleaned got drunk on midday martinis and accused her of stealing jewelry, lingerie, even groceries. Or the night Sharon gave herself the doctor's injection, and my mother held her like her own mother and had wanted to hold her the whole night, but as soon as she started to get drowsy, the medicine beginning to take effect, she made my mother leave; she didn't want my mother to be there when she died, in case there was any trouble—all she had to do was go home, be with the boys, come back in the morning, enter the apartment as if nothing had happened, and call the ambulance. My mother only told me about these experiences once there was nothing I could do, once years had passed and whatever she'd felt had already been flattened into an anecdote. It was only when she began dating Mark that she talked to me about her life after my brother and I had left Miami, how dark those years had been, how at times she really thought she might not have the courage to go on living. Life was so much better now, she'd say, like the only way to happiness was through suffering.

As she dozed, I lowered the volume of the television until it was only a whisper. Every channel at this hour played reruns of tele-novelas or dubbed American series from many years ago.

My mother told me these stories of her life because we were friends now. I wasn't like my brother, she'd say, she could tell me everything. When she told me one of her uncles had molested her and her older brother when she was a little girl, I told her nothing of my own encounters with violent men. Beneath my composed face, I was by turns sad, angry, spiteful, and hopeless. I listened to her stories and carried them on my shoulders without revealing how much it hurt to do so; I would not collapse under their weight. I couldn't. I was special. She had buried her feelings and turned her back on her own soul to raise my brother and me, and if I was the only one who could help her to face her life head-on again, then I would. We had something other mothers and sons could never have. But I understood we weren't friends, exactly. I could only tell her one half of my life, the half that was for her, to show her I was grateful and reasonable and logical and careful— everything she deserved in a son. She had no clue how many men I had slept with, or how I sometimes did it for money, or that Anais had once stayed up to look after me because I was drunk and threatening to hurt myself. I edited my life for her until it was mostly tidy, leaving only a few stains behind so that she could think she knew me. I owed her as much.

I woke up to my mother standing over me.

"I'm going to Abuela's." The sun behind her lit up her hair and darkened her face.

I groped through the sheets for my phone, but she held my shoulder down with her hand—she was holding me down, that's how it felt. "You don't want me to come?"

She paused. "I'll pick you up for lunch."

She grabbed her purse from the nightstand, went to the windows, and drew the curtains shut. Yellow light welled in the fabric's folds and seeped into the room. I thought of springing from the bed, acting excited and insisting I come with her again. But perhaps she didn't want me to come. Perhaps I was doing her a favor, giving her what she wanted, when I closed my eyes and said I'd stay.

At noon, I took the elevator down to the lobby. Armando was behind the desk, and I thought again of making small talk, asking where he lived or what he studied, but as I neared him I felt light and heavy at once, my feet and head poles apart.

I waited for my mother on the patio, where the chairs were still stacked, the tables corralled. Across the plaza, I saw the life I'd wanted to see on our first night. There was a crowd, there were noise and music. Someone had installed a giant plaster mask painted bright red and green on the nearby steps, where people poked their heads through the vacant eyes and took pictures. Locals hurried through the plaza or stopped to have lunch from the food carts surrounded by tiny stools. In the very center, high schoolers on skateboards jumped over a toppled metal barricade with loud cries and whistles. Cars and motorcycles circled the square; honks and smoke carried in the wind. Everyone in Ibagué looked like they'd been made on the same day, in the same place, by the same hands. We were short, big-nosed people with light brown skin that quickly bronzed in the sun. I scanned the faces in the crowd, wanting to dissolve into them, but had no idea how to go about doing so, not even how to take a step off this patio and join them. That was the difference between my mother and me. She did not see how she was no longer like them, how we were now both unusual here in our own ways.

I must've stood for half an hour before I went inside to ask Armando to use the hotel telephone. To make a call in Colombia, you had to press the pound sign or the star and then an area code if you were calling a landline. Or maybe I had it all backwards. I looked down at the phone and held it back out to him. He chuckled as I gave him the number my mother had sent me years ago, before she'd stopped asking me to call Abuela.

"Nelcy?"

"Who's calling?" she asked, not recognizing my voice.

"Santiago," I said, loudly. She had the radio on full blast. "Is my mother still there?"

Turning away from the boy, I pressed the receiver hard against my ear.

"She left awhile ago, mi amor."

I had no clue where my mother was, but I felt embarrassed to admit this to my aunt. The two of us—my mother and I—were supposed to be a united front.

I thanked Nelcy, took a small bill out of my wallet, and slid it across the counter to Armando.

Sitting in the lobby, I wondered if I'd heard my mother right. I was sure she'd said she would pick me up for lunch. It was noon, and wasn't that lunchtime? I was already hungry again.

WhatsApp said she hadn't been online in hours. If she wasn't with Abuela, and she wasn't with me, then who was she with? Every question fell away into another. I was sinking into the quicksand of my mind. A phrase from my childhood resurfaced: *The mother forgot she was a mother.* My mother had her own secrets; I knew this, of course, but I hadn't expected her to disappear on me. Not here, not now.

Without her, I was stranded in this moridero. I had nowhere to go. No one to see. I opened Grindr. More messages than I'd ever received in New York. Pictureless profiles were asking me if I was *pasivo o activo.* If I was *vergón,* if I wanted to *culiar* or *mamar.* If I liked *morbo.* I asked men to show me their *vergas,* their *culos* and *rajitas* spread open, loving how these words pulsed with a vulgar heat in Spanish. I sent several men a picture of my ass that I'd taken while waiting for the hotel shower to warm. I asked some men to breed me, to make me their *perra,* while at the same time I was asking other men to show me around. *¿Dónde nos podemos tomar un trago por aquí?*

Then I was back to imagining my mother in trouble. An alley. A man pressing the tip of a knife to her skull. My mother removing her diamond ring, her watch, her earrings—but my mother was fine. She had to be; this was her home more than mine. She had run into an old friend. One of her many nieces or nephews. *Mi gente.*

"I don't know where my mother is," I said to Armando.

"Want me to call her?"

"Our phones only work on Wi-Fi." Her voice echoed in my head—*I'll pick you up for lunch*—but I didn't know now if I'd heard her right or why she'd left without me.

"What do you want me to do?" He sat back down slowly and carefully on the stool, holding his phone and looking at the screen. The white light caught on his features from below, ghoulishly. Every few seconds the light on his face pulsed.

He asked me one more time what I wanted him to do.

I didn't know what to say. I clasped my hands. I wanted to run, yet my legs felt heavy as stone.

"I don't know what to tell you," said the boy.

He moved his feet farther apart and bounced his boots once, twice.

Plaza Bolívar was empty when I stepped outside. There was trash everywhere—on the steps, on the benches, at the feet of the statues. An older woman with a giant trash can on wheels was sweeping a pile of chicken bones from in front of the red-and-green mask. I peered through storefronts, looking under the arcade of the bank and the narrow alleys between the bazaars. I remembered all the nights in Miami when my mother hadn't come back from work, how my brother would say she'd flown off to Colombia without us. The pieces of this fear were scattered throughout my life, as if I had always known I would lose my mother to our homeland. What would I be without her, when she finally disappeared?

I found myself at Abuela's building, ringing the intercom.

"Tía Nelcy, it's me," I said, and because she was the kind of woman who could make gossip out of anything, I told her I'd come to see Abuela while my mother ran some errands.

Upstairs, she served me a cilantro and potato soup with strips of beef and long, translucent onions twinkling on the surface. While I ate, she cleaned, every now and then shouting to ask me how New York was, if I had a girlfriend, if and when I would see my father.

"Have you talked to him?" I asked.

"He took Valentina and her sister to Gualanday last year," she said. "He's fixed up the house with Pilar."

My grandfather's house in Gualanday, where my father and I had spent most of my summer visits, wasn't far from the city. I could still picture it: the road that snaked through lush mountains and skirted the sudden drop of the cliff face at every sharp turn—everything below densely green with life—then the suspension bridge my grandfather had designed and built over the muddy river, and finally houses clustered around the single paved road of Gualanday, where dogs lined up to bark at passing cars.

So he wasn't far at all. A fifty-minute drive at most. Tía Nelcy said he was living out there but working here in town, driving for a service like Uber ever since the engineering firm had gone under. My first thought was that we could've even run into him.

And if he was living in Gualanday, it meant the house was his now. That had always been the plan, though the day had seemed impossibly far off when I was young. Of course I'd seen photos online of him and Pilar in Gualanday, but I'd just thought he was taking more vacations now that he had someone. I'd never considered that he was actually living there, in one place with one woman. The father I knew moved around every eight to twelve months, from one project to another—now Quindío, now Putumayo, now Meta. But perhaps Pilar had changed him. She wasn't a beauty—far from it, her features were all soft, almost lumpy. The gloss of her face called to mind a loaf of sweet bread you tore apart with your fingers. There was a photo of them in Cartagena: On top of the table, next to a fried golden mojarra, rested the pile of their hands, hers covering his. It was strange, so strange, to not even know the sound of her voice. If she was living with him in Gualanday, he would expect me to meet her. Perhaps that's why I hadn't called him yet, because I knew my father would bring me to her without asking. And I didn't want to know her. I didn't want to invite another woman into my life only to see her get hurt years later. I couldn't even talk to my previous stepmother on the phone anymore. But this reason didn't seem like enough—no reason ever felt like enough—to hide from him. Whether or not I wanted to, I had to see him. He was my father and I was his only son.

The tall windows in Abuela's room were open, the sheer white curtains filled with light; every few seconds, when a breeze came in, they puffed past her face.

Abuela seemed more alive today. The right side of her jaw chewed on the air. You could almost believe she was working at a tough chunk of steak.

She was in Colombia when the stroke had come and frozen the left side of her body. She had complained every day of how she wanted to go back to Miami, how we couldn't let her die in Ibagué, but that had been years ago now. I hadn't heard any of this directly, the report came to me from my mother, who'd heard it over the phone from her sister and brothers, and sometimes their children or the children of their children—like Valentina, whom she said always gave her the truth when Nelcy didn't. What I'd pieced together: The doctor hadn't let Abuela fly back. Or maybe that, too, was made up. But it had been said enough times, by enough people, that it had become real. Abuela had her whole family looking after her in Colombia; her pension, in dollars instead of pesos, could afford her the best care in Ibagué; the list of reasons went on. What I heard in all of this, what mattered to me, was that my mother would be spared the responsibility of caring for her mother as she died. After Manuel and I had left home, Abuela stayed with my mother in her Florida home for the rest of the year to ease our leaving. When my mother got home exhausted from ten hours of looking at feces under a microscope, Abuela would be in the foyer wearing one of her monochromatic suits, ready to go to the mall, the beach, anywhere. My mother couldn't continue to take care of her alone. We had all agreed it was best if Abuela stayed in Ibagué. *We*, I thought, as if my opinion had mattered.

I talked to Abuela for a few minutes. I told her that I'd been praying for her health at church every Sunday. That I had a Catholic girlfriend who wanted to meet her. That I was doing well in medical school. I told her the version of my life she'd known before the stroke, the version that someone—I didn't know who— had made up for me. There was no telling whether she understood what I said, or if I was only speaking for myself. Her eyes were open, but today it was clear that they looked nowhere.

Behind the bed, next to the porcelain angel, sat the earring box. I was surprised to find the two pearls still wedged into the small silver cushion. Her earlobes were soft and delicate in my fingers. I unscrewed the back of her candy cane earrings carefully, as if at any moment her skin could tear. The holes in her ears stretched half an inch, giving off a spoiled stench. I wiped the oily residue that stuck to my fingers on the leg of my pants. Then I inserted the pearls' gold stems and clasped their backs shut while looking at Abuela's face, worried I wouldn't know if I was hurting her. The weight of the pearl dragged her earlobe down to the pillow. We were only dressing her up for ourselves, like there was a small chance she might come back to us. I understood why my mother wanted to be here, at her bedside, every possible second. I felt it, too, now—I was waiting for Abuela to spring back to life, to clutch her earrings, to tell me I looked pale, that I needed to eat more oranges and potatoes, more red meat. She'd ask for a mirror to check that we hadn't let her get ugly. It didn't matter if this was impossible. Imagining it was enough.

After I did the other ear, I realized I'd left the hotel without leaving a note. If my mother returned to find an empty room, with no clue of where I'd gone, she would panic. I thanked Tía Nelcy for everything and hurried back to the Hotel Ambalá. Every few steps I checked to see if Abuela's smell still clung to my fingers.

M y mother hadn't come back, Armando said, carrying a stack of chairs into a conference room. The blinding sky above the lobby lit up a circle of the floor, and I paced this circle, nervous, unsure of what to do next. I was panting like a dog after a chase.

Online again, my phone vibrated with notifications. I was on probation for not giving two weeks' notice before traveling, said the email from the restaurant. No mention of Abuela. I checked the schedule for next week. My name wasn't anywhere.

I scanned the messages on Grindr, men offering me monuments of pleasure. I held down the little orange mask on the screen and deleted the app.

Without his new number, I had to look my father up on Facebook. It could be so easy to pack my things and disappear for the rest of the week if he was really in Gualanday. I started to type: *I'm here . . .*

But this was supposed to be my special trip with my mother. I had been a good son, better than my brother, but I had turned away from her these last few years. I had called the distance many names until there was no merging back into her life. She had Mark, Abuela, her feuding siblings. I didn't know her as completely as I'd thought I did. Whatever she was doing this morning she had decided to do without me.

A fog spread through my head, then the lobby—everywhere. This was my chance to meet someone. I could distract myself for an hour. My mother would never know. I headed to the conference room, already stiff in my pants. I wanted Armando to be the most important thing in my life, at least for now. Later, I would feel ashamed, but I wasn't now; we were both trapped in this hotel, and together we could escape. My hand didn't feel like my own when I took several bills out of my wallet.

"What's this for?" He took the bills, counted them. Noticing my bulge, he grabbed it. "Not bad." He looked at his wristwatch. "Let's go fast, I can't leave the desk for long."

Armando led me into a stairwell, down a flight of stairs and a dark corridor, and finally through a door. The room was laid out like an apartment but was used as storage for the hotel, with mattresses stacked against the walls and rows of furniture covered by bedsheets. The first and second bedrooms were empty, but the one farthest back had a twin-size mattress on the floor with a pillow and a blanket. I wondered if this was where he lived—if there had been men he'd brought here before me. I knew nothing about him.

He sat on the low mattress and stripped to his socks and underwear. He looked up. "You didn't have to pay me. I'm not a prostitute."

I laughed, thinking it was funny; he didn't.

"Do you want to give me the money back then?"

He shook his head no.

I wanted to bottom, but the fact that he straddled me on the bed told me everything I needed to know. Without hesitating, I guided myself into him. I tried focusing all of myself into my penis as if to draw the blood there. Before long I was out of breath, half-hard and tired, still thinking worriedly of my mother. When my dick slid out of him again, I asked him to lie on his stomach. He rolled off me onto his back and kept masturbating. I tried lying next to him, but he didn't budge. I squeezed myself into his side, one of my legs hanging off the mattress. He pushed my hand away when I tried touching his dick. Beside him, I stroked myself quickly, trying to hide the fact that I wasn't hard anymore. I couldn't take my eyes off of him staring at his own erection.

I was back in the hotel room watching television when the phone on the nightstand rang. I found my mother downstairs, with yellow shopping bags piled around her feet, talking to Armando about the pensionados who loitered at a nearby mall's cafeteria. She was ordering an empanada when one of them—*Dios lo bendiga*—collapsed face-first into the glass display case.

"Where were you?" I asked when she finally paused. I didn't look at the boy, embarrassed at how my words had come out like an accusation.

"Just walking around. I did some shopping. I found you some new leather loafers."

"Why didn't you come for me?"

"You didn't pick up when I called earlier. I figured you'd found plans of your own."

She mimed typing on a phone screen, then winked.

I didn't tell her I'd waited for her, that I'd thought she'd forgotten me. That I'd walked to Abuela's and back. That when I'd given up, I paid Armando for sex.

For now, I laughed, and it didn't feel like I was pretending to be happy. Before running her bags up to her room, I asked: "Who do you think I am?"

SIXTEEN

By our fifth day, my phone still hadn't connected to the Wi-Fi in the hotel room. I watched my mother call my brother and Mark, and afterward, when she'd gone to sleep, I unlocked her phone, downloaded Grindr, and talked to as many guys as I could before bed.

Armando swore there was no fix for the Wi-Fi situation in our room. He'd have to call the internet company, and even then it could take days.

I told him that was unacceptable with the same coldness he'd shown after we'd had sex. I canceled the rest of our reservation and left a damning review online. My mother took the news well. The hotel was run-down. Nothing like when she was a girl.

We moved to a nicer hotel only five blocks from Abuela's, in a quieter neighborhood away from the centro. When the taxi pulled into the round driveway, she pointed to a doorway across the street. She had lived in that house when her family first moved to Ibagué from the campo. That door, she said, was where she received the news about my grandfather. I felt grateful for every day of our special trip, for everything that had brought us here. In the lobby, when the receptionist didn't want to acknowledge the online rate I'd found, I didn't relent, we got our discount, and I said to my mother: "Your son always finds a deal."

Once we checked into our new room, I told her about the bellboy, the porn on the phone, the pass he'd made at me—but nothing more.

"Descarado," she said. "That's why I don't like Colombian men, or Latino men for that matter. They lack respect for themselves and other people. Animals."

That's how it was these days: I told her a digestible piece of the whole and kept the rest—the joy, weight, and loneliness of the full experience—for myself.

"Look," I said as we stepped out onto the balcony: a view of the mountains cradling the northern edge of the city. I could almost believe our old house was just beyond the trees. "Only the best for my mother."

We were more popular than the circus. A stupid joke, but my mother laughed anyway.

For the last four days, we'd been visited by cousins and their babies dressed for us in their Sunday best; by aunts, those who were blood and those who had married one of my many uncles; by my mother's high school friends, a trio of short, riotous women who spoke in a chorus; and even by my godmother, a frail, pale woman who'd waited until the very end of her visit to ask my mother for money to keep her son in rehab.

During these reunions I was asked about my life in New York and what I was studying in school as if I were still twenty. Everyone seemed to think I was younger than I was. I gave short, vague answers to avoid explaining my current situation. It wasn't that I was ashamed, but that it would make no sense to them if I said I was making photographs and waiting tables. I didn't mind when our visitors stopped asking me questions—I felt relieved. My mother talked enough for the two of us. One second she would be laughing through the story about the time my brother took the universal remote control around our old neighborhood in Ibagué—turning televisions on and off, changing people's channels, making the volume deafeningly loud. And the next moment she would be bringing us near tears with her anecdotes of our time in America. There wasn't a dry eye in the room after she told a version of the Sharon story in which she waited through the night and made the call in the morning. Sharon was an angel now; my mother felt her presence everywhere.

Meanwhile, Tía Nelcy and Valentina, like servants, brought out pots of coffee and bowls filled with the fun-size Hershey's. Between stories, my mother patted the top of my hands, every now and again mouthing the words *mi tesoro*, though I couldn't tell if she meant me or her last story. I hadn't seen her like this, not in a long time. Here, my mother owned her life beautifully.

Friday would be our last full day in Ibagué. Tomorrow, we'd take the bus back to Bogotá, spend the night at a hotel, and fly out first thing the following morning. I'd spend another night in Miami with her and Mark before going back to New York.

At lunchtime, when the kitchen phone rang, Tía Nelcy got up from the table. It was for my mother, she said, sitting back down with her mouth stretched in an ugly grimace meant for me. I still had my doubts about where my mother had gone the other day. I wanted to catch her in a lie, in some distortion of the truth. But I knew instantly by the excessive, almost vulgar laugh—the real laugh only he could bring out of her—that it was my father on the phone. A familiar hope pierced my throat, my stomach, and stretched in a needle-thin line to the kitchen. I'd felt this same hope three years ago at my graduation, when I'd seen my mother and father together for what felt like the first time, the first time that wasn't in a photograph or in the blurry, passed-down memories I turned over and over in my mind. It hadn't even mattered that my stepmother had been there. I watched my mother and father as if I could change the past. As if I could give myself what I didn't have and had always wanted: a life that wasn't split between parents, countries, languages.

It wasn't until now, a day before our departure, my mother summoning me to the kitchen, holding the phone out, her eyes weary, that I realized how it would look—to my father, my mother, everyone—like yet another betrayal that I hadn't told him about this trip. I had been meaning to contact him after spending a few days with my mother visiting Abuela. After all, it was our first time back together in Ibagué. And I had been waiting to call him—for the moment when I wanted to see him, an undeniable feeling I imagined descending on me all at once. Even though I'd told my mother he was in Medellín with the moza, Ibagué was small, full of gossip. I had to have known someone would tell him. Perhaps I'd wanted to see if he would come looking for me. But now I felt childish, stupid. I took the phone from my mother, her eyes full of accusation, and walked through the door in the back of the kitchen into Tía Nelcy's windowless room.

"Pah-pi," I said in my lowest, deepest voice. It was the caricature of manliness that I'd used as a boy to answer his calls, only able to talk to him with the same box of old tricks. "I'm in Ibagué," I said, though he knew this, obviously. "Abuela's sick. I came with my mother to visit her. I didn't want her to be alone. The trip, everything, was very last minute." I said this as if he'd missed a small, uneventful party, like it was nothing to be upset about. I asked him where he was living, though I already knew he was in Gualanday. Soon enough, somehow, I was telling him to pick me up. If I waited any longer the feeling could leave. Of course, I didn't tell him this. All I said was: "What took you so long to find me?"

After the move to Miami, my mother had made our fathers out to be terrible men who didn't call and never sent money. She waited until I was ten to confess to me that my father had called—often, in fact. She'd wanted to protect me. My father was—I remember how she searched for the word—*irresponsible*. She recalled every time he'd said he was coming back to Ibagué from a project, only to never arrive or cancel at the last minute, leaving it to her to explain his absence to me; I didn't remember any of this myself. Rafael, my brother's father, was another story. He was twelve years older than my mother, of a different generation. Cold, emotionless. He had avoided her calls from America thinking she was going to ask him for money—money he had; he was a doctor, head of radiology—when she had just wanted to give him updates on his son. She kept this all a secret from my brother, but of course he knew. But my own father, he had called.

I never learned what had brought about this confession, but afterward, my mother wanted nothing more than for my father and me to have a relationship. Once a week, she keyed in the string of digits on the prepaid calling cards and passed the phone to me. The recording on the other side would say how many minutes I had to talk to him. It was always too many minutes. Always a chore. My father already a stranger. The only reason I took the phone was because I had to, and then as I grew older because I saw how happy my mother was when I talked to him, how it dissolved the guilt rooted inside of her. I was thirteen the first time he bought me a ticket to go back to Colombia for the summer. My brother didn't visit until he got into medical school. Only then did his father want anything to do with him.

I'd only grown more distant from Colombia since my teenage years. Gone were the summers my mother and stepmother had coordinated for me in Ibagué. Those summers with my father's brother and his two sons who were supposed to teach me how to be a Colombian boy. I never saw the middle-of-nowhere towns where my father worked; they were no place for me, according to my mother. The three or four times I saw my father each summer, we went on trips to the military country clubs in Melgar, to parks in the Eje Cafetero, to my grandfather's country house in Gualan-day. Then I was back in Ibagué helping my aunt set the table while Tío Miguel spanked my crying cousins before dinner. My father never took more than five days off from work, and weeks went by before he came to see me again. It was all brief, intense fun with my father. I went looking for men like him everywhere. But these days, my father and I were in a stalemate; neither of us had reached out to the other in over a year.

Later that day, my mother and I were having a siesta in Tía Nelcy's tiny bed when she yelled for us to come to Abuela's room. Tía Nelcy stood at the window, holding a syringe so large it looked like a toy. I glanced briefly at the plastic feeding tube implanted directly into Abuela's stomach—like a straw. Then I heard the honking myself.

We squeezed into the window beside Tía Nelcy. The small blue Renault honking all the way down the hill was my father's. He parked across the street, stuck two fingers from each hand in his mouth, and whistled up at us the way men in the campo hailed their cows when they strayed.

"Luchi," he called my mother; he had nicknames for everyone. "Come downstairs with Santo. It's been too long, I'm not leaving without a hug from you, muchacha."

"We're just about to feed Mamá." My mother, the terrible liar, hid behind a curtain panel, laughing through her fingers. She could banter on the phone with him, but only for a few minutes—anything more was too much. I assumed she felt the way I did. As much as I loved my father, he brought back painful memories and powerful feelings I found hard to revisit.

"It's true," I shouted down to my father.

"Cómo no." He sounded almost stern, but playful, too, like she was also his rebellious child. "Deje de ser pendeja, Luz Mary."

The whole block was watching us now. My father stroked and petted his cheeks like he'd shaved for the first time in years, his skin new to him. He could go too far with his games; he was doing so now. He didn't care if he made a commotion, if pedestrians or maids watched. My father was comfortable with an audience. He could've been an actor.

My mother shook her head at me from behind the curtain.

"Qué intenso." The thrill of seeing him was all gone.

She wouldn't come down—I knew this, my father knew this—but he persisted only to make her squirm.

"I'll let you off the hook," he said, after enough time and discomfort had passed. "Just this once."

My mother stopped me in the hallway before I left. She leaned out of the door so only I heard her: "You didn't tell him you were here." The lines on her forehead were creased, her eyebrows pinched, mouth strained, like she was struggling to recognize me, like she no longer knew my name. She wanted me to prove her wrong, to tell her I had called him, but I couldn't—I hadn't—and when she saw this in my face, in my silence, she said: "Pobre hombre."

She handed me a few rolled-up pesos like I was a beggar on the street. I just wanted her to say I had a choice; I didn't have to see my father if I didn't want to. One moment my mother and I were two people hurt by the same man, and the next I was a monster rejecting my father's love. She couldn't see I was only as distant from my father as she'd taught me to be. But I ran down the stairs, two at a time, toward him and away from her.

The sun on the sidewalk made me sneeze several times. Once my eyes adjusted, I looked up at the window and waved at my mother and Tía Nelcy, the biggest chismosas of them all, but they didn't go back inside.

I was thankful for whatever my father saw in my face as I crossed the street that made him stay in the car. I climbed into the passenger seat, he undid his seat belt, and, leaning back against the shut doors, we took each other in silently. He wasn't mad, not that I could tell. Even if he was, it amounted to nothing compared to how happy he looked. It'd been three years since my graduation, and though I followed him online, it was something else to see how he'd aged in person. His hair sat farther back on his head—a small bird's nest, equal parts black and gray. His face was reddish, brown, like terra-cotta, a sunbaked complexion I found strangely comforting. His mouth hung open with an almost-nervous quiver. Behind his flimsy wire glasses, his eyes were large and brilliant.

We hugged over the gearshift. It was bizarre to hold him, to be held by him. We didn't let go of each other for a long time.

Once the car reached the top of the hill, I looked back at Abuela's window. In the place my mother and aunt had stood was a single white curtain panel, billowing out over the narrow street like a ghostly, misshapen arm.

I was in a different story now.

"Bacano que estás aquí, Hijo." My father's words were simple: *It's cool to have you here.* As we drove through the centro—past Plaza Bolívar, Hotel Ambalá, the narrow alleys teeming with counterfeit vendors—I caught him up on the essential facts of my life: I was waiting tables at a fancy seafood restaurant inside of a modern art museum, thinking of going to graduate school for anthropology, living with my best friend Anais. Like the rest of my family, he didn't understand, exactly, what I was talking about. His short *hmms* only made me want to talk more. I couldn't help feeling I was trying to convince him my life was interesting, as if he were some man to win over in a bar.

At a red light he reached for my hair, took a strand between his fingers, shy at first like he was handling a tie or necklace he couldn't afford. Then he ran his hand through my hair, from the roots down the back of my head, without any doubt or worry. The summers I'd visited, when he'd pick me up from my uncle's and my hair had grown to my shoulders, he'd joked about sending me back to my mother a shorn lamb. *Tusado*, shorn, a word I loved because of him.

He rested his hand on the gearshift, and I put my hand over his like I used to. His hand was solid, dry, and smooth, like weathered stone. The only hands like his I'd held before were those of men his age in New York. How queer it was, finding this new likeness in his hands. How queer, to be twenty-four and holding my father's hand again. It did and didn't feel right. It felt better than taking my hand away. My hand atop his said it didn't matter if the last three years had made different people of us. We still had something only the two of us could understand, something beyond language; I wanted to bottle this unsaid thing so it would always be ours. This wasn't the first time I'd thought that if only we lived in the same city, if we had more than a few hours to do the work of years, if we didn't depend on phone calls and Wi-Fi connections and Facebook messages, then everything would be different. I left my hand where it was. Still, completely still.

"How's that old lady of yours?" he finally said. "Is she annoying as ever?"

"¿Mamá o Abuela?"

He laughed.

"You're right," he said, "both of them."

I managed a convincing laugh. But it made me sad, how he thought this narrative of us against my mother could still bridge our worlds. All those past summers in Colombia, when we stayed up late watching television, when we woke up at noon to eat empanadas for breakfast, when in the middle of a long, aimless drive we stopped at a roadside restaurant to drink Colombianas and devour slices of chocolate cake, he would ask: "What would your mother say?" Those long summer weekends, he gave me a new vision of the world; my mother's wasn't the only way to live. While I was away with him, I wouldn't call her. I forgot her voice, her rules. I was the one who did the forgetting. When I flew back to Miami,

I was unruly. How could she keep me from this life? With my elbows on the dinner table, I burped the alphabet. For a week, sometimes two, my father and I would have the same conversation every single night, then our calls dwindled from ten minutes to five, less and less to report each time. Soon we would hit silence in a minute. Now, almost without my noticing it, I felt my resentment toward him fill up the car. Thick, physical. We were far from those summers. I wanted him to be angry, or at least sad.

"Abuela is only bones," I said. I hadn't thought I would talk about Abuela, not after I hadn't called when his mother died, but here I was, repeating my mother's words: "I think we'll lose her soon."

I shivered, like I'd let loose a curse. I was too much like a child with my Spanish.

"Mierda. No seas pendejo. ¿En serio?" He took his eyes off the road, looked at me straight on. The joy was gone from his voice, replaced by surprise, by sorrow, by something practiced. He was used to being told these kinds of stories.

"She can't even speak anymore. On a good day she mumbles nonsense. Her jaw this morning was chewing on air"—I pressed down on his hand, wanting him to feel the rush I felt—"her brain is fried. I don't know how it happened; I can't believe it. I can only see her back in Miami, driving my mother crazy, making her go to the mall, to the doctor's, to the supermarket. Now she's in that bed. Just lying there. Barely alive—"

I paused to find the word for *stroke* or *heart attack*. But before I knew it, I'd lost the live wire of what I was saying; I looked out the window and back at my father. He was staring ahead again, his face unchanged, almost immobile, like not only his hands were made of stone. When I persisted in looking at him, he pinched his eyes and made a large, toothy frown with his mouth.

"Tenaz," he said. Another one of his words. In English, *tenacious*. But that's not what it meant, at least not to us. In this context, it meant that the situation was difficult, that it was okay, if not understandable—if not necessary—to feel devastated.

I withdrew my hand from his.

"Tenaz," he said a second time, returning his hand to the steering wheel. He suddenly seemed cold, distant, almost confused.

After a brief silence, he asked who was taking care of her. He followed this question with other equally practical ones: "How long has Tía Nelcy been with her? What about your uncle? Where was he?" and so on. He had an air of trying to piece together the whole thing, as if once he understood the story he'd be able to give me a solution. My replies changed nothing in his expression. He kept saying he was sorry. He remembered me mentioning she was sick, but hadn't known it was this serious. He would've gone to visit her, would've helped however he could, if only he'd known; he drew his shoulders slightly into himself, leaning over the steering wheel like he was pissing into a urinal.

"Tenaz," I said, finalizing the silence.

I recognized certain buildings, or at least I thought I did, only to confuse them a few blocks later with other buildings. I didn't know where we were going. As long as I didn't ask, Pilar was only one of infinite possible destinations.

"You haven't told me anything about your life," I said.

The few times I'd spoken to him on the phone I'd concluded that his life was moving along without me: He and Pilar were going on sunset walks, inviting neighbors over for dinner, taking trips with her son when he was on break from university.

He didn't speak for what felt like minutes.

"The last year has been tough, Hijo. Nobody's building anything in this country anymore and there're still hundreds of new engineers every year." He paused. "Who knows, I've been talking to an old friend with a project in Panamá."

I felt a pang imagining him in another country. Leaving Pilar, leaving her son. *How would I see you?* I wanted to ask, but how could I when I hadn't even told him I was here, when I didn't even have plans to visit again?

"Si Dios lo quiere," I said, so it shall be.

"Sí, señor."

He pointed to the Bluetooth earpiece squished into the cup holder like a snail. "I'm driving for a car service now. It's not much, but it keeps me busy."

I didn't know what else to say; I pictured Pilar's face, then him asking me for money.

"So what now?"

With both hands on the wheel, he curled forward again. "Whatever you want, Hijo."

I immediately regretted the impatience in my voice. My hand rose, forearm tensed. The pale sliver of skin below his shirtsleeve brushed against my knuckles as I snuck my hand under his locked elbow. I found myself caressing his stomach, warmth and love filling my heart. There was a strangeness to how we blurred into each other, the separation between us much less distinct in person than in my head. He flinched, folding forward around my hand rubbing his stomach. His howl, low and heavy, filled the space of the car. We had, I realized, done this in my youth. It had been the funniest thing in the world when he'd pretended I had superhuman strength.

"Let's eat," I said, playing my own stomach like a drum.

We knew touch, and we knew food. Each summer, we ate— chewy cubes of dried guava; passion fruit juice with milk or water; caldos de huevo y res; intestines filled with lard and then fried— my favorite; a cup of coffee, a roll of bread; chicken seared on the stove and served with rice, red beans, and french fries; granadillas, their seeds resembling fish eggs; mandarinas from the morning market; salty cheese, by itself or torn into tazas of bittersweet hot chocolate; crispy blood sausage and tiny yellow potatoes—my second favorite; thick potato soups made with fresh cream and pulled chicken; sancocho de gallina, the chicken's head swimming in the pot—my father's favorite; plantains and yucca, stewed—or better, fried to a golden crisp; pandebono and pan de yuca and every other pan imaginable; potatoes stuffed with ground meat and onions; arepas de maíz or choclo, or the ones carefully filled with an egg and then fried, the first bite like magic—and when we were full, we ate more. We ate as though my mother would find out and be mad at us. We ate with pleasure, with greed, with love.

"That hasn't changed," he said, his eyes pointing to my stomach.

I inhaled deeply, puffing my abdomen out like a beach ball, as far as it would go.

"¿Qué quieres hartar?"

I laughed at this word, *hartar*—to eat without rest, breathing, or thinking. To eat like pigs. It belonged with *tusado* and *tenaz* in the list of words I associated with my father.

"The place that sells chicharrones. Long as a baby's arm." I couldn't remember the name of the restaurant, but it was in Gualanday, near the house. We hadn't gone since I was very little, not since before the move, as far as I remembered. I didn't worry about Pilar anymore. If he'd planned on introducing us today, he would've told me by now.

He was looking at my face again, but somewhere past it, too, seeing me as I must have been at thirteen, back from America and eager to eat everything before me. He had a son who liked to eat, a son who was here. That was enough to make a man happy for a thousand years.

Leaving the city, I was sure I recognized a few buildings: the second-floor dentist with the neat row of chairs along a large window where I'd gotten braces one summer; the tall, skinny house shrouded in bougainvillea where I'd lived with Tío Miguel, his wife, and my cousins; the Renault dealership where my uncle kept a dusty sales office filled with European fútbol posters; the roundabout across from the bus station with the sculpture of a locomotive pointing upward, ready to soar into the sky; the fluttering string banners around the red roof of the Carnaval del Pollo, whose chicken had been my favorite, according to everyone; the love motels and warehouse discotheques at the edge of town where so many of my cousins' stories took place; the yellow plains of wild grass, the grazing cows, the empty stares of the horses along the barbed wire fences; the Andes, so blue in the distance, and their snowcapped peaks; and before I knew it we were spiraling up the side of a lush, green mountain, passing cyclists and mule-drawn carriages piled high with unripe plantains.

Sweaty, craving a breeze, we chose a yellow plastic table outside of the restaurant. We faced the road like two old men, watching the spurts of traffic: crammed buses, silver cargo trucks, tiny old cars from another century. Meaty black flies dotted the empty tables under the corrugated roof. In the back, just as I remembered it, was the glass display case half full of chicharrón glowing under a long tube of hot red light.

My father shook a toothpick out of the bottle on the table. He was used to this life. He became everyone's friend in the small towns where he worked. For many months, sometimes a year, he would make a throne out of a flimsy plastic chair and hold court at these roadside restaurants like a dignitary.

"I was thinking in the car earlier," he said, squinting one eye and poking at the air between us with his toothpick, "with your hair long, you look just like your mother." I fought the urge to perch my chin on the backs of my hands like I was in New York posing for a friend.

He went on: "My mother used to ask Luchi if Jairo was sneaking into our bed when I was away. You were too beautiful to be mine; you had to be Jairo's. The handsome one of my brothers and my mother's favorite. But Luchi was a saint. Everyone knew she went for the ugly ones. Like only the good-looking strayed." He shook his head, holding the toothpick out like a tiny pen over a mistake. "I always wished you would look like me in some way." Something in him relaxed, as if he'd been thinking those words for a long time. Inspecting his face, I wondered as I had hundreds of times if by some magic or curse my mother had stitched her face over mine and if this, too, was his punishment for choosing his work over us, for cheating on her, for being so— *irresponsible*.

He turned his neck toward the empty restaurant. The toothpick was back to bobbing at the corner of his lips. "Even at your graduation I was hoping something of me would show up in you."

He called out for Señora Carmen.

A moment later an old lady shuffled out from the back of the restaurant in hot pink chancletas. Her flat black skirt went past her knees and her faded white polo hugged her tightly.

I tilted my head forward, polite as ever: "Pleasure to meet you, Señora Carmen."

"Who is this culicagado?" She crossed her arms with all the air of an eccentric aunt. And after my father told her I was his son: "I held you when you were this big." She caught a foot of air, then rocked the empty space between her hands like a baby. She insisted I'd met her since then, too, those summers I'd visited my father. I must've been a teenager. "Yes, I remember"—she turned to my father—"when you were with the short, blond lady from Bogotá. Luz? Was that her name?"

Neither my father nor I could remember if I'd met her.

"It's okay," she said. "Everyone forgets you when you get this old."

I looked at her face, then around the restaurant. I tried to remember being here, beginning with the fluorescent chicharrón case, and then her, and this table, this road, until the memory came together, and I saw us at this very table in our wet swim trunks as Señora Carmen filled bags and bags of chicharrón, enough to feed my aunts, uncles, cousins, their children, their friends.

"—sometimes," my father was saying, "I'm surprised he even remembers *me*."

Señora Carmen brought us a basket of chicharrón and two bottles of Colombiana on a red tray. She caught my father up on the debacle with the developers flattening out the nearest mountain for luxury compounds; perhaps he could make a call to the engineer on the project or someone at the State? Since they'd started working, her pipes were only putting out a trickle.

Just before she left, she touched my hair lightly and looked at me, just above my eyes like she was about to draw a cross on my forehead. Like I was a boy of sixteen or seventeen, my whole life ahead of me. Like I didn't know how lucky I was to have this father.

Finally, she said: "He must've gotten his mother's face." My father laughed, then I laughed. After making simple animals of us, she shuffled back to her cave, also laughing.

My father was watching me closely. I picked up a chicharrón the size of a sheet of paper, snapped it in two, and held the halves up to the sun. They filled with a rich golden light, and I made a face like I was a scientist inspecting a never-before-seen specimen, my mother's expression when she discovered some new food she liked with me. Even here, I was trying to conjure her. I bit into the puffed skin, savoring the salt and fat. He took the other half, and we ate like we were being timed, the seconds counting. Golden crumbs rained down my father's orange polo. For the first time I noticed the girdle under his shirt, now as obvious as a bandage. Heads bowed, we gulped our sodas down before gasping for air. I had missed this hunger.

"How much longer are you here?" he asked, digging into his mouth with a new toothpick.

"A few more days," I said, the lie so quick it was nearly instinct. The lie sat for a second longer, and then it was another second too late to correct myself. After a week of hiding, I needed there to be more time. I felt this as he filled the days ahead with plans. We had to come back to Gualanday with flowers for my grandparents' graves. We had to have lunch with Tío Miguel and his wife, who still talked about those summers I was their third son. Some of his old construction friends were in town and would want to meet me, too. As he spoke, I looked down the road, waiting for him to get to Pilar; the landscape blended into yellows, greens, and grays. My eyes couldn't focus on anything except the pile our hands made, balmy with grease and sweat, next to the empty red tray. We were leaving tomorrow. I imagined him trying to pick me up from Abuela's in a few days but finding only Tía Nelcy in the window.

I hooked my fingers around the necks of the bottles and picked up the tray.

He repeated himself: "You can't go without visiting the cemetery."

He gave me his wallet. His big, heavy leather wallet larger than my fist.

"Sí, señor," I said softly, before walking away.

At the back of the restaurant, I set the tray down on the display case and poked my head through the doorway into a small dirt courtyard: empty laundry lines, an alberca for washing clothes, a dog bowl, a pail for water. I could hear the low murmurings of a television from one of the two doors that were cracked. When I realized this was Señora Carmen's home, I looked away. I took out the money my mother had given me instead of opening my father's wallet. Fifty thousand pesos, worth a feast for two. I didn't know how much we owed Señora Carmen, but I didn't want to talk to her again. I flattened out the bills and slid them under the tray.

"It's a shame," my father said back in the car, as if we were continuing a conversation. "Pilar is visiting her parents right now. Her father is sick."

The leather seat was burning the underside of my thighs, but it didn't take long to sink into the heat, until it was just another sensation, the pain of someone far away.

He poked his gums with a new toothpick. It was clear he'd been thinking about when to bring her up.

"I wanted you two to meet." He buckled himself in and started the car. "Maybe next time we can plan a trip somewhere together?"

The expression on his face made me want to believe I wouldn't let years pass before I saw him again. I'd come back, I'd meet Pilar, and since I had to, I'd learn to love her.

"Maybe next year," I said. "Next summer could work."

Not far from the restaurant, my father swerved up a gravel slope. A cloud of dust rose high above the windows. Halfway up the road, the wheels spun. My father pressed his foot to the gas; pebbles pinged against the car's undercarriage and the windows as if we were driving into a storm. We emerged from the dust onto a cobblestone road dotted with weeds. On the right were the wooden shacks, the abandoned railway station, the yellowing mountains. To the left stood the row houses, each door its own color—blue, green, purple, red. I imagined instantly recognizing the house, but they were near-identical: large double doors, windows with metal bars in the shape of musical notes, and small cement driveways. After parking, my father explained he often stayed in Ibagué if he was too tired to drive back. He struggled with the door, trying several keys on the lock until it opened.

My first impression once inside was of emptiness. The chairs were stacked in a corner of the living room and the television hidden under a plastic sleeve. The long tables we used to set up across the middle of the house, where we had every meal, where we played cards and Parcheesi, where my aunts and uncles and father got drunk, where I stole sips of whiskey until I was dancing to vallenatos—those long plastic tables from all those summers were gone. The wind chimes, their pendants carved into jungle animals and fruits, were gone. In place of the star fruit trees in the court-yard were metal sticks for a clothesline or hammock. The trees had to go, he explained, because their roots were messing with the foundation and plumbing. We climbed up to the pool deck, which stood five feet above the courtyard. As a boy, I would strut across the white tiles like a stage, waiting for an audience before diving in. I looked at the water now. Emerald green, eerily still, dead bugs and brown leaves drifting on the surface.

I asked my father to show me the bedrooms. Each one had two bunk beds and an empty closet; they were smaller and darker than I remembered, though he said nothing about them had changed. My father's room was at the back of the house, separate from the others. A small, old television sat on a wooden stool next to a plas-tic chair covered with unfolded clothes. I thought I spotted a woman's blouse in the pile but looked away.

I asked my father his plans for the bathrooms, for the maid's room, for the alberca, like the house was now my project. I won-dered how long I could go on asking him questions before he dis-covered I wasn't really present; how much had this repair cost, and who cleaned the pool, and how often. I converted pesos to dollars, dollars to shifts at the restaurant; I thought about how much more I would have to work if I inherited this house; and I thought about money to distract myself from thinking about Pilar; and thinking about Pilar, I distracted myself from how we were walking through these rooms, looking at everything as if in a museum—every ob-ject incredibly far away and impossible to touch.

I wanted to run around the pool screaming at the top of my lungs with a group of boys who looked like me.

I wanted to cradle a younger cousin in my arms and bring him into the middle of the water as I whispered, *Yo te tengo.*

I wanted to fan the stove at the back of the house and impress my aunts with how I diced an onion and seared a steak.

As my father locked the front doors, I stood on the roots of a tree next to the driveway, feeling like I was falling and vanishing. The house felt so empty.

One weekend in Gualanday as a child, I was getting out of the pool when my hands slipped and my chin hit the ground. Instead of taking me to the hospital, my father pressed a towel to the wound until it stopped bleeding and then bandaged me. He and my mother fought about the scar under my chin for a long time.

One weekend in Gualanday in my early teens, I was exaggerating how good life was in America to all my cousins when the hand of the boy who lived next door touched mine underwater. That night, when the power went out and we were suddenly dropped into total darkness, I took this as a sign from the universe to lean in and kiss him.

One weekend in Gualanday when I was seventeen, my father and I sat on the roots of this tree. It was Christmas, the only one I ever spent in Colombia after we'd left. I was looking at the leaves in the gutter, wondering who would gather them, and my father was crying, drunk and crying next to me, and I was afraid that if I looked at him, his sadness would clutch me. Everyone inside was yelling at the card table. It was late by then, past midnight, the hour when the vallenatos sounded sadder, becoming cortavenas. I was afraid to look up from the leaves and see my stepmother's eyes through the double doors. She had to be looking at me. She had stopped me on the way to the bathroom minutes ago; my father had another woman, she'd said, and if anyone could change my father it was me. This was four years before she fell apart in the line at Disney World. She looked and sounded how I imagined my mother had when she left my father, so I agreed to talk to him, to tell him to stop; I promised I'd do anything for her. Back at the card table I told him to walk with me. We left the game, went outside, and sat on this tree. Before I could talk, he said, *Hijo, Hijo,* as he leaned on me, already crying, and I was silent: Who would gather these fallen leaves? Who would sweep them up? Should I find the broom? He was telling me I shouldn't come back to Colombia. I shouldn't plan a life here because I would be happier in America, because I was like a bird—I could go anywhere and have anything. All I heard in his sadness was a man finding excuses to explain his behavior; a man trying to understand why things were the way they were; trying to absolve himself of guilt. *Pájaro*—he kept on telling me I was a pájaro—slang for faggot. I had been branded with this slur many times, but the humiliation I felt now was new to me. I was embarrassed for him, for myself, for everybody. He had to know that I knew what pájaro meant. I couldn't imagine telling my mother he'd said it so many times, even if all he meant—I hoped—was that I could fly. *Why be a pájaro in a cage? ¿Por qué, Hijo?* I was drunk and seventeen, and I wasn't even thinking about the future, but there, next to him in that instant, I wanted nothing more than to be here for the rest of my life. I wanted to own this house. I wanted it to be my inheritance, and I wanted to bring everyone under one roof, around the card table, the vallenatos still playing, but it was over; he'd said what he said, cast his spell, ended the illusion. And what if I wanted this? This house? This family? The questions were in my mouth, but I didn't let them out. I said nothing; I didn't lift my face because I, too, was crying. Four years later, after I'd graduated from college, my stepmother finally left him.

"When the time comes, Pilar knows what's hers and what's not," he said as he put an arm around me. I didn't know what I had to do or say to make him stop talking. "There's also the apartment in Soacha. I want to get your mother's advice on that later." The heat he gave off was so alive and his eyes were bright. I had wanted this house—the part of me that was still seventeen and crying on the roots of this tree still wanted it—but what could I really do from New York or whatever other city I found myself in?

"Que milagro!" my father said when I suggested we visit my grandparents' graves before heading back to Ibagué.

"Don't sound so surprised," I said. "I'm not always a terrible son."

The graveyard was down the road from the house. The cobblestones turned to rubble, narrowing until the road was just wide enough for a single car. On the left, inside of the shacks without doors or windows, I glimpsed children playing marbles on the ground. On the right, far below the thicket of wilderness, a parade of eighteen-wheelers silvered the highway to Bogotá.

We parked half-inside the bushes on the shoulder so motorcycles or horses could still pass. The ragged branches outside my window screeched and pushed when I tried opening my door, so I climbed over the console to get out on my father's side. I was immediately surrounded by the cries of insects on all sides.

When my grandfather passed away, I had been in Miami with my mother and brother, but mostly with Leo. My mother told me to call my father; I lied when I said I had, and the guilt tore me apart for weeks. I wasn't ready for Colombia to change without me. When my father's mother died at the end of last year, I didn't call, again. Not after my mother told me to, not after I saw the flood of Facebook posts from my aunts and uncles. I kept telling myself I would. I wasn't fifteen anymore; I had to. It would've been easier to turn away from my father's sadness had he been a terrible man, if he'd completely disowned me for being gay, if he had never called, never shown me love, if he'd forgotten me. But he hadn't treated me how he had my mother. The hurt he caused me came in small, difficult-to-articulate words and actions. It was this hurt I feared, the hurt that separated me from him. So when my grandmother died, I told myself I would call when I was ready.

My father heaved an armful of branches out of the way. Through the opening, I stepped onto the rim of a ravine full of trees and stone crosses sticking up from the ground with a mushroom white glow. The sun peeking through the leaves overhead dappled our skin like light underwater.

I went ahead of him, slowly, stepping on the roots, rocks, and small flat stretches of solid ground I could find. Halfway down, we reached a long cement rectangle. At the very bottom of the slope, the highway roared.

My father led from there, taking us to a cluster of crosses, all waist-high with scalloped edges. At our feet were the stone plaques inscribed with my grandparents' names surrounded by several others too worn to read.

He kneeled and closed his eyes in prayer without a word to me, as if I was supposed to know what to do. I bowed my head. I could almost forget all the ways he'd hurt me. At the heart of our relationship was a debt that changed hands each time we failed to be good to each other. We had passed it back and forth for years, and it had grown to an unbearable size. We would never settle the score.

My father's face, as he began to cry, looked calm, firm, full of conviction. He wiped his nose on his forearm, his breath catching with short, controlled gasps. With my whole heart I wanted to believe, and did believe, that once we got back to the car I would ask him to take us to the bus station tomorrow, tell him the truth about our departure. We could have lunch with my mother. A proper goodbye. And I would come back next summer to meet Pilar. And if there was a woman after her, I would meet her. In the meantime I would call, perhaps not every day, but I would ask about his life and tell him about mine. One day we would fill the house in Gualanday again. I could already hear the vallenatos, taste the whiskey, and all but see my father's face. We could have parties and parties.

On our way back from the cemetery, I asked my father to stop at the house again. I was surprised when he agreed to pose for me in front of the double doors.

"Put your foot there—yes—on the ledge. Look at my left ear. Now at my right elbow. Try not to smile. Just act natural."

He followed my every command.

"Place your hands on your chest. One on top of the other. Pretend you're cradling a small bird in your palms. Keep a straight face. One more," I said, spinning around with the camera out in front of us. We pressed our heads together.

"Hey," I whispered, slipping my arm around his shoulders. "Te amo, Papi."

I planted a kiss on his forehead for the last photo.

The next morning, while my mother showered, I called my father and told him we were leaving early. I had expected him to ask questions, to get angry even. All he asked was when he could pick us up from the hotel and if we had enough time for lunch; I should've been grateful for his innocence, willful or not, but it filled me with shame. After the call, my mother could tell that I was far from the hotel room. When she asked if I was okay I said I was just tired.

We drove for twenty minutes up the mountains north of Ibagué in search of a roadside restaurant with a view of the city. Each restaurant we passed was closed. The hand-painted signs said they would open on the weekend. We continued up the mountain and away from the city. The hillside thickened with fog. A light rain misted the windshield. The blue lines of faraway mountains faded into the clouds.

My mother, sitting in the back, leaned forward between my father and me to look out through the windshield. She was nervous; it was her first time spending time with my father since my graduation, and he wasn't acting like himself. She finally asked if we should turn back. Ten more minutes, my father said, we were almost near a town he knew with a good restaurant. But when we got there, everything was closed or abandoned, and after several turns down narrow streets where we could have reached out and touched the walls on either side, I realized he didn't actually know of a restaurant in this town. I kept quiet. I could see how much he wanted to give us a special lunch. My mother shifted over to the seat behind mine, silent. Every few minutes she weaseled her hand between the seat and the door, and I reached back to hold it.

We left the town and continued to ascend the mountain. In the rearview mirror, I watched my mother grip the cup holders on either side of her and close her eyes in prayer. My father was driving fast. He swerved around the bends of the empty road, and we continued to pass closed restaurants that on the weekend would be filled with parents and their children.

We ended up eating a corrientazo near the bus station in Ibagué. After the drive up the mountain, we only had half an hour to eat before the bus left. The restaurant, tucked inside an unmarked building, was where all the taxistas in the city went for lunch.

Men in sweater-vests and newsboy caps, with mustaches and little eyeglasses, crowded around the plastic tables in the dining room talking over each other. From the kitchen doorway echoed the voices of women cooking and shouting orders. I felt disoriented after the silence of the car ride.

My father sat us down at a dirty table and waved a waitress over. "Muñeca," he said to her, as if he knew her, but there was no recognition on her pretty face. He told her we didn't have much time. She wiped the table down with a wet rag that left the table stickier. My parents ordered the chicken and I asked for a steak.

My mother and father huddled over the table to talk, like the car ride was already a distant memory. The topic turned to mothers. After my father's mother died, all his siblings, even the ones who had abandoned her when the dementia was at its worst, had re-appeared to fight over the inheritance. There was the house in Gualanday, a farm in Prado, and two storefronts in downtown Ibagué, one leased to a lavandería and the other to a mattress store. My father had only wanted the house in Gualanday. He had paid for its upkeep all these years.

My mother was now telling him that my uncle, the one married to Tía Nelcy, the one everyone loved and who could do no wrong, had been found passed out in front of a bar downtown. That night he'd been carrying the money my mother sent back for Abuela's treatments, and, of course, his pockets were empty in the morning. She couldn't trust anyone anymore, she said. She wouldn't put it past them to kill Abuela to get their hands on her apartment, but alas, there was nothing my mother could do except come back and call as often as she was able to. Abuela's ninety-first birthday was next month.

I had the sensation that I wasn't there, that I was witnessing something below the surface, something I wasn't meant to see. Did everyone feel this way when they listened to their parents talk? Was this a common experience or something special? Had they always talked so openly, or was this conversation only possible because they had no obligation to each other now aside from loving me? Everything they said surprised me. These were the kind of radioactive thoughts I knew my mother buried away for a safer time. It was like I was underground, seeing where their dangerous feelings lived. And little by little I realized my parents had, in fact, never turned their backs on their souls. I was the one—the one who didn't have the courage to live with these thoughts.

"A little bird told me you went to see Hilda's farm this week," my father said. "I haven't been up there myself. She's had it on the market for a while now." He swirled the ice in his glass. "Never thought I'd see the day la Doctora became a campesina."

My mother folded her hands atop the table, covering her ring. She was looking around the restaurant for the waitress.

I asked, "A farm?"

"Let's not talk about this now," she said like someone who'd been caught.

"No, come on. What's the big secret?"

"Ayy," my father said, "looks like I stuck my foot into fresh shit." He stood before I could stop him. He scratched the top of his head until his hair stood up in a gray crest.

"Ingeniero," someone called out to my father from across the restaurant.

He looked at my mother like a child waiting for permission to leave the table.

"For God's sake." My mother sighed. "Go say hi to your friend."

I asked her what he was talking about.

"It's nothing yet."

"Mami." My face was hot, my eyes wet. "You bought a farm?"

"You know Mark isn't in the greatest health." She made a little bowl of her hands for mine, but I kept my hands on my lap. "Should anything happen to him, the house in Miami is for his daughters. And I can't go back to our old house. You know how depressed I was there after you left." She took a deep breath, unfolding her napkin and aligning her fork and knife on either side of her plate. "I have to be ready."

"Stop," I said. And I began to cry. "Why is everything about death now?"

"Be serious, Santiago," she said. "There's nothing to cry about. Honestly. We'll go see it next time."

But I cried and said: "It's not fair. We're finally together. You, me, Papi. And all we can talk about is death. Why can't we just have a nice lunch together?"

I looked around the crowded restaurant, gazing at the taxi drivers who resembled my father. There was a world in which I was just a child having lunch with his two parents; I was looking around for that world, hoping to somehow enter it. But every visit would be like this from now on. No more large reunions, no more parties lasting days. The paradise in my head wasn't Colombia but my childhood.

As I sat there, my mother stood up and put her arms around me. "You can see the whole city from the farm. We'll get you a desk and internet. I can already picture you there."

I knew she'd done nothing wrong. She was always going to come back to Colombia; she'd only left for me and Manuel. It would have only been a matter of time before she told me. But in my mind, it didn't feel fair. After everything, I was still a boy waiting for his mother to explain her disappearance.

My mother stayed in the car while we bought the bus tickets to Bogotá. My father held my hand tightly through the crowded station, as if he might lose me.

The driver of the white van let us on board. After helping my mother into the cabin, I took my own seat in front of the sliding door. My father, outside, asked if we had our phones, wallets, and passports, going down the list like he was the responsible one.

Across the open door, we grasped each other tight, then tighter. His were the biggest arms in the world, mine the softest. Every few seconds he pulled away to look at me and I squinted, the sky bright at his shoulders, thinking we might speak. There was no more time to pretend something wasn't breaking in our bodies, wanting out. I wanted to say *te amo*, again and again. I wanted to say this was a new beginning. We began to cry, silently, in the same way, as our time ran out.

My mother rubbed my back. There was a woman behind my father. I mumbled, "Papi." We broke our embrace to let the woman in the van. Forced to look at ourselves from her perspective—our noses running, our breathing heavy and hard—we laughed. My mother, stroking my back in circles, turned around to mouth some explanation to her. I wondered if my mother understood what I was feeling, but she couldn't possibly. She didn't know that at the end of every summer when my father and I had to say good-bye, it always felt like the first time. No one could stop us from crying; these tears were part of our love. As more people arrived—a handsome man with a mullet, a stocky woman doused in perfume, an old fat man in a three-piece suit—my father and I continued sobbing, not caring how we looked. We both loved someone we couldn't have in our life, whom we'd had to say good-bye to too many times, never knowing when or if we would see them again.

Once the van was full, the driver turned the engine on. Our time was over, and in a rush, I took a picture of my father framed by the van's open door.

"Call me when you get to Bogotá?"

"Si, Papi," I said, not knowing that I would forget to, first in Bogotá, then in Miami.

After my father shut the door, I waved at him through the window, and I didn't stop. My lungs filled with too much feeling, too much pressure. "I love him. I really do." I tried to keep my father in my vision—amid strangers, suitcases, crates full of chickens, women selling phone minutes—for as long as possible. "He loves you, too," my mother said, giving me a look of understanding, of wanting to understand. But even as she said, "We love you, Santiago," I was aware only of my father. Standing all alone, crying, he must have felt the sharpness and clarity of our separation the way only he and I could. He would understand, even if she never did, why I was never ready to call again.

The van turned out of the bus station into the roundabout, then into traffic, and something in me stretched, so that even if I could no longer see my father, I felt the pull of him. For a long time I had thought of my father as a horizon, as if reaching him would transport me into another world. It was easy, if not necessary, for me to think my life would've taken a different shape had I grown up here, with him, my mother, my brother—a family of four. I needed the sense of freedom I felt when I thought of my homeland, the sense that there was another life, radically different from my own, waiting for me in Colombia. There were moments in my childhood when I did find brief flashes of this freedom at my parents' sides. All of the yearning and absence at my center, all the effort and struggle of living in another country, would disappear—and if not quite disappear, then at least thin into something as sparse and immaterial as a mist—so that I felt on the verge of escaping myself.

As we left Ibagué, my mother pointed at the plains out the window—the wide expanses of farmland, brush, and mountains—when I heard a suspicious sound up front. The driver cracked the window an inch; the warm, fragrant air of the countryside streamed across our faces. I pressed against her, rubbing the side of her arm, feeling for the scar on her skin, and as we looked out past our reflections, I whispered: "Huele a bosque, Mami." I nodded toward the driver. "Vos que te cagaste." My mother pulled back from me, making a sound of playful disgust and covering her lips, but then she laughed. This was my father's joke for when someone farted in the car. It seemed to me now that I was beyond the hope of touching a horizon. There was no use in pretending I was not where I was or who I was. Transcendence never came through my father, or through anyone; there was always more distance after experiencing any person, place, or situation. Ahead of me in New York, there would still be more waking up, more working and eating, sleeping and shitting to do, because there was no end to it, life always went on, the days bled into each other, the horizon moved further afield. And it was okay, I said to myself now. It was okay because without the promise of an end, I could appreciate the inexhaustible world we made of each other; it was still there, would always be there, in some form or another—we only had to let ourselves recognize it, and in doing so, come back again.

V

The girls were kind. No rush, they said. Luz could stay at the house as long as she wanted.

Jane, the younger one, was coordinating for both sisters. At any rate, Luz couldn't afford living in Mark's house on her own; the taxes alone would bleed her dry. She had wanted to move out as soon as possible. But Jane needed time to collect the painted mallard collection, the woodcutting tools Mark had inherited from his own father, the gun safe Luz never dared touch—all the strange things her husband had loved like toys. It took Jane months to finally drive her pickup truck down from Alabama. She was his Santiago.

By the end of the year, Luz was back in her old townhouse on the lake. She spent days cleaning up after the young man from Cali. When she'd told him she needed the house back, he'd stopped answering her calls, skipped his last month's rent, and left behind half his things without telling her. She filled the house with her own furniture, but even then, she slept on the white leather couch in the living room, afraid that if she slept in her old room and bed she might never leave again.

She called her realtor, and within a week, the first offer came in from a single mother in her thirties with a seven-year-old son. Luz couldn't imagine a better person to take her place. "It's a sign from the universe," she told Santiago on the phone, feeling guilty as she added: "I can't do it again, live alone here like when you two left." The paperwork went through quickly. Now all she had to do was donate as many of her belongings as possible before the move back to Colombia.

Her last month in Miami, Luz called Freddy every night, making sure the farm in Ibagué was ready for her arrival. It was on one of these nights that she realized she called her farmhand more than anyone. The last time she had called Manuel had been to go over her social security papers. Less than two thousand dollars a month for retirement, even if she took Mark's pension, was not much to live on. Manuel had agreed and suggested she move back to Colombia if she didn't want to be poor. No help, not even a gesture, nothing. Stingy as his father. *Si no quieres ser pobre*, she repeated the words back to Santiago. It was the way Manuel had said them that had really hurt. But Santiago insisted it had been a joke, trying to soften the edges of his brother's words, though they both knew Manuel was making sums of money they could hardly imagine. Santiago, surviving off a teacher's salary in New York, had promised to help her with her phone bill and groceries and whatever else he could.

At night Mark's recriminations the day she told him she'd

bought a farm in Colombia would pop into her head: *What did she know about farming coffee? She couldn't even drink a cup without staying up all night. And wouldn't she like to be nearer to Santiago?* Mark had been seventy-five and not in great shape. It was no secret they were nearing the ends of their lives, no secret she would survive him—she was sixty-six and had her mother's genes; no one would be surprised if she lived into her nineties—and yet she'd had to plan for what remained of her life in secret. All the years she'd fought with Mark about where to retire and begged the boys to come home for the holidays, the thought of the farm quieted her mind. Her freedom didn't hinge on Mark, the boys, or anyone.

But it was no longer clear what awaited her in Ibagué. Her mother had died; her siblings were still stealing from each other; and without her job at the lab, she didn't know how she would fill her time. Perhaps after a few months on the farm, she would look for an apartment near one of the boys. Maybe near Manuel to help when the new baby came. Maybe near Santiago to be near Santiago.

For now, what remained of her furniture in Miami would go to charity or into storage for Santiago to use one day. For now, her freedom had arrived, all too fast. It was here, ready to drag her into the future.

Luz was up before sunrise. She pulled the curtains aside and slid the glass door open. The backyard stretched out before her: the brick patio sprinkled with dew, the wooden fences garlanded with black vines, the strange, dark shapes the outdoor furniture made in the dim light. She paused at the threshold of the living room like she had for all those years. The first step outside always carried the weight of traveling a great distance, and today, her last day in the house, it felt like an even longer journey. She imagined entering a room full of strangers, then stepped outside in that way. The morning was humid and hot. Her skin shed the warm yellow glow of inside, her arms taking on a silvery blue hue. In front of her, birds chased their shadows across the lake with soft little cries.

Luz was a nostalgic. She could still see the wooden porch on her parents' farm, bathed in mountain light fifty years ago when she was a girl. A wicker basket, heavy with toys, bounced on her hip as she set the little pink furniture across the creaking porch for her younger siblings. Those mornings, when she couldn't believe that something so wonderful as this hour was hers, she'd sprint down the hill, past her mother's chicken pen and her father's shed, to the edge of their farmland, and, gripping the wire fence between the spikes, she shouted her own name. Now, Luz gathered the furniture in the center of the patio, wanting to clean it one last time before the boys from the charity arrived. Nervous and excited, she recited the list of everything she was donating: the white sofa, the love seat, the dining room chairs and table, the barbecue, the bikes, the generator, the inflatable mattress. Under the quiet stars, she turned the hose on, washed the furniture, and watered the bromeliads.

For the last year the boys had kept telling her: "It's your time, Mami." They said almost the exact same things to her on their separate calls, meaning they had talked beforehand, had planned together how they would convince her to sell the house. She crossed the bricks, stepped onto the grass that marked her yard's end and the world's beginning. She felt proud of how far she had come in her life. The air thickened, wrapping around her as she neared the lake. She danced, weeds dragging along the bottom of her bare feet. She kicked her legs and swung her arms overhead hoping someone was watching her from a window. A woman in her sixties dancing alone in the morning in her backyard—what a truly strange thing to be! She knew she made quite the sight, but she didn't know why she was dancing. She didn't know why she was doing anything at all. After a little while she decided to sit. A light across the lake punched a hole through the dark. Her heart pounded so hard she could almost hear it. When another light turned on along the shore, she realized she was not ready for this to be her last day in the house. She watched the light flicker on in the children's room of the neighboring townhouse, where a Venezuelan family was now living. To her right Gustavo and Claudia, the Colombian couple who'd lived there as long as she had, switched on their kitchen radio.

The sun crested over the lake, the first light falling in long, hopeful slivers over the water and houses. The sky expanded, suddenly vast, murky, and orange. She felt untethered.

Almost twenty years ago, Santiago had pointed to the plot on the map in the sales office, tapped the blue of the lake, and said they'd found their beach.

Once a week he had made the trip with her to watch the house rise from the ground. At the gate she told him to close his eyes until she said he could open them, and once they'd parked in front of their lot, she gave him permission to see again. She wedged her shoes off, stretched her legs on the dashboard. Her little accomplice, twelve at the time, placed his socked feet over the air vents. Under the dome lights, he did his homework, balancing textbooks and ruled paper on his knees, while she studied for her laboratory technician licensing exam from the big green binder. After an hour or so she would tell Santiago to cover his eyes again—she sped past the existing subdivisions, past the single-family homes in large, lawned plots with pools and playgrounds. With his eyes shut, her little accomplice giggled at this game he no longer questioned.

As they watched the plot, the dirt, the patches of wild grass, and beyond them the lake's fountain shooting skyward into the moonlight, she couldn't help but ask herself: Was this all really just for Santiago? But with Santiago at her side, it was never long before she felt pulled into his world, a world better than hers; it was not long before nothing mattered, before everything was him. They ate cheeseburgers over napkins in their laps and took turns picking at the loose fries at the bottom of the bag. Looking out the window, they decided whose room would go where, what color would go on what wall. She wanted a hammock in the backyard; he wanted a trampoline. Sketching their dreams out across the early dark, she had the sense that they were building more than a house. How simple it had felt—to figure out her life, which was his life, their life in this way. They made plans to one day run around the living room, to one day fill the tub with bubbles and bathe side by side. One day she would teach him to dance her favorite salsas, holding his hands and guiding his feet over the carpet, the way her mother had done for her.

Every time there was another rod, brick, or pipe sticking out from the ground. Another bulldozer, another cement mixer. Everything on the lot caught the glow of Miami in the distance. It wasn't the first thing to belong to her, but it seemed to her that she had never owned anything quite like this. She had never had Santiago by her side to help her imagine a new life.

For the last three weeks, as she prepared to leave, Luz had felt overwhelmed whenever she was home. She worked extra shifts at the laboratory like she had ten years ago when she was barely staying afloat. Coming out of the lab at five in the morning, into the vast and mostly empty parking lot humming with the tall, bright lights spread across it, she sat in her car with the radio on and waited for the news to replace the music. She had to convince herself to drive home—to pack, to clean. Occasionally, because of her panics the last few months and the medicine she now took, she got tired, confused, and sleepy. She woke several hours later to a coworker knocking on her car window. How could it be this way, that her freedom felt so dizzying, cold, and strange? She couldn't understand why things weren't better. But nothing stopped her. She kept moving as she had for most of her life: Instead of a heart, there was a motor in her chest.

————

Nets of light broke across the drying furniture in the backyard. With every passing second her excitement swelled, the kind she had to share with someone, lest it grow and grow. Luz could wait no longer for Santiago to call her, for either one of the boys to remember that today was the day of the move. It was her time. She dialed Santiago first, but the recorded message said his inbox wasn't set up and the call cut off; he was probably teaching at this hour. She then tried Manuel—the hospital had set up an office in one of his spare bedrooms so he could read scans from home—but he didn't answer either. This was the worst part of life without Mark. She no longer had someone to cool the hot extremes of her feelings. By the time hours later when the boys finally called back, if they did at all, whatever she had to tell them would sound silly and ordinary. The light all gone.

Luz stepped back into the cool dim of the living room crowded with boxes. Her shirt clung to her skin with sweat. She was already tired. Even if neither of the boys had offered to help, even if neither one had responded to her messages about what they wanted to keep, she was leaving the house and going back to Colombia. How did it all mean so little to them? She was selling the house, doing everything on her own, and this newfound freedom stirred both her anger and its own powerful pleasure. Before she knew it, she was calling the gay charity Santiago had taken her to when he was in college. As the phone rang, she convinced herself it was to confirm her appointment, but deep down what she wanted was to share her excitement, to have it witnessed and fixed, before it morphed into something else—before it tipped over.

"Hello? Out of the Closet?"

Someone had picked up but all she heard was grainy silence. She pressed the speaker closer to her ear.

"I need a big truck. Because it's my time."

"I'm sorry, I didn't catch that," a man said in English, startling her. "Jeff speaking."

"Luz," she said, repeating her name slow and proud, as if it contained the entire story of her life.

"Ah, yes, Miss Luz. We have a pickup scheduled for you at noon. Does that still work for you?" His voice was bright, almost breathless. Did Santiago speak English like this in his world, too?

"My son"—she put a hand to her heart—"is gay."

"Oh. Good for him," said Jeff, before speaking to someone else in his office, his words too quick for her to keep up. Computer keys clicked on his end of the line. Near him, another phone rang. "Now is there anything else I can help you with, Miss Luz?"

She had been feeling proud as well as guilty, but now she felt a sudden collapse. She was disgusted with herself for wanting to be thought special for having a gay son.

"We went to your store once when he was in college. We browsed the shelves," she said. "He found a glass he liked, for wine. I told him he drinks too much. He needs to take care of his liver while he's young. Still, he carried it around the store until he finally put it down and said he didn't want to fly back to New York with it." She kept talking, talking, talking as if she could return to that day. "Instead, he bought a shirt that said 'Love Will Tear Us Apart' across the front. Funny thing for a shirt to say. It was a little big on him, too. And gray. The fabric would show when he sweat. He wouldn't listen, of course." She could see her son, again, when he was nineteen or twenty, saying he'd forgotten something as they left the store. "He went back inside to your clinic. Imagine that, buying a shirt and getting checked for a venereal disease, all in one place. He was always responsible about that." She had waited for Santiago in the car, wondering what it meant that he'd brought her to a store where men in makeup and wigs worked the registers, where there was a waiting room in the back full of men anxiously checking their smartphones. What response did her son want? Did he mean to scare her? To invite her into a deeper part of his world? Her mind raced from the pictures Manuel had found on the computer so many years ago, to the night she came downstairs and found Santiago having sex on the couch with the Venezuelan boy. After half an hour, Santiago came out of the store with a bandaged finger, wiggling it like it was a little man, uttering a low-pitched hello when he entered the car—still her boy. She envied his freedom. She had done her best to show him he was loved, even in the moments he perplexed and scared her. He was lucky, luckier than she'd been. She had wanted him to have a different life than hers, but she had not expected that in doing so she had given him a life that would take him away from her.

"Really lovely story. The truck will be over soon, Miss Luz."

She needed the man on the phone to ask her more questions, to really try to understand how much this moment meant to her. Couldn't he, just for a second, stop being professional? The sensation she'd fought for the last year—she didn't know what to call it—made her feel crazy and wrong again, impossible to understand. She was incomprehensible to her sons, to her colleagues, to her family in Colombia, and now to this man who was asking if there was anything else he could help her with today.

"No, thank you kindly," she said, a strange phrase, both formal and awkward, from the books of idioms Santiago had gifted her.

"Then we're all good to go. Sit tight and the boys will be over soon."

Luz moved to the bathroom, closing the door behind her. She splashed herself with water, changed into clean clothes, and did her makeup. The boys coming to pick her things up, they would have to understand. In their faces, she would recognize a piece of Santiago. And in her they would see a mother. As she led them through the house, showing them everything she was donating on behalf of her son, she would rest her hands on their shoulders, feeling something soft and living. At night, she would call Santiago and tell him in English how the boys from the charity had loved the house. They had never spoken much to each other in English, but it felt important to her now to tell him this in his language. Even if he teased her, called her *gringita*, she would go on in English. Yes, the *gay* charity, she would stress the word for emphasis, making sure he understood. All she could do was hope he would be proud of her.

Sometimes, as they drove up to the lot, Luz wished Manuel had also been in the car. But he hadn't shown any interest. The house, according to him, was just another one of her impulsive decisions. Cleaning his room one day, she'd turned on her old cassette player, thinking he was using it for a school project, when she heard her son talking, talking to himself—about his life, his loneliness. *First Colombia, now Miami?* She could never forget how the emotion in his voice cracked through the speaker. His belief that she was clueless, that she could do nothing right, made her even more sure that he felt unloved by her, that he thought she was willing to hurt him if it meant giving Santiago a better life—until she began to doubt herself. How good was she really if she couldn't hold her two boys together?

Luz had been the only person other than Manuel's wife, Xiomara, who'd come out to Ohio for his graduation from medical school. She blamed herself for not making Santiago come, for not offering to buy his plane ticket, for not calling Manuel's father to make sure his visa was ready in time—there was so much more she could've done. Her son had become a doctor in America, and no one had come.

The robed man on the stage called Manuel's name. Applause followed. As her son rose from his seat, the other students around him patted his back. He belonged to this other world now. He had a wife, a career, a future. It didn't matter that he wasn't the kindest son, that he didn't rush to her like Santiago, because he was liked, these people liked him, this world liked him. Crossing the stage, he approached the podium, his graduation gown billowing wide as he shook hands with one of his professors. For a brief moment he and the man hugged. Manuel then faced the crowd with an expression of humility and seriousness between his lean cheeks; he bowed his head, holding his diploma up high like a trophy. When he looked up his smile singled her out in the crowd—at least she wanted to believe so—shining, warm. It came with ease, the love she felt for him then, and for Xiomara, and for these small red brick buildings.

As Manuel left the stage, Luz opened her purse. Folded at the bottom were Manuel's jerseys for the Colombian national soccer team and the Miami Heat. She had planned to give them to him over dinner, but now, with one in each hand, she stood. She waved the jerseys in the air, whipping each one in circles over her head, cheering louder than anyone had the whole ceremony.

"Luz? Luz," said Xiomara, her face hidden behind the graduation program. "Luz. What are you doing? ¡Siéntate! Please."

The truck arrived at noon. She felt embarrassed when it entered the cul-de-sac, attempted to loop around, and then pulled back because it wouldn't fit. One of the men jumped out of the cabin to guide the other as he reversed toward her house. The truck inched into the driveway with a shrill, piercing beep; a black cloud of exhaust engulfed her palm trees, her orchids, but it all looked strange and unfamiliar, as if she were watching someone else's life unfold.

Luz almost forgot what was happening when the knock came at the door.

She undid the lock and turned the handle: The boys from the charity—they weren't boys at all, but fully grown men with dark gelled hair and impassive eyes. They wore loose pink shirts that said "Out of the Closet," baggy jeans speckled with paint, and steel-toe boots. The taller of the two men looked down at his clipboard, then at her.

"Luz?" He was Cuban.

She nodded. As he read something off his clipboard, she noticed his unkempt beard, the chewed cap of his ballpoint pen—but the more he spoke, the more she had the sense that he was somehow disappearing before her eyes.

"I'm sorry," she said. "Come in, please. I don't want to let the air out."

Before they could speak, she brought them into the foyer. Noticing the stacks of boxes there, she apologized again. She examined their faces; they were smiling. But they were so unlike her own sons, she could barely look at them. Their body odor, like poison, shot through the air from their already sweat-stained shirts. They were tall—their shoulders reached the top of her head, making her feel tiny.

"For you," she said, pointing at the love seat and coffee table. She continued to the dining room and pointed at the table and chairs where Santiago had done his homework. When she looked at the mirror propped against the wall, she somehow hoped the men had completely faded away, as if this move were all in her head, a brief fit of madness caused by loneliness and lack of sleep.

Within the gilt frame, the men turned around behind her, taking in the floors, the ceiling, the furniture. The looks on their faces were in a language she couldn't read.

"Sorry," she said. "The mirror, too."

In the living room, she opened the sliding doors to the backyard. Sunlight fell across the coffee table stacked high with shoe boxes and her pajamas folded on the white leather couch.

When she turned, the men stood under the archway, surveying the living room as if held off by an invisible border. Looking around, she tried to see what they saw, what story this house told of her. The flattened pillows on the couch. The ridiculous paintings from Marshalls on the kitchen walls. She couldn't remember anymore what was in the unlabeled boxes shoved under the marble counter. The men were surely asking themselves why she was alone right now, whether anyone else was coming to help her, and what life was this to live? In their own careful words, her boys had been saying she had not been living and experiencing, but deferring her life for the last year. They seemed full of new concepts and ideas about themselves and about who she was and who she should be now. They were trying to love her, they truly were, but in doing so, they had held a mirror up to her and forced her to face the humiliation of seeing herself.

She looked at the men again. If she focused on one, the other blurred. In their faces, she saw fragments of Julio, Gabriel, and

Pedro, the three men she had dated before she'd decided to wait until the boys left home, before she'd met Mark; she saw her brothers, her father, and many other men. She wanted to apologize again, but for what?

"All of this is for the *gay* charity," she said, hoping that once the word was out everything would change—the men would drop their costumes, reveal the boys underneath, boys like hers.

When nothing changed, she picked up a pillow from the couch and shielded her breasts.

"I told you we should've brought another macho," said the shorter man to his coworker, as if she hadn't spoken. He looked Dominican but spoke like a Cuban.

The taller man stared at her and asked, "Did someone die here, mami?"

His joke was a way of declaring intimacy; he felt comfortable enough to try to make her laugh. Luz gave a quick smile to acknowledge the joke. She remained stiff, though.

"What I'm saying is, this is good-looking stuff. Are you sure you want to give it away?"

"Bro, let's just get started," said the shorter one, again as if she weren't in the room. He stepped around his coworker and lifted one of the boxes under the counter. "Coño, that's heavy."

These men weren't gay. She couldn't possibly have thought everyone who worked for the charity would be, but still, she had hoped—she didn't know what she had hoped for anymore, but she felt deceived.

"Are you gay?" she blurted out.

Silence. Then the men doubled over laughing. Their laughter gripped and, slowly, crushed her.

"Do we look gay to you?" asked the short man, breathless and coughing.

"No," she said. "I don't know."

She pulled the drawstring for the blinds, and the brown slats flew farther up, clattering.

"Put that box down," she said, flicking her head at them—animals. "Start outside."

"I think she needs a moment," the short one said, punching the taller man's shoulder. "Or maybe she wants to watch us make out." He shut his eyes and opened his mouth, his tongue drawing large, vulgar circles around his lips, inches from the taller one's mouth. They laughed again. This time she didn't smile. "Mami, I'm just playing. But seriously, you need a moment?"

"This is hard," said the tall one, his voice unexpectedly low. He sounded clear and sober, like he was used to comforting distressed people. "I've been doing this a long time; I know it's hard."

The mix of laughter and concern made her chest burn. She felt her eyes open wide, her nostrils flaring. A fire spread inside her bones. She shouted: "¡Afuera!"

The men shared a glance. Their eyes said everything they thought of her. The short man snorted and the tall one smacked him before he laughed or said something.

With the pillow over her breasts, she stepped past them into the kitchen. She kept her eyes ahead of herself with a razor focus, finding dignity, at least, in being a crazy old woman. She took a painting down from the kitchen wall and read it aloud: "Today is a gift. That's why it's called the present." She placed it on the counter, then took down another painting. "May flowers always line your path and sunshine light your day.

"These, too," she said. "I never want to see them again."

From the kitchen sink, she watched the men lift the patio chairs onto their backs and carry them through the house. After a few trips, the short one walked all the way down to the lake, the top of his head just visible over the curve of grass. The tall man stood outside the kitchen window, unaware of her presence. He lifted up his shirt to pat his brow dry and there were scars all over his back—raised and thick as bubble gum—from his shoulder blades to his underwear band. She felt time stop for a moment with the vague sense that his world was so much larger than hers, larger than she could understand. She was suddenly light-headed, the sink pulling away from her as if she had stood too quickly.

A moment later, when the men came back inside, she busied herself with whatever was at hand. She wiped the bottom of the sink one more time and checked that the fridge was still empty. As soon as the men passed the kitchen, she peeked into the hallway to watch them; she didn't know what she was looking for. A part of her worried they would break or steal something. A larger part couldn't understand why they had not taken an interest in her life yet. If they only asked, she could tell them the patio furniture had been given to her by Sharon and was good as new after all these years. She could tell them a whole story about how Sharon would try to get her to smoke marijuana, how she had once nibbled on a special brownie by accident and laughed harder than ever before. She had wanted a lovely and affirming experience from giving her things to the gay charity, something to make her feel closer to Santiago, as though she was in a way passing her belongings on to his family; the thought of this as his inheritance now sounded ridiculous. She felt foolish: This was a transaction. Nothing more. The men would leave her house, drop her things off at a warehouse, and go on to another house, then another, today, tomorrow.

She had dated three men after moving to Miami but had only seen them in their own houses. There was Julio, the thirty-five-year-old mechanic who'd invited her over to watch him play Xbox, his apartment decorated with movie posters and beanbags, like a place where teenage boys would spend a Friday night. Then, Gabriel, the contractor renting an efficiency behind his brother's house—who'd thought she was in her late thirties, though she was a decade older, who'd wanted to take her out dancing and drinking in South Beach and make love to her in bathrooms or under the stars on the wet sand. She had paced these small apartments and picked at the worn shreds at the bottom of her leather purse. Sinks full of dirty dishes, laundry piled on top of kitchen counters, bills and other papers scattered across linoleum floors. Aside from those things, emptiness. The echo of her heels followed her around, making her feel tracked, like she was an animal being hunted. She remembered asking Pedro if he'd just moved in because there was only a white coffee table and a used black leather couch in his living room. "No, mami. Siete años." She didn't know how to sit comfortably inside of these houses, crossing her legs and then finding herself instinctively sliding to the floor and stretching her feet out underneath a wobbly coffee table, always thinking about what Santiago and Manuel would say about these men. Santiago would humor her and meet them with an open heart; Manuel would judge them with only a look, consider them losers, and leave before he wasted another minute of his life.

There was something grand about closing her heart off until the boys had left, but then something terribly incomplete and unreal as those first four years without the boys flew by and she still hadn't met another man. She had thought about joining a dating website and had tried, briefly, but there had been so many messages, so many men requesting pictures of her feet and breasts, of the strangest parts of her. The last thing she wanted was to become like her mother, single after her second husband and relying on her children to take care of her. The comparison, however foreboding, wasn't enough to compel Luz back into dating. She couldn't imagine going through all the small, sad humiliations of love again. The problem with loneliness was that the longer you were lonely, the less you knew how to be anything else. As she saw it, when she came to America, she'd had to fold her life and stow it away in a box, which she'd locked, then hid in a closet, and finally, she had swallowed the key; and now so much time had passed, she neither fit in her old life nor cared to wear it again. She imagined telling a man: "I lost my life in a closet."

But Mark had changed everything. She missed her gordito. Unprompted one night, she'd told Santiago that if she had to choose between Manuel's father, Santiago's father, or Mark, she would choose Mark. She didn't know why she had told her son that.

Luz had no clue how much time had gone by when the sunlight hit the side of the truck and bounced into her bedroom window. Its warmth dazed her. Around her, the empty pink room blushed.

Looking out, she saw the wooden dining room chairs in the back of the truck, their dark and twisted faces seemingly alive with pain, surrounded by her belongings.

In a moment inspired by the drama of radio plays and telenovelas, by the memories of how her siblings had fought in Colombia, by their willingness to hurt each other, she locked the front door behind the men from the charity.

When they started knocking, she was back upstairs in her bedroom, pacing the perimeter. She could hear the men laughing and knocking, laughing, knocking. The words *crazy bitch* rose above the knocks. She regretted it all. Selling the house, donating her things, moving into a new life. She wanted it all back. She wanted to wake up here, in this room. There was no doubt in her mind that these men were taking advantage of her; they had seen her as una vieja pendeja. These men didn't work for the charity. If they did, they would be like her son. They would be kind and gay and caring. But instead, they were just like every other man who'd ever tried to steal some part of her. They would fill the truck and run away with her life. They would sell it at flea markets and online.

She wished she weren't alone. She wanted Santiago. He could lighten any situation with only a joke. Or Manuel, whose cold, penetrating stare could scare away any intruder.

The line rang against her ear. Not her sons, but the charity. The same man picked up. He was trying to reassure her.

"That's Joaquin and Felix," he said. "There's nothing to worry about, Luz. They're not stealing anything. We even have cameras in the trucks. You did a good thing today." When she didn't say anything, he repeated her name. "Luz? Luz, are you there? The guys are calling me on the other line. Please unlock the door for them." Peering through the window, she saw the tall man standing in the middle of the street—he was staring up at her. She gripped her phone tighter.

What was happening to her?

Santiago had tried teaching her how to meditate when he'd visit home from college. Her lessons had begun with walks around the artificial lake, past the townhouses and the single-family homes with their sparkling pools. He strode ahead, focused and serious, while she took everything in for the first time. He must've taken this route countless times. He'd had his own universe, a secret life just outside their house. They passed an inverted rowboat covered in limpets, several ducklings huddled in the shadow across the grassy knoll. Dogs, golden and bright, barked behind white metal fences. She ran her hand over the humming green boxes full of cables and machines that held the neighborhood together. On the other side of the guard house and the gates, they sat on the lake's edge with their backs to the road. She noticed how her rainbow umbrella popped in the row of identical backyards, having never seen it from this side. He stood and stretched into the sun like a tree. He told her to listen to the sounds around them, to breathe, to relax. She thanked the birds, the trees, the winds. The grass beneath her, unusually full and stiff, seemed to suspend her above the ground. In a way, she floated.

Every three months he had returned from college a slightly different person. She missed the small, progressive growth of his personality. Now, every time he visited, he seemed molted and new. She must've been the same to him. He must've seen her as someone different each time, not as his mother, the way he told her about his online lovers and going to therapy. He talked about dislocations, which made her think of bones hanging out of their sockets, though she knew he was talking about Colombia. He seemed to be from some nobler planet, his clear voice sucking her into the gravity of its orbit. She wished she could be a fly on the wall of one of his classrooms.

He had been twelve, in seventh or eighth grade, the morning she'd left the car running, climbed the stairs, and sat down on the chair in her bedroom. This was during the time in her life when she had gone to work at four, before sunrise, and then come home at eight to take him to school. She called him by his full name, and a moment later he came to her in his baby-blue polo and checkered shoes. She made him sit on the edge of her bed and, from across the room, asked him whether he liked boys or girls.

Manuel had told her about the pictures on the computer, about the sites Santiago visited. She had known since he was little, and now she had proof, but then why had she asked if she already knew? That was the cruel part; she had thought herself brave and different, facing head-on what other mothers spent lifetimes ignoring. But she didn't know what to do with his answer, or his lack of an answer, because he didn't say anything. He looked straight at her, too scared to lift his hands from his thighs and wipe away the tears gliding down his face. Instead, his fingers clutched his khakis, digging into his thighs; it pained her to see him paralyzed by fear. The tears dripped from his chin, dotting the collar of his polo. What came next? She hadn't thought beyond herself. She didn't do anything—didn't hold him or remind him he was loved. She simply opened her bedroom door, led him through it out to the car. They fell into a silence that lasted months. For the first time, they were like strangers surrounded by darkness. She had called him years later to apologize for this, for everything, but she knew it wasn't enough; the pain she'd caused him would always be with him. He'd confirmed this when he consoled her and told her he loved her, all the words echoed from him, from a place carved by pain. Forgiveness as she needed it did not exist.

Luz stepped through the front door. The truck rumbled in the driveway, coughing exhaust. Its back door was shut and locked.

"You just have to sign this form and we can get out of here." The tall man handed her the clipboard and a pen. "You have a beautiful house," he said. "I'm sorry this was so hard for you, mami." His dark, pitying eyes pinned her down. She felt the knot in her throat loosen. She wanted to say his name but she'd forgotten it, or perhaps they hadn't properly introduced themselves; she couldn't remember at all. She signed the forms and forced a smile at the back of the truck without another word, thinking only of how the man had held her in his eyes. The truck vanished around the community pool house in the distance.

"Hola, princesa. How are you?" It was Santiago, apologizing for missing her earlier call.

"Mi tesoro," said Luz. "Better now that I'm talking to you."

She didn't mention her panic, that moment had passed. She only told him, staring into the emptied house, that everything was okay.

She continued, "I dreamed I was fighting a cow last night. I hit it in the face. It fell over and stood back up."

She kept talking and talking. As she rambled, she had the sense that she was being watched, that the tall man from the charity was still there, and that this man knew she was not very good. She began speaking in an even more melodramatic tone.

As she spoke, she remembered Colombia. She remembered lying on her mattress and talking to God at night. She remembered the porch and the butterflies. The fact that nothing had changed, that the boys hadn't come back, that they were still not coming home, that to cope, she still relied on the fantasy of their return, made her feel like she was slowly unraveling.

In what remained of the day, Luz ran from room to room, peering out the windows. Each time her voice echoed, she was startled by the words: "¡Llegó mi hora!" The rooms in which they had been a family now emanated a puzzling light. For years after the boys first moved away, she had tried to preserve the house as they had left it, hoping they would find it unchanged upon their return. Some nights she swore she saw the ghosts of her boys clattering down the staircase, tossing dishes in the sink, and flipping through television channels, fading in and out of the rooms with their translucent limbs. Now she couldn't recall how the rooms had looked just hours before. She shouted to herself and to the memories these rooms held of the boys: "¡Llegó mi hora!"

She careened now down the carpeted hallway, through the pale patch where the rug had lain, past the matted circle where the boys had long ago spilled a can of paint, to the threshold of her bedroom. The sunlit windows were hot white panels. She followed the light's path to the opposite wall, where a starbust formed on the head of a nail. She let herself stop, feeling hot and dazed. The light spun around on the nail in a vortex. She was spellbound by the shape, by this opening beyond the drywall. She was transported, reborn, which was how leaving the house was supposed to feel—when all she was witnessing was light break on a nail. This sensation lasted for seconds, or minutes; now that her time was hers, it didn't matter. She had to learn how to experience the world without Mark and the boys. Everything could be extraordinary.

As the portal on the wall finally closed, it was impossible for her to ignore how she looked, a woman staring at a nail in an otherwise bare yellow wall. She could not remember what had once hung from the nail.

"¡Llegó mi hora!" she shouted again, stomping down the stairs. And stepping out onto the driveway, into the brightness before her vision cleared, she thought that this, finally, was the end of distractions. The house, her family, everything. It had all been a distraction from herself. She sighed and felt a stillness where there had been a stirring. This was it. The moment before everything changed, before she became something new again.

Acknowledgments

This book would not have been possible without:

My mentors at Yale University: Michael Cunningham, who became an uncle to me, every step of this journey sweeter because of him; and Caryl Phillips, who intimidated me at first, with his all-black outfits and British manners, but who taught me that talent was nothing without consistent dedication.

The Lambda Literary Fellowship, where I first met Callum Angus, Brandon Taylor, and Garth Greenwell, whose belief in me opened the door to a bigger life. That week in LA changed everything.

The Iowa Writers' Workshop, from my classmates to Sasha Khmelnik to the folks of the Truman Capote Fellowship. Much love and gratitude to my teachers—Lan Samantha Chang, Kevin Brockmeier, Adam Haslett, and Garth Greenwell—and my close friends—Abigail Carney, Ada Zhang, Belinda Tang, Matthew Kelley, and Arinze Ifeakandu. You made my life easier and my writing better.

ACKNOWLEDGMENTS

The editors at *Joyland*, *Subtropics*, *ZYZZYVA*, and *McSweeney's*—
Michelle Lyn King, David Leavitt, Laura Cogan, and Claire Boyle—
who had a hand in shaping the stories that would become this
novel.

Mark Doten and Caroline Sydney, two marvelous editors and friends
who so generously read these pages and kept me going with their support.

Grinnell College, the Mellon Foundation, and all the friends who
made small town Iowa a home: Vrinda Varia, Jeremy Chen, Leah
Allen, Dean Bakopoulos, and Andreas Jozwiak. You've loved me so
thoroughly I've hardly noticed the years pass.

My agent, Jin Auh, and my editor at Riverhead, Laura Perciasepe,
who patiently nurtured this project until it was ready to meet its
readers. And the rest of team *Hombrecito*: Claire McGinnis and Nora
Alice Demick.

Too many lovers to name, but a special thanks to Roger Mathew
Grant, David Caves, and Jarrett Earnest.

The friends in New York who made me laugh and dance and eat
during those difficult and uncertain years that I was adrift: Anna
Mexler, Kyle Croft, Melissa Middleberg, Clare Mao, and the Flora
Bar crew.

My partner, R., who got me through revisions and edits in one
piece. May our love give way to new stories.

My best friends: Larissa Pham, Carl Napolitano, and Johnathan
Payne. Words can't express how much I love you, how much all three
of you are a part of me, how much you have inspired me to create. You

are the most brilliant and loving people I have ever met. You are my family, now and always.

Alex and Ed, who showed me the world when we were young and small. You gave me the love and excitement my little life lacked, and made me into the kind of person who goes out into the world and risks everything for what they want. We survived together, and we survived each other. Now I ask for everything the same way I'd ask for a glass of water. I will never, ever, not be thinking of you.

My brother and father—the first men I ever loved. Through all the time and distance, my love for you has only grown. My mother, whom I'm so proud to resemble. Thank you for playing all the roles you did in my life, always with love. You never doubted I was making something special. My first family, thank you for trusting me with our stories. Your love got me here.